THE
CIRCUS IN
WINTER

BIG CHARLIE & HOFFMAN
WITH J.H. LaPearl CIRCUS

CATHY DAY

THE
CIRCUS IN
WINTER

HARCOURT, INC.

Orlando   Austin   New York
San Diego   Toronto   London

Photo credits: Pages ii, 45, 98, 111, 137, 186, 212, and endpapers courtesy of
the Miami County Historical Society; page 1, photograph by Edward J. Kelty
courtesy of the George Eastman House; page 24 from the H.A. Atwell Studio,
Chicago, Lillian Leitzel, black-and-white photograph, collection of the John
and Mable Ringling Museum of Art and the State Art Museum of Florida;
page 80, photograph by the author; page 157 from the collection of Robert
C. Cole; page 245, photograph by Tony Hare.

Library of Congress Cataloging-in-Publication Data
Day, Cathy.
The circus in winter/Cathy Day.—1st ed.
p.   cm.
ISBN 0-15-101048-X
1. Circus—Fiction. 2. Circus performers—Fiction. 3. Indiana—Fiction.
I. Title.
PS3604.A985C57   2004
813'.6—dc22   2003025033

Text set in Meridien
Designed by Linda Lockowitz

Printed in the United States of America

First edition
K J I H G F E D C B A

For the five of us

PROGRAMME OF DISPLAYS

Weather: In the Midwest, around the lower Lakes, the sky in the winter is heavy and close, and it is a rare day, a day to remark on, when the sky lifts and allows the heart up.

—WILLIAM GASS,
"In the Heart of the Heart of the Country"

THE
CIRCUS IN
WINTER

WALLACE PORTER
— or
What It Means
to See the Elephant

CIRCUS PROPRIETORS are not born to sawdust and spangles. Consider this: P. T. Barnum was nothing more than a dry-goods peddler—that is until he bought a black woman for $1,000, a sum he quickly recouped by displaying her as George Washington's 161-year-old mammy. Barnum's business partner, James Bailey, was born little Jimmy McGinnis—an orphaned bellboy transformed into circus mastermind, a man who taught army quartermasters the science of transporting masses of men and equipment by rail. Before trains, circuses traveled by horse-drawn wagons (and were called "mud shows" for obvious reasons) and by riverboat. If it hadn't been for paddle wheels and tall stacks, brothers Al, Alf, Charles, John, and Otto Rungeling might have become Iowa harness makers, like their father. But one morning along the Mississippi in 1870, the brothers were smitten with an elephant lumbering down a circus steamboat gangplank and became forever after the Ringling Brothers, owners (along with Barnum and Bailey) of the Greatest Show on Earth.

For many years, their greatest rival was the Great Porter Circus, owned by one Wallace Porter, a former Union cavalry officer. After Appomattox, Porter took his hard-won equine knowledge, applied it to the family's business, and became, at the age of thirty-eight, the owner of the largest livery stable in northern Indiana. How he became a circus man is another story altogether.

EACH SUMMER, Wallace Porter boarded a train in Lima, Indiana, and headed due east through Ohio, Pennsylvania, and New Jersey to the strange land of a million people, New York City. He employed a number of lawyers and bankers to oversee the profits from his stables and dutifully met with them once a year to discuss markets and dividends. These obligations dispensed with, he hailed a carriage and disappeared into the swarm of the city, following the true impetus of his trip. Wallace Porter went to New York to indulge in extravagance.

During his weeklong stay, he hardly slept, so intent was he to glut himself on the city. In the mornings, he had a shave and walked along the avenues down the length of Manhattan, which, in the late 1800s, was not an arduous undertaking. He handled his business over lunch, and afterward, he visited the finest men's tailors in the city and bought new shirts, Chesterfield coats, leather boots, and bowler hats—all of which were shipped back to Lima in enormous Saratoga trunks. At night, he dined out in the best restaurants, gorging himself on pheasant and artichokes. He drowned in vintage French wines. After dinner, he took in a play or the symphony, and then, until the small hours of the night, he roamed the parks alone. In Lima, such lavishness was a mark of poor character, a flaw almost impossible to hide, which was why Porter enjoyed the brief

anonymity of the city. On the train ride back home, Porter
tallied his expenses and hid that figure in his breast pocket
like a guilty boy. He felt his thrifty father's eyes upon him,
heard his voice saying, *So what you can afford this? The money
would buy more horses, carriages, a month's worth of hay.* To
punish himself, Porter lived a spartan existence the rest of
the year, but come summer, he had to board the train, like
a fish that must spawn. Always, he returned to Indiana
feeling both completely hollow and fully sated.

The trip he took to New York in 1883 was different than
the others, because that was the year he met Irene, who
would become his wife. His banker, Irene's father, invited
him to a Fourth of July party and introduced Porter to his
guests as "my new friend, the pioneer from Indiana." Porter
looked nothing like a settler, but something about the name
itself, *Lima,* invoked the exotic and the adventurous.

The party was given on a warm summer evening. Irene's
father decked the house in red, white, and blue, and instructed the small band he'd hired to play Sousa marches
every so often to get folks in the patriotic mood. Irene descended the stairs to "Bonnie Annie Laurie" and caught
Porter's eye as he stood near the punch bowl smoking a
cigar. He was handsome in a smallish way that with his
clothes and carriage passed for a kind of elegance. When he
saw Irene, he dashed his cigar out in a cup of punch and met
her at the bottom of the stairs. He took her hand, she smiled,
and he realized then that since the war, he'd felt little within
his heart except ambition, hardly an emotion at all.

Together, they watched the fireworks display as they
ambled in the garden. "Tell me about this town of yours.
Lima." *Lee-ma,* she said.

With a smile, Porter said, "Actually, it's like the bean."

"Are they grown there?"

"It's supposed to be *Lee-ma*, but I don't think the town fathers knew that." Porter recited a list of mispronounced Midwestern towns named for faraway places: *Ver-sails, Brazz-ill, Kay-roh, New Praygue.*

Irene laughed. "Tell me about *Lie-ma*."

So he described the countryside: He lived outside town along the Winnesaw, the river that separated the northern and southern halves of Lima. He described his monthly travel circuit to check on his stables, and again, gave her a litany of town names: Kokomo, Lafayette, Monticello, Rensselaer, Valparaiso, Nappanee, Warsaw, Alexandria. Irene repeated them, like someone trying to learn a foreign language. Bursts of fireworks lit Irene's face, and Porter said, "You should travel west sometime and see a bit of the world."

It was just something to say, but Irene sparked. "What's the farthest west you've ever been, Mr. Porter?"

"Wallace, please," he said. "Leavenworth, Kansas." That was where his cavalry regiment, the Eleventh Indiana, mustered out. Almost twenty years had gone by, but he could still see the land rolling like an ocean into the blue sky. He tried not to remember other images: a barn in Alabama full of stinking, rotting, wailing men. His regiment lost 13 in battle, 161 to disease.

"I've never been farther west than Buffalo, to visit my aunt," Irene said. She motioned with a sweep of her hand. "All these people do nothing but visit one another and marry one another. They just go round and round." Irene sighed. "You're a lucky man, Wallace." He looked at his

feet, then up at the colorful sky, trying to gather his courage to ask to see her again the next day. But Irene said it
first. "You'll have to come back tomorrow and tell me
more." She put her hand in the crook of his arm.

Already, Irene loved Wallace Porter, or knew she would
love him. But she also knew this: When men steer women
through crowds, they need to believe they are at the helm.
Women must apply subtle, imperceptible pressure with
their fingertips. In this way women lead while appearing to
be led, This is the way of the world.

NEW YORK courtships were customarily long affairs, drawn
out over years at times, but Irene would have none of it.
When her father protested about how the hasty marriage
would look, she laughed and said, "What do I care? I'm
going to Indiana." They married two weeks after the party
and boarded the train for Lima. The return trip became a
makeshift wedding tour with extended stays in the finest
hotels in Philadelphia, Cleveland, Louisville, and Cincinnati. They went sightseeing, played faro in riverboat sa-
loons, dined out until they ran out of restaurants, then
moved on to the next city. In the Pullman, Irene held
Porter's hand but rarely took her eyes from the landscape
unfurling beyond the window. To her, the Blue Ridge were
the Alps, and the Ohio River might well have been the Nile.

As they neared Lima, Porter saw the flattening land full
of corn with new eyes. He thought for sure that upon arrival, Irene would find the town and his house (and by ex-
tension, himself) too simple, too crass. How could he tell
her the truth? He was a longtime bachelor who, after late
nights spent poring over figures, often slept at his livery

stable. Despite the furniture and rugs, his home was nothing more than a farmhouse, plain and simple. Porter delayed their arrival there by driving through town in the still-warm September twilight to show her his stables, Robertson's Hotel, the millinery, and the dry-goods store. They passed some of Lima's most well-appointed houses. He'd been inside them, of course, but Porter existed on the fringe of Lima's best circles, the aging bachelor invited to large Christmas parties, but never to lunch, never encouraged to drop by. Surely, he thought, Irene would change that. By the time he turned toward home, darkness had settled down from the trees onto the grass, and cicadas were singing. Neighboring farmhouses—windswept and peeling by day—glowed rosy at night with lamps burning in the windows. Irene drowsed happily as he guided the horses down River Road, which tunneled under the green-black trees lining the Winnesaw River.

At her new home, Irene inspected the sitting room and dining room by the light of a kerosene lamp. She stared at the black kitchen stove and announced that she full well intended to learn its mysteries. Of the four upstairs bedrooms, two were full of clothes, furniture, and paintings—Porter's accumulated New York booty, much of it still in trunks or wrapped in brown paper. Irene laughed. "The king's treasure rooms," she said. Another room Porter used as a study; pipe smoke had worked its way into the walls. She walked on to the simply equipped bedroom—just a dresser, nightstand, and a bed draped with a patchwork quilt.

Porter went to the window to pull down the shade. In the glass, he watched his new wife unfasten her gloves and take down her hair, then remove each piece of clothing:

dress, bustle, corset, stockings, chemise. Irene welcomed the night; she had been preparing herself to sleep in that humble bed, in that modest house, for a lifetime already. In the morning, she'd ask her husband to take her for a ride; they'd go until his horse tired then choose a fresh one at one of his stables and ride on, like the Pony Express. At that moment, there was not a single thing lacking.

But what Porter saw reflected in the shivering glass was a woman too lovely for that humble bed in that modest house. He blew out the lamp and said, "I'm going to build us a new place."

"I like this house."

"We need a bigger one. For children."

That night, Porter built a house of words: cut-stone paths crisscrossing the lawn, weaving their way around trees and an English garden with a lily-padded pool. A two-story gray mansion with three white columns and twin verandas half hidden in ivy and rosebushes. For Irene, he would make a temple, a repository of his New York excess and hungers.

He could not see that she was tired of temples. Neither knew that already she was dying. There was a lot Wallace and Irene Porter could not and would not see.

ALTHOUGH HE pleaded with her, Irene refused an invitation to join a local ladies' circle. "I've had my fill of circles, thank you very much."

Although she pleaded with him, Porter refused to allow Irene to accompany him on the road. "Some of these towns don't have proper hotels," he said.

"I don't mind boardinghouses. Aren't there other women at these places?"

Porter looked at his shoes. "There are women, yes. But no ladies."

He relented, however, when business took him to Chicago or Indianapolis. There, he bought Irene tokens of his affection: rugs, coatracks, clocks, crystal chandeliers. She accepted these gifts with despair and stored them in her husband's cluttered treasure rooms. To Irene, a chair was the price of a rail ticket, a dresser was a week's stay in a hotel, and with each purchase, the broad future she'd imagined shrank just a little bit more.

Construction of the mansion began in the spring of 1884. Porter chose good ground—a grassy hill a few hundred yards from his farmhouse. From that vantage point, he and Irene would be able to look out over the countryside and the Winnesaw River. Each night, he read mail-order catalogs in bed, choosing what furnishings to order. He asked her what she preferred: Chippendale or Hepplewhite? Pineapples or grapes as a scrollwork motif? Red portieres or white? Invariably, she chose whichever was cheaper and plainer. One evening the subject was bathtubs. "This one will do just fine, Wallace," she said.

"But it's not nearly as big as that one," he said.

"Choose whichever you prefer then."

"It's important to me that you like it."

Irene smiled. "Don't be silly, dear. What's important is that *you* like it."

Even though it smarted to hear her say that, he could not stop spending money on the mansion. Its unfinished skeleton appeared in his dreams, and every night, he walked through its bones.

IRENE HAD SPENT much of her first fall behind the reins of a small buggy, taking long, solitary drives until daylight gave out. Then her first Indiana winter arrived. She paled indoors, and by summer, she was still a tint of gray. Gradually, she began keeping to the house, rarely venturing farther than the front porch. One night after dinner, Porter found Irene there, embroidering in the bright glow of the setting sun. He said, "You don't look well, Irene. Are you feeling all right?"

"I can't seem to get warm," she said, "even sitting here in the sun." It was August.

He asked her in a near whisper, "Is it a child?"

Irene smiled into her lap. "Perhaps. I'm seeing the doctor tomorrow."

But the doctor said no child grew in Irene's belly. "Plenty of time," he said, and blamed her pallor on the adjustment to a Midwestern climate. "It will pass."

Then one morning Porter woke up in a shaking bed. Irene lay on her back, panting, wet with sweat despite the chill that had crept in overnight. Her body was a curled fist, and her own fists were digging into her belly, her eyes shut tight. He tried to straighten her, but the pain had locked her muscles in that pose. He repeated her name, kissed her palm, but in return got three long fingernail scratches down his cheek. When it was over, Porter laid a wet washcloth over her forehead, and Irene opened her eyes. "What's happened to your face, Wallace?" she said, taking the cloth from her head and daubing it at the hardening blood on his cheek.

"I got scratched I guess."

"Yes, well, stay clear of whatever it was next time," she said without looking in his eyes. Because she had seen fit to warn him off, he knew this had happened before.

By the next winter, Irene's gray skin stretched tight over sharp bones. Blue veins pulsed in her thin flesh. The fits of pain came with no warning; the beast fed on her and stole quickly away. Irene asked Porter to keep the lamp burning all night long, and he obliged, although it bothered him that his presence alone was no longer enough to sustain her. He asked, "What's wrong?" She said, "Nothing." She said, "Nerves." She said it would pass. Irene made herself a cocoon of their quilt, and when she did have to leave her bed to eat, bathe, or use the water closet, she moved slowly, almost in stealth, as if she was trying to sneak past her pain. One night as he shadowed her through the house like a ghost, she crumpled on the floor. He carried her limp body back to bed.

For too long, Porter had abided by her desire to pretend nothing was happening, but finally, he could no longer pretend. The next morning, he shook her awake. "I've had enough," he said. "You will see a doctor."

Irene yawned. "Why?"

"Stop it, Irene. This isn't going away. I thought it would, but it hasn't."

She kissed him on the cheek. "Well, honey, if it would make you feel better."

Doctor after doctor came by train. From the hallway

outside the bedroom, Porter heard them murmuring, asking Irene where it hurt. None was ever present, though,
when a spell occurred. The doctors opened the door, rubbing their beards or their heads, whispering that they
wanted to open her up, some to look at her liver or her in-
testines, others her heart. One even thought the problem
was her lumpy skull. It was the ague, some doctors said,
caught from one of the mosquitoes hatched in the fetid
summer waters of the Winnesaw. Others called it severe
dyspepsia or yellow fever. The last doctor, the best in the
country, came by train all the way from Boston, and even
he was puzzled. All of them left (as a kind of apology) pills
and syrups. The castor oil and calomel turned her stomach
inside out, so Porter threw them out and began spooning
tiny drops of morphine and laudanum onto her tongue.
She slept soundly, at last. The bottles stood like sentries on
the bedside table, guarding her from the beast's return.
Teaspoons became tablespoons. Trickles became rivers. She
was flooded with opiates, floating away.

Then it was spring again, and he was no closer to finding a cure for Irene than before. Porter mounted the stairs
to wake her from a nap and found her already up. The red
curtains were open, and she gazed out the window at the
unfinished mansion on the hill.

Without turning her head, she said, "They'll be coming
back soon, I suppose."

"No, the doctors are gone."

She pointed out the window. "I meant them."

"Next week. Foreman says it will be finished before the
snow flies."

"Yes, I'm sure it will." Irene said, "I never wanted it."

He sat down on the bed. "I didn't know that." Even as he said it, Porter knew it wasn't true.

Irene's laugh was brittle. Turning her head from the window, she said, "I married you because I wanted to live differently. I wanted my life to be an adventure, but you wanted me to live as I was accustomed." She spat the last word from her mouth.

Porter felt his failure sitting like a gargoyle on his heart.

"You must promise me you won't let those doctors operate. They don't know what they're looking for anyway. I can just see them gathered around, cutting here and there. A bunch of pirates digging for treasure without a map."

Porter didn't recognize the cynical, sharp-edged woman in the bed, but he gave her his word. It was, after all, the only thing she wanted from him.

THIS IS HOW Wallace Porter became a circus man, but not why.

Not long after the doctors stopped coming, the Hollenbach Circus Menagerie came to Lima, a locomotive followed by fifteen red and yellow railcars. They pulled into the siding along the Winnesaw, and the overalled roustabouts led twenty horses needing new shoes to Porter's livery stable on Broadway—conveniently only a block from the railyard. It would be a fateful day.

Porter hadn't been out of the house in over a month, leaving his stable manager to attend to his daily business affairs. The winter days had flowed one into the next and nothing had changed except the color fading from Irene's face. When Porter sat in her room, he talked to her whether she was asleep or not. He imagined his life devoid of Irene's illness. In that other world he maintained in his head, he discussed financial transactions with his banker, bartered with a hostler over the price of a new foal, exchanged pleasantries with Irene as he took his dinner alone in the kitchen. One night as he inspected the building site, he finally heard himself chattering away and began to fear for the state of his sanity and soul. He woke Irene and said, "Tomorrow I'm going into town. Will you be all right alone, or do you want me to send someone out to sit with you?"

Irene shook her head.

"You don't want me to go, or you don't want someone to come?"

She nodded her head yes.

"I'll leave your lunch next to the bed. You won't even have to get up."

Irene squeezed his hand. Only then did he realize that he hadn't heard her voice in weeks.

The next morning, Porter rode into Lima, inhaling deeply the wet spring wind. He saw the circus train sitting on the siding as he came into town, and not long after he arrived at the stable, a stumpy, balding man in an unkempt suit walked into his office. "Excuse me," he said, taking off his hat. "Clyde Hollenbach of Hollenbach's Menagerie." He pointed his walking cane. "I've got me some horses need shoeing. Folks say this is the place for it." He dressed in black, like a minister turned to the Devil—florid, rumpled, and red-eyed. His breath smelled of whiskey, his clothes of smoke sunk into the threads.

"Are you here to put on a show?" Porter asked, but the man shook his head no. Circuses passed through Indiana sometimes, stopping in South Bend, Fort Wayne, and Indi-

anapolis, but never before in Lima. Too small to attract a
big enough crowd, most likely. Over the years, Porter had
read news stories about Barnum bringing Jumbo the
elephant from England, and just two years earlier, Tom
Thumb had died with sweet elegies printed in most every
paper.

Hollenbach lit a cigar but didn't offer Porter one.
"We're due in Carolina in three days, but these horses need
tending to. Normally, I've got my own men to do the work,
but I'm a bit shorthanded this season." He puffed at his
cigar and stared at the wafts of smoke drifting in the air.

"Things are slow now. We could have all those horses
taken care of by tomorrow," Porter said.

"Fine." Hollenbach stood to leave.

"Where are you going to put all the animals? All the
people? If you don't mind my asking."

Hollenbach waved his hand. "Oh, we'll find us a lot to
make camp. Sometimes I board them all in hotels and
stables, but..." He didn't seem to know how to finish.

Porter understood that money troubles don't only
show up on ledgers, but also in the smell of whiskey and
worry on a man. Hollenbach's eyes were slightly frantic,
and his fingers twitched and twiddled. What the man
needed, he decided, was a good lunch.

At Robertson's Hotel, Hollenbach ate the beef stew and
Boston brown bread offered, but seemed to enjoy the
scotch more than the food. By the end of the meal, Hollenbach was soused. "Take it from me," he said, "this is the
craziest business there is. Sucker born every minute, my
foot. I'm the sucker!" He brought his fist down on the
table, shaking the dishes and glasses. "Damn that Barnum

anyway. I read that book of his and should have known
better."

"Known what better?"

"A man can't expect to get anywhere in life when his
livelihood rests on the actions of those he cannot control."
Hollenbach slugged the last few fingers of his whiskey in a
single gulp and poured himself a fresh glass. "They get sick.
Have babies. Get lazy and pull on the wrong rope and
down it all comes. And what can I do about it? I pay these
people a decent wage. They have a place to sleep, and believe me, it's a better life than some of them had before."
Standing up from his chair, Hollenbach said, "Allow me the
honor, sir, of showing you what I'm talking about."

They stepped out into the muddy street and walked
down Broadway to the river. The railroad tracks of the
Chesapeake & Ohio snaked along its banks. From the siding, the smell of campfire smoke and roasting meat drifted
toward them. Porter wasn't listening to the circus proprietor's complaints, only the fiddle music ahead. The rising
steam from cook pots smelled of mysterious spices, and he
inhaled deeply the aromas of cooked meat, animal dung,
moldy hay, and liquor. The circus people gathered in warm
circles, spoke toasts with rough tongues and laughter. The
doors of the railcars yawned open like black mouths, and
from within, yellow and green eyes blinked, animal or
human Porter could not discern. The circus people called
out greetings to Hollenbach, who raised his hand and nodded in return. As Porter walked through the siding, he
found a certain respect for the man beside him, who despite his swilling and swearing, made his way among this

strange retinue like a general making a friendly inspection
of his troops.

At the edge of the camp, an elephant stood swinging
hay into its mouth, rocking back and forth, clanking the
chain around its foot. Hollenbach approached its trunk.
"This is George, the only elephant left. A good worker. Had
to sell the rest. Cost too much to feed." George's skin
sagged from protruding bones and Porter stroked the
knobbly, bristled hide. One ivory tusk was tipped with a
gold ball, the other was broken off, "from lifting tent
poles," Hollenbach explained. Porter didn't know anything
about elephants, but he knew when a creature was on its
last legs. In the war, he'd watched three horses crumple beneath him, one from musket fire, two from starvation and
exhaustion. George's sad eye fixed on Porter like a plea,
and he had to look away.

Hollenbach led Porter to his private railcar, his name
painted in gold on the sides. The car was a modified Pullman
done up in red velvet and mahogany, complete with a sleeping berth, woodstove, and armchairs. They passed the rest of
the afternoon drinking more whiskey, smoking cigars. Hollenbach confessed there was not even enough money for
next month's hay and soon he would have to sell his circus.
The silence of the previous weeks had made Porter hungry
for the sound of a human voice, even if it was Hollenbach
lamenting his financial woes. He kept the thought of Irene—
alone and curled in pain—in the back of his brain for as
long as he could. The darkening sky said it was after five,
and he was waiting for a lull in the conversation to make his
departure when there came a loud rap at the door.

"Come then," Hollenbach roared.

The door opened, and a black-haired woman stepped into the light of the crystal sconces. She wore a white dress with a shawl draped over her shoulders and bowed slightly to Hollenbach, then to Porter.

"What is it, Marta? So late."

The woman, Marta, bowed again. "My baby is sick, sir," she said, the English correct, but thickly accented. "He needs a doctor."

Hollenbach sighed and rubbed his forehead. Porter set down his glass and spoke, looking first at the woman's eyes. "I know a doctor. Byrd. Very good, and *reasonable.*" The last word was for Hollenbach, whose head was still cradled in his hand.

"I thought your mother could cure these things, Marta?" Hollenbach looked at Porter. "Her mother knows magic. Chants and such. I had to let our croaker, Doc Miller, go at the end of last season, and Marta's mother has done almost as good a job. Right?"

Marta kept her eyes lowered and clutched her shawl more tightly. "She's been cooking the broths all day. Nothing works for him. I thought you should help." Marta looked up then, her eyes narrowed into slits, and Porter understood that Hollenbach was responsible for the child beyond his duties as an employer.

Hollenbach missed Marta's look, but not her meaning. He kept his eyes on his drink. "How is he? The baby."

"He makes noise when he breathes and will not eat." Marta's voice was flat.

"Well then, tomorrow morning take the baby to this Dr. Byrd, and tell him to send the bill to me." Hollenbach puffed on his cigar and blew the smoke toward her. "Normally, I'd have to deduct some from your month's wages for this, but I'll let it go this time."

She said nothing and was turning to leave when Hollenbach said loudly, "Porter, do you know how our Marta earns her keep?" Marta stopped still, facing the door. "Turn around dear and show my friend your secret." His voice trembled with a subtle menace, but it was the money, Porter decided, not malice making Hollenbach take it out on the girl.

Marta came to him, whipping off her shawl with a flourish and covering her hands. Her eyes were closed as if she were praying. "Lift the shawl and, without looking, take my hands."

Hollenbach laughed. "She's a mystic."

Porter did as she instructed and grasped her fingers. Her hands were wet, but soft, which surprised him, because he'd imagined that the hands of circus people would be rough with calluses and rope burns. Working hands. There was something odd about her hands, too, the feel of them squirming in his, that he could not place.

Marta threw her head back, exposing the curve of her throat. Around her neck she wore a beaded necklace cinched tightly. Porter felt silly but tried to smile. Marta's eyes opened suddenly and she pulled her hands quickly away. "You should not be here. Go home."

Hollenbach rose out of his chair. "Why?"

"The one he loves is very sick. His hands should be taking care of her now."

Porter shook Marta by her thin shoulders. "How did she know this? Have you seen the doctor already? Or someone in town? What kind of game are you playing?" As he shook her, the shawl fell to her feet, and then he saw her hands, thin and blue-veined with gold and silver rings encircling each finger. Porter turned her hands palms up, then palms down. On one, he counted seven, on the other eight. Fingers.

"The extra ones are not mine," she said.

He couldn't take his eyes off her hands. "Whose are they?"

Marta motioned to Hollenbach with a nod of her head. "They are his mostly, but I think they are part in this world, part not. They tell me things to say, and mostly, they are true."

Without even a word of good-bye to Hollenbach, Porter ran out of the Pullman, dodging smoldering fires and canvas tents until he reached his stable and whipped his horse home to the dying Irene.

FOR THE LUCKY, death is a slow, quiet fade. For the rest, death humiliates, leaving us screaming and praying, covered in sweat, blood, and excrement. Dying, the final throes of it, is a messy business. Irene wanted to save her husband from this. So she staved off death, waiting for that window of opportunity when he might leave her alone. The soul is a funny thing. It can be saved and lost, fed and consumed, and sometimes, at the very end, it can be ordered to do our bidding.

In later years, when people asked Wallace Porter what possessed him to buy a circus, he told them, "I'd been to see the elephant, that's why." Those who did not know him well assumed that, like the Ringlings, he'd seen a pachy-

derm somewhere and been bitten by the showman's bug.
Those who'd heard his story about George the elephant's
accusing eye believed that he bought Hollenbach's Menagerie as a humane act of goodwill. But others recognized
the phrase from the days when gold miners and home-
steaders headed West and Union boys headed South.
Going to see the elephant meant you were going over the
wall, into the cave, across the mountain, into the dark
night beyond the firelight's reach. When you returned—if
you returned—you said, "I've been to see the elephant."
Some things once seen cannot be said, and so we say we've
seen the elephant instead.

DURING THAT LONG moonlit ride, Porter didn't pray. He
stormed at a gallop to the dark house and saw Irene standing at the bedroom window, waving down to him as she
once had, and he thought, *The witch was wrong. I'm a fool
running all crazy out here.* He looked up again and saw it
wasn't Irene, but the reflection of the moon shimmering in
the window. Porter threw open the front door and ran up
the stairs.

Scattered on the floor were shards from an amber
bottle, its contents already soaked into the rug. The lamp
next to the bed had long since run out of oil. Caressing
Irene's cold hand, he told her about Hollenbach, Marta and
her fifteen fingers, George, and the circus people he had
seen. As he worked a brush through her tangled nest of
hair, Porter pictured his still-unfinished mansion. For the
first time, he saw himself living there alone, floating ghost-
like from room to room, visiting the intended nurseries
and playrooms full of trunks, broken furniture, dust, and

cobwebs. He saw the fields around his mansion gone fallow and brown, the barns abandoned, the tulip poplars bare.

Irene had fouled herself, so Porter placed her slumping form in an armchair while he changed the bedding. He cleaned her with water from the basin, and as he drew the cloth between her soiled legs, he knew he would never have a child, never find the courage to marry again. Irene lay naked on the bed, her skin bluish white, dry, and scaled. He found a jar of salve and rubbed it into her skin. As he anointed her belly, he felt a knot as big as an apple in the pit of her stomach and kneaded it with his fingers, tracing curves and ridges. This apple had been a pea on their wedding day, but Porter had no way of knowing that. He thought: *Instead of a baby, I planted this in my wife's womb, this beast which fed on her blood. It was inside her all the time.* He dressed her in a fresh nightgown, got into bed beside her, and slept.

When he woke, the morning light glowed behind the drapes. Leaving Irene, he watched the sun rise over his land and the Cunningham farm beyond. The sky was cloudy purple, turning pink at the edges, and across River Road, flowed the sluggish Winnesaw. Far off in the distance, he heard the long, slow pull of a train whistle and wondered if Hollenbach and his troupe might be leaving already. No, he remembered. They had horseshoes to tend to, Marta's baby to take to Doc Byrd, and surely Hollenbach was in no hurry to begin a season when each day he would sink deeper into his financial hole.

Porter saw it then, a vision clear as the sun: his name on a dozen railcars, Irene beside him in a private Pullman as they chugged across America, a circus king and queen.

She was smiling and squeezing his hand, just as she had two years ago on the wedding train from New York. Then he saw his land overrun by elephants and bears, clowns romping in the grass, acrobats dancing in his trees. In his head, he tallied it up. He knew what price his stables would fetch, but how much would a circus cost? Animals and tents, calliopes and wagons. Circus people, all of them. And barns and bunkhouses to put them all in. Porter parted the red velvet curtains, and sunlight streamed into the dark bedroom. He stood back from the window to show Irene this new life. "Look," he said, almost bowing. "Look at what I'm going to do."

JENNIE DIXIANNA
— or
The Secret to
the Spin of Death

WINTER IS a long circus Sunday, a time for rest. To fill the cold months, the Great Porter Circus & Menagerie held nightly poker games in the cookhouse of its winter quarters in Lima, Indiana. The wind outside howled across the plains and whistled through the walls. In the corners of the room, snow gathered like dust. The players drank cheap whiskey from tin cups and sat at a round wooden table placed so close to the potbelly stove that it seemed like another player. One February night, the competitors were proprietor Wallace Porter, his friend and local businessman George Cooper, elephant keeper Hans Hofstadter, and this night, a rarity—a woman. High-flying Jennie Dixianna joined the men in a flourish of feather boa.

Jennie played cards with a sweet, demure bluff that masked her skill. This sleight of hand had taken her far in life and was perhaps her greatest talent, more so even than her acrobatic act, the Spin of Death. To all appearances, she looked dainty, frail, and reticent, but once she entered the hippodrome and threw off her Johnny Reb robe, her mettle was clear to see—lanky sinews wrapped tight over hard bones. But also, Jennie possessed that certain magic that makes men reach out their arms, grasping as though blind for the fragile handkerchief dipped in rosewater dangled before them.

"Well boys," she said, "Let's see, how about seven-card stud? Aces wild, and what do you call those kings with the knives in their heads?" Jennie's eyes widened as she scanned the table.

"Suicide kings," Porter answered.

"Oh, yes. I always forget that."

Each time she took a gulp of the fiery whiskey offered her, she crinkled up her face in disgust. And kept on drinking. Jennie cooed her way to winning a large portion of the pot and called it beginner's luck. In the lantern light, her blond hair glistened like flax, and as the hours passed, the men's eyes drooped while hers flashed dark diamonds. When the rising sun poked fingers of light through the holes in the walls and under the door, Jennie Dixianna sat triumphant behind a pile of gold and silver coins, a shimmery film of sweat on her face. George Cooper tipped his chair back to smoke a cigar, winking at Wallace Porter as he turned to escort Jennie back to her bunkhouse.

"Where did you learn your cards?" Porter asked, his eyes straight ahead, a smirk on his lips.

"What do you mean?" Jennie asked, puzzled.

"I'm on to your little secret. You hide it well, but you're not an amateur." He was smitten with admiration.

Jennie gave a small, knowing laugh. "I've seen a good bit of this country, Mr. Porter. You pick up useful tricks. I won't apologize for that."

In a flash, she'd turned the tables and put him on the defensive. "Yes. Well," he said. Jennie was looking at him frankly, all the falseness she'd displayed in the card game gone.

They stood at her stoop, shivering in the early morning cold. Hans Hofstadter stomped by on his way back to his bunkhouse next door and glared at Jennie. He'd lost a good bit of money that night and, more than likely, was not looking forward to telling his wife, Nettie. Hofstadter entered his bunkhouse, and a second or two later, they heard a metal pot flung against the wall. Then the screaming in German.

Jennie pouted. "That's just fine. I'll not get a wink of sleep."

"Are they that bad?" Porter said. "I've heard stories from the men."

"Worse. I must find another place to rest my head." Jennie placed her black-gloved hand on Porter's arm. She looked past the winter quarters to Porter's mansion sitting on the frozen hill in the distance.

"Oh," he said, and stepped back.

Jennie took her hand away with a laugh. "Good night, Mr. Porter. Good morning. Whichever you prefer." She raised her skirts and stepped into her bunkhouse and, with a heavy clunk, shut the door in Porter's red face.

WHEN ASKED, Jennie Dixianna said she'd been born in a swamp and had walked out of the water, wholly made, draped in moss. "I am an American Venus, delivered from the gods," she said. There were grounds for believing her.

Her act was a variation of the Spanish web. First, she climbed a rope, which slithered snakelike between and around her legs as she rose higher. At the top, she fastened a small loop tightly around her wrist, held the rope at arm's length, and posed in graceful relief. The finale of her act was a series of full swings high above the hippodrome. The ringmaster announced:

"LADIES AND GENTLEMEN! HIGH ABOVE THE CENTER RING, MISS JENNIE DIXIANNA WILL NOW PERFORM HER FAMOUS *SPIN OF DEATH!* TONIGHT, SHE WILL ATTEMPT TO BREAK HER RECORD OF FIFTY TURNS, POWERED ONLY BY THE STRENGTH OF HER ONE DAINTY ARM. COUNT ALONG WITH ME AS JENNIE DIXIANNA TRIES TO BEAT HER OWN WORLD RECORD!"

Jennie suffered from chronic rope burn on her wrist, a constant open sore that, when not in the ring, she hid with her long black gloves. Every one of her performances broke the wound open and left the rope stained red. Audiences gasped and cheered when Jennie descended from the rope, hand over bloodstained hand. The circus people feared that she would wear her flesh all the way down to the bone, and that one night, she'd fall from the sky, leaving nothing in the spotlight but her hand still clenching the rope. Doctors said she'd die, not of a bloody fall, but of gangrene. They prescribed poultices and foul-smelling salves. Jennie scoffed at them all. "I can stop my own blood, and every night the flesh of my wrist grows back," she said to the astonished circus people, who half believed her. Surely, they thought, no mortal could withstand so much pain.

Jennie Dixianna could have been as young as eighteen or as old as forty, and depending on the quality of light, she looked anywhere in between. She never revealed her age, and some of the circus people believed she cast spells and swallowed bitter pills to change her age at will. Sometimes, Jennie took a lover—a wagon painter or calliope player— and during the brief time of their affair, Jennie's appearance would soften or harden to accommodate the shape of the man she'd taken. These men walked around the winter quarters in a drunken stupor, hardly eating, stumbling through their duties until she tired of them and banished them from her bed. The circus people grilled these lovers for her secrets. *Does she stew up potions? Does she sleep human sleep? What does she eat?* But these men never spoke of her, neither fondly nor harshly, and for months afterward, they moped about, shaking their heads, cleansing themselves of her charm.

Jennie Dixianna knew about Wallace Porter's dead wife. A year earlier, he'd held a boisterous Christmas party in the mansion, the first time his friends, business associates, and circus employees all commingled. Jennie wandered into the study and saw Irene's portrait over the mantel—a small woman white to near translucence with black moon eyes, steady and sad.

"The rosy cheeks are a bit of painterly license, I'm afraid. She was dying, even then." A woman stepped into the room, her fairness shimmering in the firelight, a young girl standing in the folds of her burgundy velvet dress. "I'm Elizabeth Cooper," she said, her chin jutting. "My daughter, Grace. My husband and I are friends of Mr. Porter."

Jennie introduced herself and offered her hand, but Elizabeth ignored it, fussing with the lace bow in her daughter's blue-black hair. Jennie turned her gaze back to Irene's quiet and determined face. "She died some time ago I understand," she said.

"Yes. It was quite a blow to our dear Wallace. I don't know that he's ever gotten over it."

Jennie smiled. "Perhaps it's time for Mr. Porter to stop mourning her," she said, and left the room.

Since then, Jennie had spent many nights darting from shadow to shadow, following Porter on his solitary sojourns around the winter quarters. "Checking on the stock," he always claimed, but his dark-rimmed eyes told a different story. She saw the pain in them, in his stoop, his gait. While others felt sympathy for him, Jennie felt only disdain. She wore her wound like a talisman bracelet, a secret treasure. Surely, Jennie thought, much could be gained from a man so weak of heart.

But the night of the card game, Jennie discovered that Wallace Porter could not be won the usual way. He'd seen through her simpering and believed he'd found her truest self, but Jennie was layered like an onion, skin over skin over naught. With a flick of her festering wrist, she could be any woman at all: mother or shrew, whore or lady, sister or siren. She knew what sort of woman Wallace Porter desired. He wanted a ghost. It was no trouble, really. She'd played spirit made flesh before.

A FEW DAYS AFTER the card game, Jennie watched Wallace Porter sneaking into the practice barn a few minutes before her usual arrival time. He'd been doing some checking, the circus people told Jennie. Playing cards with the roustabouts, asking about her without seeming to ask about her. No doubt, he'd learned that she didn't practice the Spin of Death during winter, preferring to use those months to rest her weary arm and let her wrist heal. Instead, each afternoon she performed a regimen of stretches and acrobatic flips to stay supple.

When she opened the practice-barn door, she felt Porter's presence immediately—in the corner amid a tangle of unicycles and bicycles, crouching behind a wall of juggling pins stacked into a pyramid. After stoking the iron stove, she hung her overcoat on a nail and changed her mud-clogged boots for a dainty pair of dancing slippers stuffed in her coat pocket. She stretched close to the stove, her smoky breath drifting around her shiny face. Slowly, layers of clothes fell away—sweaters over shirts, pants over pants—until Jennie Dixianna appeared wearing nothing but a pink leotard snug as flesh. She hurled herself headlong down the length of the practice mat in a flurry of flips and twists. When she practiced or performed, Jennie felt herself to be both solid and liquid, malleable enough to be poured into impossibly shaped molds and solid enough to withstand any force. After an hour, she was soaked through and flung herself onto the mat, panting.

Not for a single moment had Jennie forgotten her audience, and so she was not surprised when she heard a smattering of applause from behind the juggling pins. In his zeal, Porter's hand must have nudged the pyramid, which came crashing down around him. By the time the clatter subsided, Jennie was mostly dressed, wrapping a scarf over her wet hair. Cheeks flushed, she checked herself in a broken mirror that hung by the door, and speaking to the glass, said, "I'm ready when you are." Tiptoeing through the pins, an abashed Porter took her hand.

Evening was setting in. The low-hanging, scalloped clouds foretold heavy snow, and slivers of ice stung their faces as they rounded the corner of the practice barn and walked into a wall of wind. Slowly, they climbed the hill to Porter's mansion.

"That was magnificent, Miss Dixianna," Porter said.

"Thank you, Mr. Porter."

Dropping her hand, he wound his scarf over his mouth. "Dixianna," he said, speaking through wool. "A curious name. I've always wondered, where did you come by it?"

"It was my mother's name," she said, looking away at the snow glowing blue in the changing light.

JENNIE'S FATHER, Slater Marchette, was lucky to have survived the war with the Yankees, but he came home forever changed. He left a hard board of a man, but returned to his water oak–shaded shack in the Alabama bayou as soft as oleander, a sap given to weeping and hand holding. Slater hugged his wife and daughter so tight they lost their breath, and all that night, the house shook with his fierce love. After dinner, he danced and stomped, and once Jennie was sent to bed, he rocked the floors and walls, shouting his wife's name over and over.

Slater spent six months walking home from the war, carrying nothing in his haversack but scroggling apples and an unblemished Confederate battle flag, which he hung on the wall of his home as if it were a priceless painting. After a time, he found work on a fishing boat in Bonsecours Bay, but came home each night to braid Jennie's hair and kiss his wife's growing belly. The night the baby came, his wife screamed and swore while he filled cook pots with her blood. "Quick," he said to Jennie, "run and get Sister. Tell her your mama's bleeding to death. Hurry."

Sister wasn't family; she was a conjure woman who lived in a tin shanty just down the shell road. While he waited, he used every blanket, sheet, and towel to staunch the blood. When Jennie and Sister finally arrived, they found Slater awash in red, his wife blue-white and draped by the flag—the only piece of cloth left in the house.

Sister clasped her leather-lined hands. "I don't understand. It didn't stop." She explained then that there was a verse in the Bible with the power to stop blood. "Only a few know which one it is. You say the person's name and read the passage." Sister looked at Jennie, then at Slater. "What your wife's name?"

Through tears, he said, "Annie. Anna Marchette."

"That explains it then," Sister said, shaking her head. "Your daughter said her name was Dixie Anna. That's what I told God."

"A pet name," he cried.

Jennie had never heard him use any other.

Slater Marchette buried his wife, his darling Dixie Anna, under a shell mound with the baby still inside her. Jennie was six.

SO, JENNIE became a walking phantom, the living receptacle of unlived lives. Porter ate dinner that night with three women: his star acrobat, Jennie Dixianna; her mother,

Anna Marchette; and (at long last) his wife, Irene. She walked through the halls of his mansion as if she'd always lived there with him, and for the evening, he allowed himself to believe that Irene had never died at all, that this woman moving familiarly from room to room was Irene, and that this was just another night in their long and happy marriage.

In the sparkling candlelight, Porter swirled scotch in his crystal glass and read aloud the letter he'd received that day from old Clyde Hollenbach. After Porter bought Hollenbach's circus, the old showman and Marta, the Fifteen-Fingered Lady, had settled on the beach in California. *"Two children,"* Hollenbach wrote, *"twenty fingers. All is well."* They toasted Hollenbach's jolly circus family with red wine. After dinner, they listened to Strauss on the Victrola and floated across the room, staring with far-off eyes over each other's shoulders, moving together flawlessly by mere touch.

Then they retired, undressing wordlessly, back to back. Porter blew out the lamp, and they climbed under the chaste white sheets and turned to each other without passion.

HALF-ASLEEP, Jennie heard a voice say, "You are my sweet, my little Dixie Anna." It was her father, back from the boat, smelling of fish, sweat, and whiskey. In a minute, he'd start plaiting her hair while her mother fried mullet, and after dinner, when they thought she was asleep, the house would start its swaying. Jennie felt his hands, then more. She kept her eyes screwed shut, held onto the image of her mother smiling. She was twelve now, not six.

One day, her father got so drunk he fell off his boat into the Gulf waters. After swimming to shore, he decided a change in vocation was needed, a job conducive to benders. So, he bought spades and shovels and went out each day in search of the pirate Jean Lafitte's hidden treasure. Legend had it that Lafitte had spent one winter hunkered down nearby in a secluded shanty, hiding from the Spanish navy, and as a precaution, had buried a fortune in the sand.

By now, Jennie was the man and woman of the house: cook, farmer, laundress, barterer. Sometimes when she was hungry, she went down the road to Sister's. There was always food on the stove, and Sister paid Jennie to collect ingredients for her conjure balls and charm bags—horse hairs, fire ashes, snake skins, cedar knots. People came from as far as Mobile and Pensacola to buy them. Jennie tried to save the money for winter—stashed in her mother's keepsake cigar box—but more often than not, her father would return from treasure hunting hung over and empty-handed, find the money, and buy himself another drunk. She'd begun wearing her mother's old dresses, and at night, her father buried his head in her calico lap for consolation. Sometimes, when blind drunk, he came home a buccaneer, one of Lafitte's Black Flag men, and called her Veronica, his Creole mistress. "I gave you the map," he'd say, giving her a teeth-rattling shake. "Tell me where it is!" He'd rip her dress open, drag her by the hair before he fell on top of her. He always cried, during and after. Jennie never cried.

WALLACE PORTER made love in the dark.

Jennie was careful that first night with him. Barely moving while his lips traced her cheeks, she imagined herself dead, a cold body under examination. She could not imagine herself a virgin and strike a pose of timidity, because she could not remember ever being so pure. Jennie knew that to work her bed magic on Porter would send him reeling, and later, he would feel ashamed and blame her for driving out the animal in him. This had happened with other men who left before morning, and always, she awoke to find everything from their pockets heaped on her dressing table: silver coins, fraternal rings, watches, and (sometimes in their haste to leave her) wallets stuffed with bills, calling cards, even tintypes of their families. Jennie kept this bounty locked in a cedar box, her wintertime savings account. She wore the key around her neck. In his sleep, Porter touched the key, but Jennie moved his hand from her throat to her breast.

At daybreak, Jennie woke up alone in Porter's bed. Out of habit, she looked over to the dressing table and was relieved to find it just as it had been the night before. On the pillow next to her, she saw the note. *"Checking on stock. Breakfast at 8. Love, Wallace Porter."* That he'd signed his note so formally, with first and last name, made her laugh. She pictured him chewing on his pen, *Love, Wallace* staring at him from the white page and at the last minute scrawling *Porter* as an afterthought. Jennie rose from the bed, folded the note, and tucked it into her pants pocket where she hoped Porter might find it later, peeking out like a secret sign between them.

Jennie stood shivering before a full-length mirror, but her skin warmed with quiet heat the more she looked at herself. She was a stomach sleeper, and so knew that what she saw in the mirror—taut legs and buttocks, a cascade of blond hair—was what he'd seen that morning. To see herself head to toe was a rare treat. On the road, Jennie applied her makeup with the aid of a small mirror mounted into the lid of her Saratoga trunk. No full-length mirrors were allowed, since glass of any kind was a liability in railroad travel. When they made stands in cities, Jennie frequented department stores, not to shop, but to see herself fully. Standing before Porter's looking glass, she decided that what she wanted from this man was her own private Pullman car with her name painted boldly on the side for all America to see. Inside, it would be lined floor to ceiling with mirrors, and before each of her performances, she would stand in the middle of her car, costumed and beautiful, and know before she stepped into the ring exactly what the crowd would see. Jennie Dixianna was a star, one who suffered for her brightness, and she saw herself as deserving not only of her own railcar, but also of the power of prophecy.

Jennie pulled on her tights, her layers of clothes, wishing she had a nice dress to wear to breakfast instead of mannish pants. Deciding to leave her hair loose and long, she left her hairpins on Porter's dresser for him to find later. A maid would probably find them as well, but Jennie wanted to leave a mark, a whiff of indiscretion. She heard a noise from the window and peeked outside. A carriage driver sat stiff-armed at the reins, nose red, breath billowing from his mouth. A foot of snow had fallen overnight, and the horses stood to their fetlocks in heavy, wet snow. Elizabeth Cooper stepped lightly out of the carriage, followed by her daughter, Grace. They visited the winter quarters frequently, Jennie knew. Like a doting father, Porter took the girl on endless tours of the winter quarters to watch the performers, trainers, and animals. Perhaps, Jennie thought proudly, she'd made Porter forget he'd arranged a visit.

As Jennie descended the stairs, she heard the front door opening and closing, and called out, "How are we this morning!" Halfway down, she stopped. "Oh, I'm terribly sorry. I thought you were Mr. Porter."

Elizabeth stood frozen in the foyer, her eyes wide. "Excuse me. Where is Wallace?"

"Checking on the stock, I think."

Silence. Elizabeth lowered her gaze to her hands nestled in a gray muff. Jennie crossed her arms and propped herself against the newel post. Grace stepped forward. "You're Jennie Dixianna, the acrobat."

Jennie offered her hand. "That's right. I don't think we've ever met properly. And you are?"

"I'm Grace. Cooper." She shook Jennie's hand limply.

"Ah, yes. Your father is a friend of Mr. Porter. Doesn't he run that carriage business?"

"Cooper & Son."

"You have a brother?"

"No."

Jennie laughed. "Then why would he name his company that?"

Grace's brow creased. "I don't know, ma'am," she said finally. "I'll have to ask."

Jennie laughed again, like a string of tiny bells pealing.

"It was his father's business, if you must know," Elizabeth said. There was no mistaking the look in her eye— bright green jealousy. She grasped her daughter's hand. "Dear, please go find Uncle Wallace for me. He must be down at the barns." Once Grace was out the door, Elizabeth said, "Please tell Mr. Porter that I will be waiting for him and for Grace in here." She walked into the study, closing the door with a restrained click.

Jennie opened the front door and breathed deeply, letting the cold seep into her lungs. The snowfall the night before had been heavy, but the morning was crisp, blinding blue and white. The sounds of the morning were clean as ice—the squawks of hungry birds in the snow-tipped trees, a lion's roar from the barns. In the distance, she saw Porter trudging up the hill with Grace. He made slow, careful progress, like a man trying to cross a river of ice cracking with spiderwebs, like a man who wasn't sure if he wanted to get to the other side.

AT NIGHT the water cried. Sister told Jennie that long ago, Spanish priests used baubles and rum to lure the Biloxi Indians to Christ, away from their goddess mother. She rose from the sea, beckoning to her children from atop a mountain of wave and foam, and the Biloxi rushed into the sea to beg her forgiveness. She spread her arms, scooped them up, and took them with her to the bottom of the Gulf. Sister said, "The sea's brimming with failed mothers and their sorry children. All of them crying, and their tears lap the shore."

Jennie was sixteen when she finally told Sister. All of it. Saying nothing, Sister lit a lantern and motioned for Jennie to follow her into the night. They made their way through fields of sea oats to the site of her father's latest dig—a long trench cut into the beach. In the moonlight, Jennie saw shovelfuls of sand shooting out of the hole to the familiar beat of her father's grunts. Sister picked up a shovel, swung it over her shoulder like a spike-driving hammer, then handed it to Jennie. Sister whispered, "Your mama wouldn't have it no other way."

Because he stood below her in the trench, because it was dark, Jennie saw no blood, not even the look on his face. "Hear that," Sister said. Jennie heard nothing but the sound of the waves, and Sister said the water had ceased its crying. "Good sign," she said. They tossed everything in the hole with him—whiskey bottles, shovels, tinned meat, his tent and blanket, even the blackened logs from his campfire—and the earth obliged, swallowing Slater Marchette whole.

Later, Sister took a pair of scissors to his Confederate flag and fashioned a costume that bared plenty of midriff and thigh. She told Jennie a circus was showing up in Mobile. "A pretty little white girl like you, they'll snatch you up in a minute." When Jennie protested that she had no special talent, Sister opened the thin pages of her Bible and pointed to the verse that had nearly saved her mother's life. "You know this, you can do anything, child."

She became "Jennie Dixianna" the moment she signed her first performer's contract. Jennie Marchette was a dirty flopsy doll buried deep in the sand.

WALLACE PORTER visited Jennie Dixianna's bunkhouse that night and found her bundled up with quilts at the fireplace. Porter knelt down and put his head in her lap, massaging her sinewy thighs. He covered the pink bracelet scar with small kisses—in a few months, the Spin of Death would begin and her wrist would be red, always red. "How do you do this, every night," he asked.

Jennie kissed him softly and quickly, like a butterfly landing and fluttering away. She poured them each a glass of wine. "Some morning you had."

"Yes." Porter looked at the floor like a guilty boy. "I'm sorry if I was the cause."

"I forgot they were coming."

"What did you tell Mrs. Cooper?" Jennie asked, but she already knew the answer. She'd heard their angry whispers through his study door.

"What women you bring into this house is your business. And God's," Elizabeth had said, "but how could you expose my daughter to this?"

"I haven't exposed her to anything." Porter's tone was soft and soothing, like a man calming his angry wife.

"What happened here last night, Wallace? Don't lie to me."

"Nothing at all. Miss Dixianna and I were discussing her contract when the storm started. I couldn't very well send my star acrobat out into the blizzard to freeze to death, now could I?"

"No, I suppose not. But, Wallace, would you be involved with her? With a woman like that?"

Porter said nothing for a few seconds. Then, finally, he'd answered. "No."

Now he was in her bunkhouse, in her brass bed, and after they made love, Porter fell into a fitful sleep, suspended between wakefulness and dreams. He was immobile, his eyes pasted shut so he couldn't see, only feel,

Jennie straddling him. Then she spoke, she commanded, although her lips never moved. And Porter answered.

Do you love me?

Yes.

Have you loved Elizabeth?

Yes.

After Irene died? In your grief, you went to her?

She came to me.

She comforted you. Eleven years ago.

Yes.

And since then?

Nothing. Not once.

He woke before dawn. Jennie was already up, sitting beside him in a red robe. "Good morning," she said. "That must have been some dream you were having last night."

Porter groaned. "I didn't drink that much, did I?"

Jennie rubbed his temples. "You were thrashing all around and mumbling about love and secrets." She kissed his forehead. "I hoped you were dreaming of me."

"I was, I think. I don't really remember."

Porter left at first light, stumbling out the door like a blind man without even kissing her good-bye, but she knew he would return. Jennie Dixianna remade her bed with fresh sheets, sprinkling them with perfume. Pumping a basinful of water from the spigot, she washed herself in the firelight's glow. Water splashed onto fireplace bricks, sizzled, and disappeared.

Clean and naked, she took her cedar box down from the mantel and opened it with the key around her neck. Jennie counted the silver (twenty dollars and two bits), polished the rings (worth at least two hundred, she guessed), and tallied the paper (five crisp ten-dollar bills). The last she folded into a monogrammed money clip gleaned from a stoop-shouldered drummer she'd met in a St. Louis hotel, the one who'd asked if he could watch her use the chamber pot. Jennie surveyed the remaining contents: A to-do list written in a wife's delicate script. *"Coffee. Sugar. My laudanum. Your headache powders. Sally's penny candy. Potatoes."* A punched ticket stub. A folded-up family portrait *"The Hartley Family, Mendota, Illinois, 1866."* Penciled doodlings of strangers' faces. A priest's Bible. Did it belong to the one who'd wanted to have her in switched-around clothes—he in feather boa, she in collar and robe? Or was it the priest who liked to play with candles? Jennie thumbed through the Bible, smiling at the underlined fire and brimstone passages, and let her finger rest on Sister's secret verse.

And then Jennie wasn't in her bunkhouse, but back in that rarely remembered Alabama shack. Her past was a black cat that wanted to sit heavily on her heart, but most nights, Jennie kept the cat shooed away. How had it gotten inside? Perhaps it was the flicker of firelight, the opened box, the smell of clean skin. For a moment, Jennie was a little girl again, sitting on her mother's lap, looking down into a cigar box full of mementos (long since bartered or lost). Dixie Anna Marchette was telling her the story of her life one button, one bauble, one pressed flower at a time.

And then the box in her lap turned to cedar, brimming with paper and silver. It held nothing of her inside, nothing of Jennie Marchette. That girl was long gone. Years ago, the battle flag outfit had turned to tatters, and she'd burned it without a single regret. Instead of personal keepsakes, Jennie Dixianna's box contained the flotsam of men's pockets,

the skeletons that hung like ghosts in their back-hall closets. This was her story—a collage of broken glass from a
thousand shattered bottles, and each new shard made her
stronger and more beautiful. Jennie placed a slip of paper
inside the cedar box, "*Checking on stock. Breakfast at 8. Love,
Wallace Porter,*" and then she whispered inside. "Wallace
doesn't know, and Elizabeth will never tell, but Grace
Cooper is his daughter." Tomorrow, she'd ask Porter for a
big tin washtub, later a feather mattress, and slowly work
her way into a mirrored Pullman. If they failed to appear,
Jennie would play her ace. But in the meantime, she
closed her treasure chest and locked it for safekeeping.

THE LAST MEMBER
OF THE BOELA TRIBE

Chapter the First
How Bascomb Bowles Went from
Honey-bucket Boy to Pinhead

"HONEY-BUCKET BOY" is a sickly sweet euphemism for the men (mostly Negro) whose job it was to clean the pots into which steamboat passengers (mostly white) pissed and shit. Bascomb Bowles was such a boy. Born on a Georgia cotton plantation to a slave woman (father unknown), he and his mother moved to the promised land of Paducah, Kentucky, after the War. Having attained her long-cherished freedom, Bascomb's mother promptly died, leaving her fifteen-year-old son to find his own way in the world. He found a job cleaning honey buckets aboard the *Bayou Queen*, a steamboat paddling up and down the Ohio and Mississippi Rivers. He performed his duties faithfully and well until a steamy August morning in 1875. The *Bayou Queen* safely in port, Bascomb donned his Sunday best and walked into Paducah to see his first circus, a three-ringer making a two-night stand. The name of the circus was the Hollenbach Menagerie & Highway Hidalgos. In his pocket, Bascomb carried a sandwich wrapped in paper; he didn't know for sure, but he figured the candy butchers and concession stands served only whites. He was right about that.

But what Bascomb had no way of knowing was this: The circus proprietor, Clyde Hollenbach, needed to expand his sideshow displays from the Dark Continent. P. T. Barnum was at that time making a killing with a new curiosity—a pinhead named Zip, What-is-it? Supposedly, a party of big-game hunters had captured Zip while searching the river Gambia for gorillas. There, they found a new race, Darwin's missing link, naked people swinging from trees like monkeys. But Hollenbach knew it was all ballyhoo, just another one of Barnum's humbugs. He'd recently hired Barnum's disgruntled boss canvasman who'd told him the secret: Zip was actually a simpleminded Negro from New Jersey named Billy Jackson who was born with a small pointy head that—once shaved but for a topknot—appeared vaguely simian. The fellow earned about fifty a week, most of which was sent to his mother. Hollenbach marveled at the ingenuity of the gaff: take a Negro with a funny-shaped head, stick a spear in his hand, drape him in faux leopard skin, and voilà!

So he searched for his own Zip, What-is-it? and found a likely candidate touring with the Diamond Show, a Sioux billed as the Aztec Princess. Upon further examination, Hollenbach discovered the princess was actually a man, a fellow too feebleminded to unbuckle his belt or unbutton his trousers. The sideshow manager, sick of changing his charge's soiled pants, had taken away his underdrawers and fashioned a large skirt that could be easily lifted and lowered when nature called. The manager shook Hollenbach's hand and said, "The trouble with pinheads is most of them's retardates. If I was you, I'd just find a regular colored and shave their head and nobody'd know the difference anyway. It'd be a lot easier." Hollenbach agreed.

For weeks, he'd been trying to make a female Zip from materials at hand, namely his Zulu Queen, a black woman of enormous proportions named Pearly. Her "act" consisted of long periods of imperious sitting on a bamboo throne. Once a day, the sideshow lecturer announced:

"LADIES AND GENTLEMEN! AS THE SUN SETS, THE TIME HAS COME FOR AFRICAN ZULUS TO PRACTICE THEIR MOST ANCIENT RITUAL. GATHER ROUND AS OUR ZULU QUEEN PERFORMS THE FAMOUS FERTILITY DANCE!"

When a sizable crowd had gathered, Pearly would lumber down from her perch and initiate a series of jerking movements that quivered her loose folds of flesh. Despite her willingness to engage in this undignified display, Pearly would not consent to become a pinhead. "My contract say what I gotta do, and that's all I gotta do," she said. "I can read, you know."

On that August morning in Kentucky, Hollenbach was desperate for a pinhead and miserably hot. He walked heavily, like a man lumbering along chest deep in water. A handful of dark faces dotted the circus midway, but Bascomb's was the first he saw. Mopping his brow, Hollenbach walked right up and offered this perfect stranger a job.

Since his arrival on the lot, Bascomb had seen quite a few Negros. Roustabouts driving tent stakes to the beat of an old railroad worksong, slopping water into elephant drinking tubs. Down at the railroad siding, he'd even seen the circus version of himself, a young boy emptying the lavatory buckets from the Pullman sleeping cars. "No thank you, sir," Bascomb said to Hollenbach, bowing a little. "I've got me a job already."

Hollenbach explained he was looking for a star, not a roustabout. "I'll make you famous, boy. How do you pronounce your name?"

Bascomb hoped this wasn't some sick, cruel joke. "Bowles," he said. "Like this." He cupped his hands together.

Hollenbach took the cigar from his lips and stared into the air, talking to himself. "Bowles. Bowl-zuh. Bow-uhl. Boo-lah. Bol-lah." Hollenbach snapped his fingers. "I've got it." He raised his silver flask in a toast to himself, took a swig, then pointed at the sideshow banner line of canvas posters. "Ladies and Gentlemen! May I present—Boela Man, the African Pinhead!"

"Sir, I ain't from Africa." Bascomb paused. "I mean, I never been there." He didn't even want to ask what a pinhead was—it sounded painful.

Hollenbach clapped him on the back. "These rubes don't know Africa from Oregon," he said, jerking his thumb over his shoulder. Three white men were gathered around a grifter's carny stand, losing money as fast as it appeared from their overall pockets. "All you gotta do is act like you're from the jungle. Growl at the white folks. Scare 'em a little."

Bascomb nodded. No one had ever given him permission to scare white folks before.

"I'll pay you ten dollars a week," Hollenbach said.

Ten dollars a week! And all he had to do was shave his

head and wear funny clothes. Hollenbach said his services would be required in the sideshow tent—two shows a day—plus the occasional stint as a rigger during the big show. All circus personnel paraded through the tent for the opening spectacles, and he'd be especially needed during the Moorish Marauders of Hassam Ali and Down in Ole Virginny, whose themes required every dark face Hollenbach could muster. He'd have his own berth in the Pullman car for Negro employees—good accommodations, considering some roustabouts slept two to a bunk. Three squares a day in the cook tent. And he'd see the country, not just the same old river towns from a steamboat deck, but any town in that ever-growing web of railroad tracks. Bascomb didn't hesitate to sign the contract Hollenbach offered him—he put his X next to the X on the dotted line.

Pearly shaved his head, escorted him to the costume tent to be fitted for his African garb, and introduced him to the other sideshow performers, explaining the differences between them. Raju the Sword Swallower and the contortionist Mr. Rubber were working acts. Slappy the Seal Boy was a genuine freak, born with flipperish arms and legs. Koko the Tattooed Lady was a made freak, a woman with a map of the world etched on every inch of her skin. Ching the Human Pincushion wasn't a freak at all, Pearly explained, just a practitioner of an ancient healing technique. Satan's Child was a fake freak, a mummified baby with goat hooves sewed onto its hands, lying in a black coffin. "This is the Pickled Punk," Pearly said, leading him to a glass jar. A two-headed fetus floated in amber fluid, two sets of arms locked in permanent embrace.

Bascomb touched his topknot, which stuck out like a stumpy tail. "Where will I be?" he asked, scanning the raised platform inside the sideshow tent.

"Oh probably right next to me so I can keep an eye on you." She squeezed his arm. "I've been fooling these people a long, long time, honey. It ain't hard. Just act like a monkey that fell out the tree, and white people'll eat it up for sure." Pearly chuckled, a wry snort. "Way I see it, a nickel's a nickel. Dollar's a dollar. I'd be a blue bug if that's what they wanted to see, stupid fools."

That night, Pearly shared all she had with Bascomb. They told each other how they'd gotten from where they started (cotton fields, both of them) to where they were, drinking rum from tin cups, staring into a warm fire with money in their pockets and the world to see. When they retired to her tent, Pearly shared her cot, drawing him into her voluminous softness. It seemed a small price to pay—a shaved head and a few moments of benign humiliation each day—for this new life he'd been blessed enough to walk into, and he rejoiced to think he might never empty another honey bucket in his life, nor would his children, if he played his cards right. As he lay next to his Zulu Queen, the Boela Man listened to the night, sounds he knew by heart—bugs and birds and dogs—followed by the call of elephants and lions. Together, they made a music that stirred him, and Bascomb wondered if he'd unlocked a dimly remembered past deep inside.

Bascomb married Pearly within the year, and Hollenbach rejoiced: Circus marriages were a great boon for business, and this one, like the union of Tom Thumb and

Lavinia Warren, was voluntary. The Boela Man and the Zulu Queen were married over a hundred times: the first time in a small church, and then again and again and again during the big show. The bride and groom entered the hippodrome astride elephants, attended by Bengal tigers—a magnificent opening spectacle with fifty native dancing girls and fifty jungle drummers in bone necklaces. Problem was, Hollenbach didn't employ a hundred Negros. Some colored roustabouts were called in from driving tent poles for the spec, but the rest were white circus people in blackface.

They waited for children. Bascomb joked with Pearly, suggesting that perhaps her makeshift Fertility Dance was actually the opposite, an accidental Curse of Barrenness. Finally, in the thirteenth year of their marriage, Pearly bore a son they named Gordon, royal prince of the Boela Tribe of African Pinheads.

Chapter the Second
How Gordon Bowles Came to Know More
Than He Ever Wanted to Know about Elephants

GORDON LOVED elephants. From his voracious reading, from pestering elephant handlers, he knew that the African elephant has bigger ears, more toenails, and a different trunk tip than the Asian elephant. He knew female elephants spent two years pregnant, and that their nipples were between their front legs. He knew they ate 150 pounds of hay a day, plus an occasional watermelon for dessert. Walking trunk to tail, they had his mother's brand of lumbering grace, a proud and floating fatness. He admired the dexterity of the elephant's trunk—part nose, part hand—a versatile appendage which could also be (depending on the circumstances) cowboy lariat, swath-cutting scythe, water bucket, showman's hook, lightning bolt, mother's hand, flyswatter, trumpet, crane, or exclamation point. Sometimes, a trunk could be a billy club, a loosely held weapon capable of knocking the wind—even the life—out of a man.

He favored an Asian elephant, a bull named Caesar with gold balls on the tips of its tusks. Caesar's trunk, Gordon believed, was a third and more powerful eye, a cable that closed the incredible distance between its head and the earth under its feet. On the road, troublemaking boys often threw handfuls of whatnot into the elephant stalls: peanuts mixed with coins and bottle caps. Caesar could sift and sort with its trunk—suck up the peanuts, deposit the money into the pockets of the keepers, and blow the bottle caps back in the boys' startled faces.

Gordon grew up in Pullman cars and the sideshow tent, but he spent each winter in a kind of normalcy, rising from a trundle bed each morning in a bunkhouse. His parents, Bascomb and Pearly, nursed coffee at the kitchen table, flames licking logs in the fireplace. Some mornings, he pretended this was a different life—a cold winter morning in Kentucky or Ohio or Pennsylvania, perhaps—the life he might have lived if his father had only turned Hollenbach down that day in Paducah. But then the chow bell would ring, calling them to the cookhouse for breakfast, and in the distance, he'd hear a lion roar good morning. Elephants ambled by on their way to the river for a bath, and so Gordon knew he'd risen at the winter quarters of

the Great Porter Circus, which had purchased the Hollenbach menagerie and properties not long before he was
born. This was Lima, Indiana, hometown of proprietor
Wallace Porter, who had a sweet spot for children and allowed Gordon unlimited access to his private library and
elephant barn. All summer, Gordon longed for November,
the time when his family let their hair grow (Pearly had finally consented to shaving her head for the sake of family
solidarity) and packed away their leopard-skin robes. In the
winter, he could talk to his parents without having to
grunt, amuse himself without having to throw sawdust. He
longed for cold and snow the way schoolboys long for summer—winter freed him from the circus.

BE WARNED. This isn't a pretty story.

In the spring of 1901, an outbreak of influenza hit
Lima and the winter quarters, sending many to their beds,
including Gordon. In a fevered haze, he heard the commotion of April 25—the arrival of wagons, men yelling,
horses galloping, guns firing. A knock on the door. Voices
whispering in the kitchen. His mother stroking his arm,
telling him not to worry. There'd been an accident. In the
afternoon, Gordon awoke from a nap and heard his mother
in the next room saying, "What will become of Nettie? Poor
woman with a brand-new baby." *They're talking about Hans
Hofstadter,* he thought, the ill-tempered elephant trainer
who sometimes shooed him out of the animal barns with a
pitchfork. He had a wife, Nettie, and a newborn son, Ollie.

"Porter will keep her on somehow, I'm sure," Gordon
heard his father say. "Can't say as much for that elephant."

They rehashed what they'd heard: Hans Hofstadter was dead, beaten and drowned in the river by a bull with gold-tipped tusks. His assistant, Elephant Jack, had arrived in the midst of it, a helpless witness to Hofstadter's attempts to escape. To atone for his tardiness, he'd taken the first shots at the offending elephant—Caesar. Out of ammunition, Elephant Jack had called for reinforcements; they were out there now, putting the elephant down.

At suppertime, Gordon pretended to be asleep when his parents checked on him. As soon as they left for dinner at the cookhouse, Gordon dressed quickly and snuck outside, following the sound of gunfire he'd heard in the distance. Caesar's path was easy to follow—a broken fence in the camel lot, enormous footprints heading toward a stand of trees. The toppled elephant lay on its side in a fallow field surrounded by a posse of men holding lanterns, guns, and rope. (Gordon wondered why they'd brought rope—to catch it? To hang it?) They stood shifting on their feet, crunching the frozen earth beneath them. Elephant Jack was recounting what he'd seen at the river. Hofstadter tossed ten feet in the air, his slow swim back to shore, and Caesar's final trick—holding the struggling keeper underwater. Gordon peered around the men's legs and saw Caesar, head and body bullet riddled, eyes shot out and crying blood.

Gordon recognized some of the men from the winter quarters, but some were unfamiliar, local farmers who'd volunteered, he thought, not so much to protect their homes, families, and livestock from a rampaging animal, as to have the opportunity to act like big-game hunters. Now that it was done, the hunters stood contemplating their kill, discussing, estimating, speculating: the number of shots fired ("somewheres around two hundred," a man said); the amount of strychnine ingested, concealed in three cored apples ("enough to kill five or six horses," said another); the length of the unsheathed penis lying like a dead snake on the ground ("Three feet," Elephant Jack said, slicing it off with his knife. "Good leather for tanning"); and the value of Caesar's sawed-off tusks ("five thousand bucks, give or take a few hundred"). Gordon tasted bile in his mouth and swallowed hard.

The men then turned the discussion to cause and effect. What made the elephant turn on Hofstadter after many years on the road together?

"A few weeks ago," one handler said, "I saw a wet spot on the side of his head." This musky oil meant Caesar might have been in musth—a condition not unlike a dog in heat—which produced in male pachyderms a powerful, dangerous want.

"Hofstadter'd been down for a week with this flu," someone else said. "Maybe the sickness changed his smell. Spooked the elephants?" Gordon heard affirmative grunts around him.

"A week chained up in a smelly barn probably didn't help matters any," the general agent, Colonel Ford, said, cutting an angry glance at Elephant Jack. During Hofstadter's convalescence, the assistant had been free from the keeper's watchful eye and had neglected his duties— he'd thrown new hay on top of moldy old, failed to remove the leg irons once a day to exercise the elephants.

The reporter from the *Lima Journal* pointed to Caesar's lolling tongue with the toe of his boot—the pink flesh marred by black circles, the exact circumference of a lit cigar. "Hofstadter enjoyed a cigar," someone said. Nobody said anything, which told Gordon that it was the correct explanation. Hofstadter had instigated his own brutal demise.

Gordon looked up and prayed for Caesar's enormous soul. Did elephants go to heaven, he wondered, or did they return to the land from which they'd been taken as calves? Maybe they went home in the holds of magic ships, like the ones that brought them from Africa and Ceylon and India. He felt a nudge at his shoulder. A Negro handler named Sugar offered him a swig from a bottle of whiskey. Gordon expected it to taste good, like liquid butterscotch. Instead, he gagged on the first sip—flames burned his mouth and throat, then embers glowed in his stomach. It wasn't the same fire, not a cigar's orange coal, but it was all he could stand to know of Caesar's pain.

During all the commotion, no one noticed Elephant Jack stuff his hand deep into his pocket. No one saw him make a fist around his cigar. No one had ever caught him in the elephant barn during his benders—he was a simple man, but a mean drunk, given to torment and torture. Either way you look at it—the week of neglect or the cigars—Hofstadter's death was on Elephant Jack's head. He knew it, but he stared at the ground and kept it to himself.

The article written up by the *Lima Journal* reporter made no mention of Elephant Jack's dereliction of duty, nor the cigar burns. The headline read:

ELEPHANT IS KILLED
CAESAR IS BROUGHT TO JUSTICE
Pays the Penalty for the Murder
of Hans Hofstadter with his Life
Elephant Jack Pursues the Beast
to the Fields and Shoots Him

Chapter the Third
How Verna Bowles Learned about
the Relative Nature of Beauty and Truth

LIKE A LOT OF people, Wallace Porter went belly up in 1929.
The years that followed were thin and mean, and finally in
1939, he had to sell everything to the Coleman Bros. Circus, who opted not to renew the contract of the Boela
Tribe. It was no great matter. Three years earlier, Pearly's
heart had burst like an overfilled balloon, old Bascomb
was in failing health himself, and Gordon (a reluctant performer but loyal son) was more than ready to leave the
tribe. Like many other retired circus people, the Bowles
men moved into Lima and bought a house. Every day, Bascomb sat on the porch swing like a lifeless dog, his dull
eyes watching cars pass by. Try as he might, he couldn't
come to terms with his stagnant life.

He died soon after.

Gordon married Mimi, a woman large in spirit and
small of frame, a former vaudeville dancer who gave lessons in town. In the last months of her pregnancy, Mimi
had to carry her enormous belly around like a rock in a
sling. Their daughter, Verna, was a fourteen-pound baby.

Mimi died soon after.

By the time Verna was born, the Great Porter Circus was long gone, but the stories remained. Her father saw each empty barn and corn-stubbled field as a historical monument, marked *Something Happened Here.* Always, he spoke of Lima's days gone by with great solemnity, even sadness. Verna felt that for every story he told (and there were many), there was another just behind it, one he'd never tell. He kept the past divvied up inside—the one he spoke of, stored in a red and gold music box that played cheerful calliope music, and the past he hid in a padlocked black trunk, stashed in a rarely used closet of his heart.

Verna bore no resemblance to her pretty, petite mother. She cursed her nappy hair and stout body. In the fifth grade, she bloomed to a whopping size 34DD, and her breasts laced themselves with stretch marks. Ashamed, Verna developed a slump-shouldered stoop and went on crying jags in the bathtub. Her father, bless his heart, did what he could to make her feel better. He said, "Verna, honey, there isn't just one kind of beauty."

In aught nine, he said, the Congolese Women toured with Porter's circus. While on African safari, some frog named Guy Farlais had stumbled upon a remote tribe of nearly naked Congolese who, lucky for Farlais, spoke a kind of French. The women had lips like duck bills—from infancy, girls of the tribe wore saucers in their lips to make them bigger and more beautiful. Farlais promised the chief untold riches if he'd lease twenty women to him for a tour of Europe and America. He billed them as "The Greatest Educational Attraction of All Time!" and made a tidy profit for himself and Porter.

When the Congolese Women first saw the Boela Tribe's

black faces, they'd gestured wildly toward the horizon, speaking in a strange tongue Gordon couldn't understand. They cried a lot, especially when they saw Porter's one African elephant, Sambo. Stroking his bristly hide, the Congolese tugged on the elephant's chains, sending a plaintive wail into the sky. They missed their children back home ("nearly a hundred of the little monkeys," Farlais laughed). Each night, they danced and sang before boarding the circus train. The Congolese taught the Boela Tribe this number; Porter loved it and called it "The Ceremonial Hunting Dance," but Gordon called it "The Lost Child Dance"—African mothers calling to their children far across the ocean.

"Those women must have been some kind of ugly." Verna said.

"Not to their husbands," he said matter-of-factly. "It's like how Chink men likes little feet, so if they wants their daughters to find a good husband, they bind up their toes till they can barely walk. I seen some once. Mrs. Ching. Her family was acrobats that trouped with us. Had feet curled up like fists, but she wasn't nothing but proud." He thought this a better example of cross-cultural beauty than the Hottentot Venus—in her tribe, women hung weights from their privates, stretching them like earlobes until the skin flapped at the knees.

"Whatever happened to them? The Congolese."

Gordon shook his head. "Porter sent 'em home. Eventually. It's a horrible thing, taking things away from where they belong to put money in a man's pocket." His eyes were far away.

Verna never told her father this, but sometimes she

wished that the Congolese had been forced to stay. Maybe in the sideshow, she could have been "The Ugliest Congolese Woman!" Maybe there, standing next to saucer-lipped women, she could have been beautiful.

HER FATHER worked for Ollie Hofstadter (son of Hans the elephant trainer), who'd opened his own business, Clown Alley Cleaners. After school, Verna met her father at the store, and every day Mr. Ollie said, "There's my big gal, the spitting image of her grandmother," like it was a compliment to be compared to Pearly (Verna had seen pictures). But even his insensitivity couldn't keep her away from her bedroom window on summer nights. That's where Verna sat listening to the snatches of stories floating up to her from the porch below, where her father and Mr. Ollie often sat passing whiskey between them. One night toward the end of a bottle, Mr. Ollie took a familiar story (his short-lived clowning career) all the way to its never-before-spoken end—the night he killed his best friend, Jo-Jo the Clown.

Their act was pretty standard. Big guy (Jo-Jo) terrorizes little guy (Mr. Ollie). Tables turn. Little guys gets revenge. *Laughter!* They'd done it hundreds of times, but that night they were drunker than usual, so drunk that Jo-Jo forgot to put on his wooden wig. When Mr. Ollie struck Jo-Jo's head with the hatchet, he felt not the familiar *stick* into the wooden wig, but rather a sickening *give*. Jo-Jo fell into the sawdust. *Laughter!* Clowns emerged with a stretcher to carry Jo-Jo away, but they'd grabbed a prop stretcher by mistake—they lifted the poles, leaving him on the ground. *Laughter!* The spotlight followed Mr. Ollie as he ran across the center ring crying, tripping on his big, floppy shoes. *Laughter! Applause!* He waited for the band to play Sousa's "Stars and Stripes Forever," the circus emergency song that would prompt the ushers to clear the tent, but instead, they broke into "Strike Up the Band."

Mr. Ollie sighed. "It was all my fault."

"Now, he was drunk, too," Gordon said.

"Still." A long pause. "Whose fault was it my father died?"

Another story she'd never heard before. Verna heard ice tinkling against glass, then another long swig. The two men on the porch were quiet for a long time.

"I know he died down at the river, but no one would tell me much else," Mr. Ollie said. "My momma never spoke of it, except in these nightmares where she talked to him in German."

"What'd she say?"

Mr. Ollie sighed. "I never learned German."

Silence. Finally, Gordon told him. Like this:

Hofstadter arrived the morning of April 25, 1901, still sick from flu, smelling of sweat and camphor. Elephant Jack, his assistant handler, was nowhere in sight—sleeping off an all-night drunk. He'd taken a vacation in Hofstadter's absence, and the barn stank of moldy hay and dung. The elephants tugged on the chains eating at the flesh of their tree-trunk feet, a sign he'd neglected to remove the leg irons each day and walk the elephants around the paddocks. Their trunks swung hypnotically, heads rocking back and forth, the malady of boredom. Hofstadter chomped an unlit cigar in his furious jaw. Unlocking the chains, the keeper hustled the elephants out of the barn to the river for a bath.

He was standing on the bank when, out of the blue, Caesar picked him up with his trunk and tossed him ten feet into the air. Hofstadter landed with a smack in the middle of the river. His head struck a rock, and that was it.

"It was quick," Gordon said. "He didn't feel no pain. It was bad luck is all. A hoodoo."

"No wonder Elephant Jack took such good care of my momma and me," Mr. Ollie said. "He neglected the animals and spooked them. My mother always told me circus animals is cared for the very best. I guess that wasn't always the case."

"No, it wasn't," Gordon said quietly.

Mr. Ollie thanked him and teetered home.

Later, Verna found her father in the kitchen. "Grilling," he called it—cracking eggs into a skillet with potatoes, onions, and leftovers. Plopping down into a kitchen chair, she felt a whoosh of air from the cushion, the sound of the fat woman settling in. Even alone in the kitchen with her father, she was embarrassed, overwhelmingly aware of her body. She wished, along with her size, she'd also inherited Grandma Pearly's renowned self-assuredness.

Gordon joined her at the table, squirting ketchup on his concoction. Finally, she had to ask him—how old was he when Mr. Ollie's daddy died? He put down his fork. "You been snooping again, girl?" Verna hung her head. "Lemme tell you something. Lemme tell you the truth." Gordon told her. Like this:

Once while playing in the elephant barn, he'd watched Hofstadter put his cigar out on Caesar's tongue with a sickening sizzle. He saw Hofstadter die that day at the river, watched Caesar take revenge—and was glad. Hofstadter hit the water, but he didn't die instantly, like he'd told Mr. Ollie. It took a while. The elephant held a thrashing Hofstadter at the bottom of the river with his feet and tusks. After, Elephant Jack found him underwater, his eyes and mouth wide open, his curses floating helplessly down the Winnesaw River. The bullhook—bent into a sad C—was still clenched in the keeper's angry fist. He saw what came after. Two hundred bullets and seven poison apples. Elephant Jack's knife. Caesar's penis and its intended use. Black circles on a pink tongue.

Yes, yes, yes. All Gordon actually saw was Caesar's corpse—after the fact. But understand: Over the years, he had lost the ability to separate what he'd seen from what he'd heard, what he knew for sure from what he'd surmised. In his mind, he *had* been there, hiding in the hayloft watching Hofstadter brand Caesar's tongue, standing on the banks of the bloody Winnesaw. He saw these things clearly, like photographs in his head.

Verna cried, regretting that she'd prompted her father to open up the dark box. "You don't want to tell Mr. Ollie his dad was a bad man."

"He's my friend. He loves his daddy, and he'd never believe any different anyway." Gordon rinsed his plate in the sink. "Sometimes you run across a man whose granddaddy kept slaves. Just you *try* telling him what my daddy told me about that, what his mama told him..." He couldn't finish. "Time for bed," he said.

The next day, Gordon took Verna downtown to the Lima County Historical Museum. A few months earlier, the local historical society had turned the old Robertson Hotel into a makeshift gallery. He escorted her through the crowded displays of Indian arrowheads, pioneer butter churns, and circus artifacts. Finally, he led her to a raised pedestal in a far corner, upon which sat a large animal skull. Without being told, she knew it was Caesar's.

"Read that horseshit." He pointed to a framed clipping gone yellow with age.

ELEPHANT IS KILLED
CAESAR IS BROUGHT TO JUSTICE
Pays the Penalty for the Murder
of Hans Hofstadter with his Life
Elephant Jack Pursues the Beast
to the Fields and Shoots Him

She touched a bullet hole on the skull. A voice yelled, "You! Girl! Don't touch that," and Verna snatched her hand back. The woman who'd rung up their quarter admission peered over her spectacles. "You should tell her what happened," Verna said to her father, glancing at the woman.

Gordon dismissed her with a waved hand. "She don't care. The truth ain't nothing but a lie that folks learn to live with."

GORDON DIED when Verna was nineteen. She inherited the family fortune: her mother's Victrola and red tap shoes, the mortgage on her father's house, the unpaid loan on his car. To help her out, Mr. Ollie gave Verna a job at Clown Alley Cleaners doing alterations and working the steam-iron press. For a short time, Verna became known in Lima for her generosity—she gave freely of her food and whiskey and cigarettes and bed and breasts—and some men took what she offered. It wasn't a bad life, considering what she had to work with, but secretly Verna mourned. She dreamed of the old circus days, longing for the steam locomotive and the romance of cinder, for the sweet promise of escape. Sometimes, she wished it was a hundred years earlier and old Hollenbach was still around to save her. For the time being though, she'd have to make do in a world without sideshows.

Chapter the Last
How Chicky Bowles Avenged Caesar and Found His Place in the World

VERNA NAMED her son Charles Bowles, but his teachers insisted on calling him Chuck. In grade school, the kids called him *Up Chuck* and *Num Chuck,* which inevitably led to *Dumb Chuck.* The girls called him *Chuck Chuck Goose* and flapped their arms and honked. The boys called him *Fuck Chuck* and *Chuck Sucks,* until one boy stumbled upon *Chucky,* which started a new theme: *Yucky Chucky, Sucky Chucky, Chuckman, Duckman, Fuckman.* When they ran out of rhymes, they just called him *nigger.* Nothing much rhymed with it—bigger, jigger, digger—so they left the word alone, all by itself.

Verna hated the name Chuck. She called her son Chicky, because he was such a tiny baby, her little baby chick. But year after year, he stayed small, his body refusing to grow. In fairy tales, Chicky saw others like him: fairies, elves, goblins, gremlins, gnomes, and hobbits. When he was ten, the doctors gave him a name: *achondroplastic dwarf.* The kids at school would find other words: *Shrimp, Teeny, Tiny, Lucky the Leprechaun, Munchkin, Shorty, Shortstuff, Pee Wee, Pipsqueak, Tattoo, Baby, Itsy Bitsy, Runt, Half-pint, Junior, Mighty Mite,* and *Gary Coleman.*

Over dinner, Verna told her sometime boyfriend Reggie (Chicky's father) about the doctors' diagnosis. Despite Verna's reassurances that Chicky's size wasn't his fault any more than hers, Reggie shoved himself back from the table and slammed out the screen door. Standing in the backyard in the fading summer light, he threw up his arms and screamed, "What do you expect from a family of freak-show niggers?" From the bedroom window, Chicky watched his father sitting in the backyard, smoking cigarettes one after the other, flicking them like fireflies into the air. In the small hours, he heard the screen door squeak, footsteps coming up the stairs. He closed his eyes and waited for his father to come rub his back—sometimes, once in a while, Reggie put Chicky to sleep like this—but he fell asleep waiting. In the morning, Verna awoke to a half-empty closet and her grocery money gone. They cried for a while, then went downstairs to make pancakes.

IN THE TENTH grade, Chicky wrote an essay for school about the history of dwarfdom. All of his findings were true, albeit somewhat monstrous and bizarre. His teacher, Mr. Flowers, suspected the entire paper was fabricated, but because he'd always felt sorry for the little guy, and because he didn't feel like checking Chicky's sources, he decided to "let it slide." Mr. Flowers gave the paper an A and felt better about himself for having done so.

The Pros and Cons of Being a Dwarf
by Charles Bowles

There are many cons to being a dwarf. In
ancient times, dwarfs were left outside to die,
either from exposure to the cold and heat or from
being torn apart by wolves. Sometimes they were
sacrificed to the gods so the tribe could get rid
of its sins. In some parts of the Orient and South
America, small children were captured and placed
in small crates—their heads free outside the
boxes, their bodies crouched inside. For years,
the makers fed the children's mouths and emptied
their wastes through small trapdoors. Over time,
the children became like root-bound plants. When
fully grown, the children were freed and taken
away to some faraway land, "found" in the woods
by their own makers, who displayed them in freak
shows as an ancient race of being never before
seen on Earth. Once in ancient Rome, the dwarf
population decreased. A ruler who loved to be
entertained by dwarfs decreed that a small
percentage of newborn children should be deprived
of vital nutrients to stunt their growth.

Things didn't get much better as time went
on. In the Middle Ages, monkeys and dwarfs were
both considered subhuman and were kept chained at
the sides of rich noblemen to provide amusement
for the court. Peter the Great and Catherine
de Médicis bred dwarfs in barns, like dogs in
kennels, trying to find the perfect strain of
dwarf playmates for the royal family. Adolf Hitler

exterminated dwarfs to rid German society of their
tainted genes. Before they were sent to the gas
chambers at Auschwitz, Hitler hired artists to
sketch dwarf bodies. The drawings were categorized
as scientific findings and filed at the Bureau
of Race. Also, dwarfs die in the womb from
therapeutic abortions.

On the bright side, there are some pros to
being a dwarf. An old story says that dwarfs were
formed by God's hand from the leftover clay molded
around Adam's rib to make Eve. In ancient Egypt,
dwarfs were honored: the gods Ptah and Bes were
dwarfs. A wealthy Egyptian dwarf, Seneb, and
his normal-sized wife and children were buried
in the famous tomb at Giza. The cult of Isis
associated dwarfs with fertility, depicting them
with large phalluses!

There were many famous dwarfs in Europe, such
as Jeffrey Hudson who was presented to Queen
Henrietta, wife of Charles I, inside a cold pie.
Hudson dueled normal-sized men over beautiful
ladies, carried important messages for the queen,
and advised the king on matters of state. During
the French Revolution, a dwarf spy named
Richebourg let himself be carried around like a
baby in order to smuggle messages back and forth
between aristocrats. It is rumored that the
classic baby face—the Gerber baby—is actually a
drawing of a midget named Franz Ebert. Throughout
time, there have been lots of famous little
people, such as Aesop, Attila the Hun, Charles III

of Italy, Toulouse-Lautrec, the Lollipop Guild,
Billy Barty, Herve Villachez, Grumpy, Sneezy,
Sleepy, Happy, Dopey, Bashful, and Doc.

Maybe the most famous little people in American
history are General Tom Thumb and Lavinia Warren.
Invitations to their wedding were very popular in
1863. On their honeymoon tour, the couple visited
the White House as the guests of Abraham Lincoln,
who couldn't take his eyes off Lavinia because she
looked just like Mary Todd, only shorter. When the
president asked the general his opinion of the
Civil War, Tom Thumb replied, "My opinion is that
my friend Barnum could settle the whole affair
in a month!" Midgets and dwarfs aren't allowed
to join circuses anymore, so many of them have
retired to Gibsonton, Florida. The local post
office there has installed a "Little People Only"
line with steps leading up to the window.

In conclusion, I have shown that while there
are some drawbacks to being a dwarf, history shows
that if given the chance, dwarfs can contribute
greatly to society.

Because his legs were too small to climb steps easily,
Chicky rode the short bus, the one for kids with disabilities.
Painted on the side was LIMA COMMUNITY SCHOOLS, NO. 5,
but Chicky wished they'd just write RETARD BUS since
that's what everyone called it anyway. Each morning and
afternoon, he joined his fellow passengers: Three-Fingered
Louise with a shriveled-up hand like a claw; wheelchair-
bound Aaron the Always Crying Boy, whose mechanized

elevation into the bus—a long and noisy procedure—never failed to attract passersby; and Lonnie the Masturbator, with crossed eyes, red pimples, and a hand that wouldn't quit. Sometimes Chicky wanted to tell the bus driver, "Just keep driving." The Retard Bus could travel cross-country, just like the trains that once carried his grandfather and great-grandfather. They'd stop in some podunk town, parade down Main Street, and in the evening, display themselves in all their imperfect glory under canvas and harsh lights.

But Chicky knew this would never happen. Times had changed. People still looked at freaks, but not like they once had, with amazement and mirth and awe, but with something worse—the quickly averted gaze of shame, the teary-eyed glance of pity. When he stood waiting for the Retard Bus, when he walked down the street with his mother, when he paid for gum at the B&B Grocery—Chicky felt Lima watching him. Instead of court jester, he was the poor, poor poster boy.

Chicky got off the Retard Bus at Clown Alley Cleaners to wait for his mother, but mostly he went to sit on the counter and listen to Mr. Ollie's circus stories. Like the time Annie Oakley shot a quarter from between his fingers at forty paces. The time Lima made the front page of the *New York Times* because Rasputin's daughter was mauled by a lion out at the winter quarters—she'd escaped Russia by joining the circus after the Mad Monk's assassination. As Chicky got older, Mr. Ollie's stories got bawdier, full of genitalia and deformities. The severed finger floating in cloudy formaldehyde Wallace Porter passed off as Napoleon's pecker. The drag queen named Monte Alto who danced the hoochie-coochie dressed as "Monsieur et Madame," a fake hermaphrodite. The Four-Legged Woman named Trixie with the legs and lower torso of her parasitic Siamese twin sticking out of her stomach. Mr. Ollie looked to make sure Verna was out of earshot. "Trixie and her sister was both fully operational," he said, chucking Chicky on the shoulder, "if you know what I mean."

Chicky did—sort of. He was a very innocent sixteen.

One day, Mr. Ollie hustled Chicky back to his private office. An old daguerreotype hung on the wall—a skinny fellow walking next to an elephant during a city street parade. "This here is my pop," he said. "He died when I was only a wee babe."

"My dad left when I was ten," Chicky said, remembering the screen door slamming.

Mr. Ollie touched his shoulder and told the story of his father's death, the version he'd heard from Chicky's grandfather Gordon while they rocked on the front porch all those years ago. Chicky had never heard it before.

"I don't tell many people that story," Ollie said, looking at the floor.

"That's the skull down at the museum." Chicky pointed to the elephant in the photograph.

Mr. Ollie nodded. "I heard they did that. Never been able to bring myself to go down there and see it myself." Opening his desk drawer, he pulled out a leather drawstring pouch and withdrew a sliver of yellowish bone. "I do have this though. Ivory. A piece of that elephant's tusk. Elephant Jack gave it to me when I was a little boy. A memento, he said. Something to remember things by."

On the slow walk home, Chicky told his mother about

the mean bull elephant that killed Hans Hofstadter and the tusk in the pouch, but she stopped him midway and told him the real story, the one her father had told her that night in the kitchen, so long ago. "My dad told me Elephant Jack cut off that poor animal's pecker intending to make purses and wallets with the leather." She shook her head. "I'll bet that pouch ain't rawhide."

"I touched it," Chicky said, stunned.

"Well, now you know not to."

Chicky looked up. "Mama, should we tell Mr. Ollie?" He meant the pouch, everything. Verna stroked his head. "Sometimes the truth don't set you free, honey. Sometimes it's the very worst thing."

AFTER HIGH SCHOOL graduation, Chicky started collecting disability. He gave Verna most of his check and spent the rest at Snake Eyes, a downtown bar. The clientele consisted mostly of laid-off railroaders, bankrupt farmers, and members of the Sons of KY, a biker gang who wore the Confederate battle flag emblazoned on their hogs and jean jackets. Chicky shouldn't have been allowed in the door—he was underage, not to mention black—but he'd become a permanent fixture of the place, its mascot and inventor of the Chicky Dance, a variation of the Chicken Dance he performed atop the pool tables. Marty Cutter, a regular, said it was a good-luck dance—IU usually won if Chicky danced before Big Ten games.

Sometimes Marty offered Chicky ten bucks to be his human ashtray—follow him around all night with a beanbag ashtray plopped on his head. Other times, Buddy the bartender gave Chicky free beers if he'd circulate during happy hour with baskets of french fries and onion rings on his head. Business boomed, and Chicky was in bliss. He basked in the spotlight, proud to be known as a funny guy, a useful guy. If one night he failed to show up, people called him at home, begging him to get his ass down to Snake Eyes.

At Chicky's twenty-first birthday celebration, Marty Cutter asked Chicky if he could balance a mug of beer on his head. Chicky did it, no problem. As he retrieved his drink, Marty looked down at Chicky's head, which was directly at crotch level. "Damn Chicky, too bad you ain't female. And white. Or I'd have to marry you."

A Son of KY clapped Marty on the back. "You got that right, man."

Someone called out, "Who says you gotta marry someone who holds your beer and sucks your dick?"

Laughter.

Buddy leaned over the bar. "Way I heard it, Marty don't even care if it's white. Or female."

Marty went red. Everyone knew he'd served five years at Pendleton for breaking and entering—a fairly long stretch. They laughed uncomfortably and returned to their drinks, casting sideways glances at Marty when they thought he wasn't looking.

When Chicky went to take a leak, Marty said, "You know what I heard. Chicky hangs out up at the park at night. In the *restrooms.*" Rumor had it the gray cinder block bathrooms at Winnesaw Park were queer hangouts.

"That's bullshit, Marty," Buddy said, wiping the bar with a mildewy rag.

Marty crossed his arms. "At my parole meeting, a deputy told me they picked him up in there during a drug bust." His story was a complete fabrication, but Marty figured no one would willingly approach Johnny Law to check. "Mark my words," Marty said, "Chicky's a swisher."

When Chicky emerged from the bathroom, Marty yelled, "Jesus Chick, took you long enough. You keepin' company in there or what?" Everyone laughed uncomfortably and returned to their drinks, casting sideways glances at Chicky when they thought he wasn't looking. He laughed, but didn't get the joke. For the rest of the night, no one asked him to do the Chicky Dance or put anything on his head, so he went home early, a little deflated.

The next night, a winter storm warning was in effect, more than ten inches predicted. The first flakes floated down like dandelion fluff. When Chicky walked into Snake Eyes, the temperature inside was warm, but the reception was ice cold, nothing but turned backs and hard stares. Undaunted, Chicky clambered up onto a barstool, plunked down a dollar bill, and asked Buddy for a draft. The bartender stood with folded arms and didn't move.

"Hey. Can I get a drink or what?"

"Depends," Buddy said, finally walking over. "Are you gonna fix what you done. Or what?"

Chicky looked around. Everyone was staring at him, except for Marty Cutter whose eyes were fixed on the black-and-white above the bar. "I don't know what you're talking about, Buddy."

"Lemme show you then." He walked around the bar, yanked Chicky off his barstool, and shoved him outside

onto the sidewalk. They walked into the alley that ran
alongside Snake Eyes. Buddy was in shirtsleeves, his arms
and nose flushed red in the cold. "What the hell do you
think you're doing writing shit like this on my place?"

There on the brick wall. Spray painted. GAY POWER. A
foot and a half off the ground.

"I didn't do this, man." Chicky looked around ner-
vously. A few guys had followed them into the alley.

"Don't give me that shit, Chick. It's a perfect match."
Buddy thrust him toward the wall. The graffiti just met
him at chest level. "I don't want to see you around here
anymore. Got me?"

Marty came out, mug in hand. "Probably has AIDS or
something." He started to take a drink, then seemed to
think better of it and threw his mug at the words behind
Chicky. Shattered glass settled on Chicky's shoulders like
icy snow. "Like that kid over in Kokomo trying to go to
school and spread it all over."

"Ryan White," someone said.

Marty nodded. "Yeah."

A Son of KY pulled a knife from his boot. Chicky
scanned the cold, hard faces of the men surrounding him.
They stood shifting on their feet, crunching the frozen
earth beneath them. Clouds of warm breath spilled into the
sky. Chicky felt tears coming and ran out of the alley.

"Don't y'all come back now, ya hear?" Marty said.

For the rest of the night, the snow fell thickly, coating
the streets and sidewalks that Chicky roamed. Last call in
Lima was at one, so he stood across the street from Snake
Eyes, hidden in shadows, to watch them all stumble into
their cars and fishtail it home. Then, Lima was silent but for

the buzz of streetlights. Stop signs shook in the increasing wind, and stoplights swayed pendulously, their green, yellow, and red faces clotted with snow. Chicky turned toward home, his heart so despondent he doubted his ability to put one foot in front of the other.

Two blocks later, he passed the Lima County Historical Museum. He'd toured its contents on numerous school field trips, passed it almost every day without noticing it really. Tonight though, Chicky saw that they'd moved the elephant skull from its pedestal and placed it in the display window. They'd framed the 1901 newspaper article, and for the first time, he stopped to read it, starting with the bold headline:

ELEPHANT IS KILLED
CAESAR IS BROUGHT TO JUSTICE
Pays the Penalty for the Murder
of Hans Hofstadter with his Life
Elephant Jack Pursues the Beast
to the Fields and Shoots Him

Chicky stared into Caesar's eye sockets, empty for almost ninety years. There was no picture accompanying the framed story, but Chicky could see it anyway: a posse of men full of drunken self-importance surrounding the wounded animal, taking potshots. How many people had read this clipping and believed it, he wondered. Caesar wasn't a murdering beast any more than he was what Buddy and Marty thought he was. His great-grandfather hadn't been a Boela Man, or even been a real pinhead! Lies, he thought. The world was a web of lies—written on walls and in newspapers, sitting under museum glass, and worst of all, lodged deep inside people's heads, impossible to remove.

But maybe not, Chicky thought. He took off at a run toward home, but returned dragging his old Flexible Flyer, a blue saucer sled. In a nearby alley, he found a brick and flung it through the plate glass window of the museum. There was no alarm, no one around to hear the glass shattering or Chicky's grunts as he scooted all that remained of Caesar onto his sled, no one there to watch a black dwarf dragging a sled laden with an elephant skull down Broadway toward the Winnesaw River.

At the riverbank, he gave the sled a shove. It skimmed over the ice until it reached the still-flowing middle. The weight of the skull sank the sled like a bowl in dishwater, and in a second or two, Caesar was gone. Chicky knew the museum would still try to tell the story, repeating all the same inaccuracies, but without the skull, fewer people would stop to listen. Maybe in another ninety years, no one would remember at all. He could paint over the words in the alley, but not the rumor, and Chicky had no intention of waiting around ninety years for it to go away.

IN THE NEXT day's paper, the theft of Caesar's skull made the front page:

CIRCUS ARTIFACT NABBED
FROM LOCAL MUSEUM

No suspects were reported, and the curator said: "It's an unfortunate loss, but not that unfortunate. We acquired the skull from the Indianapolis Zoo in 1955 to provide a historical display to accompany the story of Hans Hofstadter. The stolen skull actually belonged to a much smaller female elephant. We've contacted the zoo, and another skull should arrive within the next few months."

But by the time the paper hit the stands, Chicky was already headed South. He'd hitched a ride on a snowplow out to the truckstop on the highway. There he found a trucker heading to Florida. Interstate 65 from Indianapolis to Louisville was down to one lane, and the herd of semi trucks inched along single file at barely thirty miles per hour, but Chicky didn't care. He was too busy picturing himself in the Gibsonton post office, stepping up to the window for midgets and dwarfs, and mailing Verna a Sunshine State postcard. *Dear Mama, You'd love it here. Love, Chicky.* When he walked down the street, he'd say good morning to the Alligator Man and Monkey Lady and Lobster Boy, and they'd say, "There goes Chicky Bowles, the Last Member of the Boela Tribe."

THE CIRCUS HOUSE
— or
The Prettiest Little Thing
in the Whole Goddamn Place

WHY DID SHE fall in love with Colonel Ford? This is what Mrs. Colonel thought: It was the War Between the States. It was nothing but boys and old men to look at for months at a time. It was his uniform. It was his orders to report back to the front and the subtle way her people encouraged quick marriages to keep up morale. It was being fifteen.

But this is how she told the story: She was only fifteen the first time she saw him—at a cotillion to raise money for the cause. He was only a captain then, dashing in his gray uniform and muttonchop whiskers, galloping up the shaded drive. All the other girls wanted to dance with him, but he followed her with his eyes the whole night. He knew when her cup of punch was empty, and a new one appeared in her hand, like magic. When he finally asked her to dance, she refused, but he persisted. And so she danced with him, and he whirled her away. After a week-long courtship, they married.

There you have it. The good part anyway.

In 1900, Wallace Porter, proprietor of the Great Porter Circus & Menagerie, hired the Colonel out from under P. T. Barnum's nose, but the Colonel took the job as general agent with Porter only on the condition that his wife, Mrs. Colonel, would have a decent roof over her head. For twenty years, she'd accompanied her husband on the road, spending her days cooped up in hotel rooms and her nights trying to sleep in Pullman cars. "I'm tired of traipsing around like a gypsy," she'd complained. A week later, a telegram arrived from Wallace Porter that read, "MADAM YOU WILL HAVE YOUR HOUSE   STOP".

On a hill overlooking the winter quarters was Wallace Porter's mansion, two-storied and three-pillared. But once, he'd lived at the bottom of the hill in a clapboard farmhouse. It had stood empty for sixteen years, abandoned to the wind and rain. Sparrows nested under the eaves; at dusk, they rose from the trees like a wave against the sky and descended on the house for the night.

Porter ordered a group of roustabouts to fix the house and drive the birds away. The men knocked down the nests under the eaves with long-handled brooms. Inside, they cleared away the cobwebs draping the doorways and the piles of mouse droppings. The milky light filtering through the clouded windows lit up a universe of floating dust motes. For days, the roustabouts wore bandannas like masks, lifting them to their eyes to rub away dirty tears. While Colonel Ford tended to his business in the barns or in Porter's mansion, Mrs. Colonel flitted through the house in her black lace dresses, shaking her black parasol at the roustabouts like an angry señorita.

ONCE THE HOUSE was restored to order, Mrs. Colonel spent her days strolling through the winter quarters, paying visits to the circus people. All those years alone, she'd dreamed of a home to furnish, a porch where she could sit on hot summer nights, a landscape that changed only with the seasons, and most of all, a circle of intimates to entertain and amuse. This was the life Mrs. Colonel had been raised to lead. She decided, *My husband mostly runs this circus, and that makes me First Lady, of sorts.* She knew the duties this role required: entertaining, taking up causes, providing a woman's influence, softening the circus's rougher edges by genteel example.

Each day on her stroll through the winter quarters, she brought with her a loaf of bread, a cake, a plate of cookies, and one by one, Mrs. Colonel visited the bunkhouses of the performers. "Now that we're to be neighbors," she'd say, "we'll want to get acquainted." Startled by her cordiality, the circus people scrambled to serve her tea in chipped cups. The Hobzini Sisters, Bareback Riders and Equestrienne Beauties, were still lounging around in their nightgowns well after noon. They took turns escaping to dress, put up their hair, and dot their cheeks with rouge. The Fukino Imperial Japanese Acrobatic Troupe smiled and nodded their heads in appreciation when Mrs. Colonel spoke, although they understood no English, a fact Mrs. Colonel chose not to notice.

After the elephant trainer Hans Hofstadter was killed by one of his bull elephants, Mrs. Colonel asked her husband what was to become of his widow. "I suppose we should keep her on in some way," he said, "after what happened." A few days later, Mrs. Colonel paid a condolence call. She found Nettie Hofstadter half dressed, nursing her newborn son, Ollie. Mrs. Colonel asked, "Would you like to work for me? I could use the help." Nettie looked up then, her eyes blank. Mrs. Colonel leaned in closer. "It'll be better than working in the cookhouse or sewing. The Colonel and I weren't so blessed, so it will be nice to have a child around." Mrs. Colonel touched the down on the child's head. Nettie said without enthusiasm, "Yah. I work for you." Mrs. Colonel hugged her. "We have to take care of one another, don't we?"

The next day Mrs. Colonel visited Jennie Dixianna. The acrobat answered the door in a red satin robe, hair snarled, eyes puffy and bruised. Mrs. Colonel was going to apologize for disturbing her until she smelled the sour whiskey on the acrobat's breath. A ruby bracelet hung around Jennie's wrist, and Mrs. Colonel bent slightly to get a better look, but found that it wasn't a bracelet at all, but an open wound with jewels of blood. "I wanted to pay you a call, but I see you're indisposed at the moment. I'll be on my way then."

That night in bed, she asked the Colonel about Jennie's wrist. He described her aerial act, the Spin of Death: "She spins herself around in a blur of red, white, and blue for the finale. Chronic rope burn on the wrist, and I can't get her to wear a glove. Doctor says she'll die of gangrene eventually, but I don't believe it myself." He rolled over, his back to his wife, and a few minutes later began to snore. Mrs. Colonel considered sending over a salve, but decided against it, remembering the loud slam of Jennie's bunkhouse door.

WITHIN TWO WEEKS, Mrs. Colonel had visited every bunkhouse but one, a small cabin on the far side of the winter quarters, half hidden by trees. She heard no sound within and was turning to leave when she noticed a blanket draped over ropes strung from the eaves. Behind the curtain, Mrs. Colonel found a young man sleeping in his suit, collar unbuttoned, an open book on his chest. Mrs. Colonel studied him carefully, noting his smooth pink cheeks, aristocratic nose, curly brown hair and long fingers. He reminded her of a sleeping prince from fairy tale books, perfectly formed and beautiful. Most circus men, Mrs. Colonel had found, were either hulking brutes or skeletons with bad coughs. *Oh, but this one,* she thought, *this one is a gift from God.*

He awoke then with eyes wide. Mrs. Colonel said, "I beg your pardon. How rude of me."

The man jumped up and straightened his coat. He closed a small suitcase sitting on the chair next to his bed. Before the lid snapped shut, Mrs. Colonel caught a glimpse of starched white shirts and long underwear. "Please excuse me," he said. "I wasn't expecting company."

"I'm Mrs. Colonel Ford. The Colonel is my husband," she said drawing out the last word, *huzzz-band.* She offered her limp, black-gloved hand.

"Jeremy Trainor. Painter." He bowed ever so slightly.

Mrs. Colonel noted how gently he'd taken her hand, as if it were a flower he didn't wish to bruise. She thought a firm handshake very common. "I brought these," she said, pulling out a bundle from her drawstring bag. "Peanut butter cookies. I'm trying to acquaint myself with everyone."

Jeremy Trainor asked, "Won't you have a seat?" but Mrs. Colonel blushed, since the only place to sit was on his bed. He offered her his arm. "On second thought, please join me, my lady, on the veranda." She laughed. They spent the better part of the afternoon sitting on the bunkhouse stoop, eating the cookies and talking. He'd been with Porter's circus for over a year, painting the advance posters and touching up the calliopes and wagons with gilt daubings. He shared the bunkhouse with six other men, carpenters and blacksmiths, coarse and crude. They found him sissified, so he'd strung up the partition to keep himself separate.

Mrs. Colonel sighed. "I did the same all those years traveling on trains, but I suppose I've resigned myself to the fact that these are my people now." She told him how she'd ended up the wife of a circus man—the Waltz at the Cotillion Story—and he told her how he'd ended up a circus painter. He had been raised to farm his family's patch of stony soil. As a child, he'd drawn pictures in dirt and ashes, the only medium available. But when his father and brothers saw his work, he was whipped and sent to his room without supper. "I ran away two years ago to be an artist, and look how far I've gotten."

Mrs. Colonel remembered then that first ladies performed another important function. She said, "I have a whole house in need of an expert's hands. It's just the thing to get your career off the ground." Their relationship began that day, that old and regal association called patronage.

INSTEAD OF WALLPAPER, Mrs. Colonel Ford wanted to cover the walls of her house with murals by Jeremy Trainor. "Imagine," she said. "Floor to ceiling. Every wall. It will be magnificent." She sent a note to Jeremy, and the next morning, she waited for him on the porch. A fog had risen from the Winnesaw, and she saw him walking through that low-hanging cloud, dressed in overalls. Mrs. Colonel imagined all those winter days, standing at the foot of his ladder, sending up words of praise. She imagined for a moment that the young man walking through the mist was actually her lover. It had been years, even decades, since she'd felt that old ache, and it surprised her that her body was still capable of producing such a want.

Inside the parlor of ghost furniture, they drank coffee and discussed what Jeremy would paint. "I thought a nice lawn scene would work well in the dining room," Mrs. Colonel said. "Lords and ladies. Croquet. As a girl I visited a plantation in South Carolina that had a fox hunt." Her expression turned dreamy, faraway.

Jeremy shifted in his chair. "I was thinking of something more local, like the circus."

Mrs. Colonel laughed. "You already paint the circus."

"I want to do portraits, paint the landscape." Jeremy Trainor swept his hand wide across the room.

"I thought you weren't fond of the land?"

Jeremy took a sip of coffee. "I'm not fond of *farming* the land." He sat forward in his chair, elbows on his knees, staring earnestly into the eyes of Mrs. Colonel. "I have a vision."

She patted his leg. "Well, honey, of course you do."

He took Mrs. Colonel's hand and squeezed it softly. "I paint posters. Do you understand?" She did not, and Jeremy explained that when the circus paraded through towns, he saw people along the sidewalks sitting on his posters. "They fold them like accordions and fan themselves." Later, he said, the posters littered the streets and fluttered on fence posts. The wagons he painted chipped in

the wind and rain and had to be restored with the same
colors year after year. "But your house will last," he said.
"It's very important to me."

Mrs. Colonel swallowed hard. "What would you start
with?"

"Hofstadter and the elephant."

She knew that at least one room of her house would be
dedicated to the memory of the elephant keeper and the
awful circumstances of his death. *Oh dear,* she thought.
What will the Colonel think?

The Colonel was not amused. He bellowed and roared.
"This idea of yours has gone far enough. I'll not have my
house turned into a maudlin museum by some two-bit
artist." Mrs. Colonel tried everything. She stroked his
hands, played their favorite waltz on the Victrola, held the
match as he lit his pipe, and brought him brandy sours, his
favorite drink, on a silver tray. All the while she spoke in
soft tones about increasing the value of the house, about
posterity, but the Colonel would hear none of it.

Mrs. Colonel nurtured her longing in private. She took
naps every afternoon with the door closed, and before
sleep, imagined the Colonel had relented. Jeremy came to
the house each day to paint and to see her. She acted the
story out in her head, complete with dialogue, long afternoon teas, shy looks, and passionate embraces. Often when
she awoke, she found that her hips moved of their own
accord.

Finally, she resorted to the means by which she usually
got her own way; she locked herself in the bedroom and
refused to open the door, even for meals. She sobbed and
choked on tears. The Colonel couldn't understand what

was so important. "Why are you doing this, dear?" he asked, standing at the door on the third day. Neither of them had ever held out so long.

"You said I could decorate the house however I wanted. You've never let me cultivate myself. Never."

The Colonel finally relented. "It will look godawful hideous, but have your way."

He was right. The house would be hideous, but that was no matter. Mrs. Colonel knew her body was doughy and shapeless, her hair grayed. She could never hope to seduce Jeremy. *He will never love me, but if I let him paint,* she thought, *he will at least have to appreciate me.*

THE FOLLOWING WINTER, Jeremy began, as he'd said he would, with the death of Hans Hofstadter. Mrs. Colonel brought an easy chair into the study and sat amid the tarps and ladders. She allowed herself only momentary touches— a pat on the arm to call him to lunch, a stroke of his face to wipe off flecks of paint. He painted the brown Winnesaw, the trees, the gray sky, the elephant that held a small man in its trunk and lifted him like a prize. The keeper's red shirt was the only bit of color on the entire wall. When Nettie finally realized what the mural depicted, she yelled something in German that Mrs. Colonel couldn't understand. She refused to enter the room again and later forbade Ollie to enter as well. But for years, Mrs. Colonel would sometimes catch him in there, staring at the death of his father.

Each time Jeremy finished a room, Mrs. Colonel stuffed a roll of bills into the chest pocket of his overalls and turned her cool, powdered cheek to him for his thank-you.

From the window, she watched him trudge home through the evening snow. She imagined him lying awake in his cot, hands folded over his chest, waiting for the snores of his bunkhouse mates to begin so that he could steal into the night to bury her money, their money, in a secret place.

It took him two winters to finish the first floor. In these rooms, Jeremy painted exactly what lay on the other side of each wall. The side of the house that faced the winter quarters was a mural of the barns—zebras and elephants ambling in their paddocks, camels grazing in fallow cornfields, horses going through their paces in practice rings, and enormous cats jumping through fiery hoops. On the side of the house that faced the countryside was an Indiana winter—clods of earth powdered with snow, the sky gloomy and oversized. So accurate was Jeremy's work that during the winter, if Mrs. Colonel squinted her eyes almost shut, the effect was as if there were no walls on the first floor at all. But in the summer, she was left in the lonely house of winter walls broken by window squares of green.

THIS IS WHY they call it the heartland:

In the summer, the fields on either side of Mrs. Colonel's house glowed a brilliant green, rippling in the wind. The air stretched above like miles of blue canvas, and Mrs. Colonel pictured a center pole rising up from Indianapolis's Monument Circle to hold up the endless sky. Sometimes as she sat on her front porch in the evenings, Mrs. Colonel felt her heart swelling up as big as the horizon. Only then could she say that Indiana was almost as beautiful as her Virginia. During these lonely months, Mrs. Colonel fancied herself shipwrecked and stranded. Outside her windows was a green ocean dotted by islands of trees, and on each island stood a farmhouse, sheltered from the sun and the prairie winds by those blessedly spared shade trees. Each island looked remarkably the same, and sometimes she thought about walking off the porch, diving into this ocean, and swimming to the next stand of trees. Maybe there, she'd find another woman waiting for her men to return, a woman as heartsick as herself.

THE THIRD WINTER, Jeremy started on the upstairs and decided to devote each room to a different performing act— the Fukino Imperial Japanese Acrobatic Troupe, the Great Highwire-Walking Worthingtons, even the Boela Tribe of African Pinheads, whom he brought to Mrs. Colonel's house, "for sketches," he said. Colonel Ford came home one afternoon to find the Boela Tribe sitting on his sofas, drinking from his crystal. Bascomb Bowles, the elder of the family, was stooped over the pianola, plunking out "Amazing Grace." "For god's sake," he told his wife later, "did Jeremy actually have to bring them here?" Mrs. Colonel secretly agreed, but Jeremy was insistent. For a week, she kept watch for the Colonel while Jeremy studied the Boelas in an upstairs bedroom, which he locked at the end of the day. "A surprise for you," Jeremy said. "My masterpiece." When he finished, he covered her eyes and led her into the room. "Voilá!" The room was a jungle of vines and trees, glowing eyes peering out of the night, and around a fire danced the Boela Tribe in loincloths and bone necklaces, shaking spears. Mrs. Colonel almost fainted. When the Colonel saw the room, he screamed, "Holy Mary, Mother of God!" and stayed up all night whitewashing the walls. To spare Jeremy's feelings, she kept the room locked from that day on. "The Colonel is quite progressive on the Negro question," she explained, "but this might be too much for him, I'm afraid."

After the Boela Tribe incident, the Colonel almost put an end to the painting, but Mrs. Colonel assured him their bedroom would be to his liking. She invited Jeremy to dinner so they could discuss the matter. "Why are you asking me my opinion all of a sudden," the Colonel asked, pushing back his plate and lighting his pipe.

"I assume," Jeremy said, "you'll want something you don't mind looking at a lot."

Mrs. Colonel said, "Yes, what would you like, dear?"

The Colonel took two thoughtful puffs off his pipe. "The prettiest thing in this whole goddamn place is Jennie Dixianna. If I'm going to have to look at something every morning, I'll look at her." Then he stood and left the room.

Mrs. Colonel felt her face pinching and tears welling up, but she kept her composure in front of Jeremy. "I believe that I'd like you to put Alberto Coronado on the other wall of the room. His triple somersault is just lovely. Yes. That will do nicely." She walked to her bedroom, slamming the door behind her.

The east wall of the Ford's bedroom captured the somersault in all its stages: Coronado posed before takeoff with the trapeze bar in hand; Coronado in midflight, tucked and spinning; Coronado triumphant, hanging in the strong arms of the catcher. "See how lifelike it is," Mrs. Colonel said to her husband, pointing out the raven hair and mustache, bronzed skin, and tight leotard. The Colonel only nodded his head.

That night, the Colonel walked into his newly painted bedroom and sniffed. "I can't sleep in here. The smell makes my head hurt." For a week, he tested the room every night, and still found the smell too strong. Then, he did away with the formality of testing the room altogether and continued sleeping in the Fukino room. By the time the circus left that spring, Mrs. Colonel had grown accustomed to the spacious bed in her half-painted room.

Dear,

Hope all is well with the show. It's been most quiet around here, with notable exceptions. Nettie's boy Ollie is getting to be a handful. Yesterday, he broke the antique vase. Nettie gave him a good lashing. Caught him drawing on the walls in the study, but didn't tell her. You know how she is about the study. Weather humid, but not bad for this time of year. Hope you've been enjoying good weather on the road. I will write more next week.

Fondly,
Your loving wife

May 21. Radford, Virginia. Population 4,000. Found an empty lot on top of hill, one-half mile from town. Rain and thunderstorms all day. Miss Stella Hobzini lost her balance in the tandem horse race over obstacles and fell from her saddle. She hurt herself severely and had to be carried to her dressing room. Parade at 12 o'clock. One bandwagon, mounted people and elephants only. One show. Attendance good. Traveled forty-three miles on N&W. Overall, show going well. Will write more later. [unsigned]

HERE ARE A few things you should know about the above correspondence:

1. The second letter is a copy of the May 21 entry in "The Great Porter Circus Route Book," a daily record kept by the Colonel for business purposes.
2. A comparison of the Colonel's letters to his wife and his route book entries reveals this method of correspondence had been his practice for years.
3. Mrs. Colonel had always suspected as much, but the diligence it took him to copy his entry twice had always satisfied her as a kind of romance.
4. Despite their mutual promise to "write more later," during the 1904 circus season, this brief exchange between the Colonel and Mrs. Ford constituted the sum total of their communication.
5. Neither one noticed.

WHEN FALL CAME, Jeremy returned with a sketchpad full of Jennie Dixianna. "I watched her a great deal this season," he explained to Mrs. Colonel. "I wanted to capture her act and her passion." Mrs. Colonel tried to smile when she saw the cream-colored pages full of the blur of Jennie's act, but covered her mouth when she saw Jennie Dixianna's bare back as she soaked in a washtub. Jeremy's voice was level. "Miss Dixianna was kind enough to sit for me a few times. I found it very helpful. I think the Colonel will be pleased with the results."

The next week, he worked on the west wall almost constantly, and for the first time, the Colonel took an interest in Jeremy's work, offering suggestions and praise. Like the painting of Alberto Coronado, Jennie Dixianna was represented more than once. Climbing the rope to do the Spin of Death. The Spin of Death itself. Standing in the sawdust, her ruby bracelet thrust in the air, receiving applause after her Spin of Death. "I'd like to bring her here," Jeremy said one day, "for a final touch up."

On the appointed afternoon, Colonel Ford burst into the house a half hour before Jennie arrived to change his shirt. When Mrs. Colonel walked into the living room with the tea tray, she found Jennie seated between Jeremy and the Colonel, laughing with her head thrown back, one hand on the Colonel's knee and the other on Jeremy's. Mrs. Colonel plunked the tray down on the table and sat in a nearby armchair. After listening to the three of them chatter about the last season on the road, Mrs. Colonel rose from her seat. "Gentlemen, I think Miss Dixianna has business to attend to?"

"Yes, of course," Jeremy said, taking the hand of Jennie Dixianna, helping her rise from the couch. Colonel Ford reached for her other hand, but when he caught Mrs. Colonel's stare, he touched his pipe instead. Jeremy and Jennie mounted the stairs that led to the bedroom.

The Colonel and Mrs. Ford munched cookies and sipped tea in the darkening room. Neither rose to light a lamp nor spoke a word. For the next half hour, the house was completely still until they heard the steady thrump and squeak of the bed above their heads. They lifted their eyes and studied the ceiling together. Mrs. Colonel sobbed into her cupped hands, but the Colonel did not rise from the sofa to comfort her, nor did he charge up the stairs and stop what was going on. He clenched his pipe between his teeth and spat out the word "whore," which only made Mrs. Colonel cry harder.

NO WOMAN sets out to make a fool of herself, but it still happens. All the time. A girl marries but forgets why. She wants to remember, but her husband has forgotten as well. They grow apart. A new man appears. Suddenly, she remembers love; it is a bird inside her heart that flies out the top of her head. Then, she remembers lust; it is a bird inside her womb that flies out between her legs. Her need for this new man makes her do foolish things, and the man knows this. He isn't worthy of her loyalty, her love. He is weak, lured away by money and a scheming temptress. For the first time in her life, the woman understands why someone might commit suicide, because there are days when her humiliation is so total it seems only death can take her far enough away from it.

Sometimes the woman dies. If she lives, sometimes she leaves her husband, but not always. Sometimes he leaves her. It's the same old story, but as often as it's been told, only one version ends with walls like those in the house of Mrs. Colonel Ford.

DESPITE HER PLEADING, the Colonel refused to let her paint over the murals. "We spent a small fortune on these walls," he told her. "You get what you pay for in this life."

A few weeks after Jeremy Trainor disappeared from the winter quarters, Mrs. Colonel snuck into her bedroom and caught the Colonel dancing in front of Jennie's wall, his arms outstretched, eyes closed. Despite his wide girth, the Colonel still waltzed as smoothly as he had the night of the cotillion, when she'd refused to dance with him until she could no longer bear his ardor. *You are the prettiest little thing here,* he'd whispered in her ear.

Mrs. Colonel knew the form he envisioned before him was Jennie's and not her own, but she moved softly into her husband's outstretched arms and matched his step. In that brightly painted bedroom in Indiana, many miles and years away from that night in Virginia, the Colonel and Mrs. Ford swayed to a lost song, weeping together at how little difference time made.

WINNESAW

— *or*
Nothing Ever Stops Happening
When It's Over

TWO MILES OUTSIDE Lima, the Winnesaw Reservoir sits, a big brown puddle of river water, backed up and stagnant. I've seen it in spring, all that Winnesaw lapping against boat docks and half-submerged trees. The trapped reservoir water still smells of river, and I cannot help but think of the Flood of 1913. It's the same water probably. Surely in all this time, the river has run its course and found its way back here to our dam, the way old elephants return to their own boneyard to die.

The Winnesaw River nearly broke its banks every year, which was maybe why we weren't expecting it in 1913, the year the rains came so fast there wasn't time to sandbag the banks. We were living out by the winter quarters then, me and my husband, Charles, and Mildred, who was just a week or two old. Charles was doing work for Wallace Porter, building his circus wagons and animal cages, sometimes cutting curlicue designs on the staircases of Porter's mansion.

Porter had been friends with my parents, so I knew about his wife, his great love, dying on him. He said he'd never marry again. He was small and bone thin, the kind of thin people turn when they stay up all night worrying and forget to eat for days at a time. He had tiger eyes, tan and gold and green, but they were rimmed by dark circles, so the eyes sunk in and you caught yourself sometimes leaning forward to look into the hollows. His eyes were the only sad thing about him though, because he carried himself like a gentleman, all poise and polish, right down to his voice, which was the same for respectable folks like my parents as for the gypsies and strange rabble who ran his circus, the circus he bought with the money after he'd sold the biggest livery stable business in northern Indiana.

Understand, I lived through the Flood of 1913, but also I was living near the winter quarters, where I could hear the animals screaming, where, after the waters went away, all the carcasses rotted in the fields where they'd settled, like the gray open-eyed fish you'd find in a dry creek bed.

In 1913, Porter practically owned the town. He bought about a hundred acres along the Winnesaw River, built a bunch of barns for all those animals, and built himself a mansion on the top of a hill with white columns and stained glass windows. Since his wife was gone, Porter lived up there all by himself, except for the maids and butlers, of course. Some said that at night he'd go down the hill to the winter quarters and play poker and drink with the roustabouts, or sometimes they'd find him in the barns, watching the animals mate. He said to Charles once that he was just making sure that the mating was getting done, that things would keep on going. Charles even heard that sometimes Porter would get all hot and bothered watching those animals and he'd pay calls on the star acrobat, Jennie Dixianna, who had a bunkhouse all to herself.

Maybe he did and maybe he didn't. It was never any of my business, but I believe what Porter told me once. "Grace, what I always wanted was to have many children, to scatter my name like those proverbial seeds in the wind, but God didn't make that possible for me, so I'm just going to make something on this earth really big and put my name all over it."

Most people simply buy a company or make a doodad and go about making a name for themselves that way, but Porter was different. Around here, people use that word *different*, like a slur, but he was the better side of different.

I came from money, but I married for love, so Charles and I didn't have much. Our rented house was awful plain, so Porter loaned us some old furniture from the bunk-houses, a ratty davenport and a stained mattress. Charles stayed up late into the nights, making us chairs and a head-board by the light of the kerosene lamp. A few weeks later when I found out Mildred was coming, he carved a cradle, and after she was born, he painted it sunflower yellow. The rains started while I was still weak and shaky from the birth.

The rain never let up, not for a whole week. At first, the water covered the backyard, creeping up the back steps, one by one, and then spilled its way through the door and into the kitchen, where I was standing at the sink. The water rushed in like the tide, but instead of soothing me, the cold Winnesaw grabbed my ankles with frozen hands, sending icicles shooting up my legs. Charles found me there, shrieking, holding my nightdress up out of the water. He carried me upstairs, sloshing in his big boots through the living room while I cried for him to save the

only nice things we had, my mother's books and my photographs, which were floating around the feet of the
kitchen table. Charles piled sandbags around the doors, but
it didn't do any good, so he brought up all the food and
blankets and the soaked things. I placed the books and
photographs on the bed and watched them swell and curl
while Charles rocked Mildred in her yellow cradle.

After the second day, when the water was a quarter
way up the wall on the first floor, Charles and I saw a
dinghy across the widening river set out from Brown's
farm. Charles waved a shirt out the window, and the two
men inside the boat waved their hats. But the river was
churning brown rapids and an uprooted tree tossing in the
water capsized their boat. They grabbed the tree and went
floating on by us. Charles and I watched them from the
bedroom window and neither of us said anything.

That night, the animals screamed. Lions and tigers were
roaring to be let out of their cages. The elephants blew their
high-pitched cry through their trunks. Over the pounding
of the rain, I heard water lapping against the house, as if we
were on a boat going down the Congo River, and in the
jungle on either side of us animals were clawing each
other's backs in the darkness. We heard men yelling, and although we could not make out the words, the tone of their
fear and their frantic attempts to get the animals free echoed
in the night. I got out of bed and opened the window to
pitch-black and saw jewels in the trees, the yellows and
greens of squirrel eyes and possum eyes and snakes, too,
blinking into the river that wouldn't stop coming.

I slept in fits and starts, and when I opened my eyes at
sunup, I saw what looked like a snake climbing over the

windowsill. I screamed and woke Charles, who walked to the window with a shoe, but then he laughed and told me to come see. A big bull elephant from the winter quarters had stuck his trunk in the window, and when he leaned against the house, his shivers sent vibrations running through our feet. The water covered his legs and was starting to come up his body, and his eyes, brown like a horse's and fringed with long lashes, kept looking at us, like we were at fault. Until then, I realized, his life had been one of show and strain in return for human kindness and some hay. I couldn't stand to see him look at me, pleading. I sat back down on the bed and took Mildred up in my arms.

"Charles," I said. "Give him some food. Bread. Do something."

"What do you want me to do, Grace? We need all our food."

"Make him go away then," I said.

So Charles threw my hairbrush hard against his back, but the brush just glanced off and floated away.

He sighed. "I can't make him leave. Maybe he'll go by himself."

But he didn't. The baby wailed in my ear, and the elephant bellowed all day long and shivered the house and I couldn't look out the window at his eyes all afraid of cold and death. The elephant's trunk poked around the windowsill, like a tongue licking the corners of a mouth. Towards noon, Charles remembered a straw tick mattress in another room, slit it open, and fed the straw to the elephant out the window; but there wasn't much and the elephant just wailed louder when the straw was gone. By five, bitter cold water almost covered his back. Both the elephant and the baby stopped crying, and then there was only the silence of waiting and the steady thump of current against the house.

Charles stood at the window. "He's just standing there with his head down. He knows it won't be long."

And about the time the sun went down, the trunk slipped off of the windowsill, and I got up, too, and watched the elephant sink down into the brown water. There wasn't a splash, just a swallowing up and a big spray of his last breath of air.

I kept Mildred away from the window all that time. There are some things children shouldn't see, even as babies. People think they can carry on in front of their babies as if they aren't even there, like they won't remember. But they do, because it's like planting a kernel that one day explodes and the memory comes rushing back and fills their heads with revelations of things long forgotten. See, I don't think that we live just once. We live when things first happen and every time we remember that first time, we live it again.

I thought the elephant had floated away in the current, and I imagined his gray bulk bumping off underwater trees, a rollicking tumble, head over tail in the brown water. But the darkness outside and the thick brown water shrouded the elephant completely. He sank below our window and never moved, and when the water finally receded, he would still be there, stiff and cold and so big that, even lying on his side, he was almost as tall as Charles. With our team of horses, Charles had to drag the elephant far enough away from the house so that we could burn him.

But right then, I didn't know that the elephant's body was under my window because the sky was dark all the time, gray and brown, the same as the water that was all around us. Everything flowed, sky and water and time itself, so you couldn't tell the difference between each day, or even where the water ended and sky started.

The second or third day, a log floated in the front door and started banging away at the piano. Charles laughed at first and said the old piano had never been in tune anyway, but after a couple of hours of the *bang-bang-bang*, he stopped making jokes. The piano was only partly covered by water, and the log, pushed in a steady, thunderous rhythm by the current, struck the keyboard in random chords. Every hour or so, the current shifted the log to a different set of keys and a new song banged out to the beat of the river.

Finally, Charles said, "I'm going to float the piano out the front door. I can't stand the racket."

But I cried and said, "Don't. I'm too weak to help if you get into trouble. We'll put little pieces of cloth in our ears and it won't be so bad."

The earplugs worked for Charles and me, but not for the baby. She kept pulling them out and wouldn't stop crying long enough for me to feed her and give her something to take the place of the tears. The water continued to rise, lapping against the pictures hung on the downstairs walls and coming slowly up the stairs. Then the bangs and chords changed and the sound came from underwater, so it sounded like you were swimming in a pond, listening to someone playing piano on the bank while you were underwater. Charles and I took out our earplugs, and even though the plunking was muffled, Mildred still cried, wailing, gulping air and tears.

That night, the sound of the underwater music drifted into my sleep and I dreamed I was playing the piano in our sunken house, moving my arms and fingers through the sluggish Winnesaw. Charles stood beside me, clapping the beat of the current on top of the piano while Mildred squirmed out of his arms and floated up and up, her white baby gown trailing like wings behind her.

I sat straight up in bed then, awakened by Mildred's screams. I shook Charles awake and told him about my dream.

He rubbed his head. "Maybe we're going crazy. From the din."

"We can't stop the noise and we can't make her sleep."

"Well," Charles said, "there's the brandy."

He got a bottle of apple brandy down from the closet and soaked his handkerchief in it and stuck it in Mildred's mouth, rewetting the cloth every few minutes, and she sucked enough of it to finally fall asleep.

Some days later—I say it was two, but Charles always swore it was only one—we were awakened by calls of "Hello in there" coming from outside our window. The rain had stopped, and Wallace Porter had sent some of his roustabouts on a raft made out of the side of a circus wagon. Charles rigged a rope with the sheets and lowered Mildred in her cradle, then me, then climbed down himself. And wouldn't you know that as we rounded the front corner of the house, we heard the piano shatter blessedly apart and watched it float in pieces out the front door. Charles and I cried and hugged each other, pointing to the piano shards and laughing like crazy people, which I suppose we were, from no food for days. We sat there on the raft, listening to no rain hammering the roof, no baby crying, no piano plunking, no elephant bellowing, just the miraculous quiet of the current.

The men who saved us were strong from raising tents and sweeping barns, but they had dark circles under their eyes, dead eyes in sad faces that hardly nodded to us before they started heading toward the winter quarters. Charles asked, "What's happened to everything?" But they didn't reply, so Charles grabbed a plank of wood and started rowing, trying to keep us on course. I sat at the front of the raft and stared into the muddy water where faces of the dead floated up to say *Help me, please.* But it was too late, I knew, and their faces sank back down into the mud. Some of the faces were folks from town, but some were strangers and I wondered how far they had come down the Winnesaw and how far they would go before they would finally stop and how would anyone know who to send them back to?

Animals from the menagerie floated around us or were snagged in branches, and dogs and cats and cows, too. A horse tried to swim to us, eyes wild and blowing water out its nose. Charles threw a rope around its neck and tried to carry it along, but later the rope was pulling straight down, like we'd caught a big fish, and he cut the line off with his pocketknife.

Something big and gray moved below the surface, so I leaned over, when a big burst of air and water in front of me wet my face and I was looking right into the eyes of Wallace Porter's prize hippopotamus, Helen. She circled us once and sank back underneath the raft. One of the roustabouts stopped rowing and said, "Maybe she will live," and that's all any of them ever said the whole time we were on the raft.

We rowed into the winter quarters and saw Porter's house sitting grandly on an island in the middle of swirling water and most of the animal barns half drowned. The roustabouts set us down on the island and the maids ran down the hill, wrapped the three of us in blankets and helped us toward the house. One woman gave sandwiches to the men, who ate them without speaking and set off again to look for more faces and drag them back to Porter's house.

We found Wallace Porter in his study, which smelled of cigar smoke and whiskey. He was drunk and delirious, talking to God about judgment. When he saw us, Porter wiped his hands down the length of his face and said in a solemn voice that there was food in the kitchen and plenty of rooms to sleep in. I couldn't stand to see him like that, with so much gone, so Charles and I turned and left his study. We ate some soup in the kitchen and gave Mildred some milk and slept and slept. When Charles woke up, he said, "I dreamed last week all over again," and I told him I'd done the same thing.

Finally, the sun came out, and at first, I thought there was no way in heaven that the earth could soak up that much water. I never did think all that water came from the sky anyway, because it seemed like most of it sprang up from holes in the earth, from a China flood many years ago, a slow tide always moving through the earth. Sometimes I think nothing ever stops happening when it's over. Maybe the Winnesaw Reservoir we have now is nothing more than that same flood from 1913, come back to see us again.

When the water was gone, Wallace Porter opened the front door and Charles and I walked with him down the drive and across the field toward the winter quarters. There were no sounds at all, not even birds, and for a moment, I felt as if the only people alive on the earth were those who'd made it to Porter's house. We could barely take a step without moving branches out of our way, walking around uprooted trees, wagons, roofs, barrels. Everything looked as if it had been boiled and burned and tossed in a tornado, settling down like silt wherever it was.

This must be why the animals were scattered over the fields in the strangest poses, their eyes open and looking up at the flat sky. An elephant lay on its side, big chunks of its hide gouged out, but the blood had all flowed away somewhere. A Bengal tiger hung by its hind legs from a tree down by the river, caught up in the branches. We walked into the gorilla barns and found three dead, trapped in their locked cages.

That day, every time I turned away from death, there was another carcass, another body, and I'd start shaking again. But I don't think I was as sad as Porter was when we walked into Jennie Dixianna's bunkhouse and found her pinned to the wall, trapped by her brass bed. Charles and I walked back outside, where we heard Porter crying, moving the bed to set her free.

I whispered to Charles, why didn't she just swim away? Charles had no answer until Porter let us in and we watched him pick up all the empty whiskey bottles scattered over the floor. When his arms were full, he looked

around, as if for a trash barrel, and seeing the state of the
room, started crying. Her face is still with me, gray like fire
ashes, with leaves and branches twined in her hair like she
was some kind of brownie or fairy.

Charles carried her body up to Porter's house and I
asked Porter what we should do about all the carcasses. He
sighed like a man letting go of his last breath. "Burn them.
Tell the men to cover them in kerosene and burn them."

Maybe if we'd had one of those backhoes, like the ones
they used to dig out the reservoir, we could have buried
them in one mass grave and erected a cross to mark the
place. But we did what we could. We set all the animals on
fire, then closed all the doors and windows in Porter's
house to keep out the smell, but the stink of roasted, rotten
flesh seeped in through the wooden shutters and under
the doors, and none of us could eat for those two days.

When we walked outside again, all the skeletons were
charred black in the sun, not an ounce of flesh left on
them. No one knows what Porter did with the skeletons,
and most don't care, as long as the bones of the past are
sunk somewhere for good. Eventually, though, everything
is revealed, floating on the water's surface or tossed on its
receding shore. Maybe Porter tossed the bones into a ravine
covered now by the reservoir, and one day some shiny ski
boat will run smack dab into an elephant's ribcage and
wonder how in the world that happened. I'll tell you how.
Flesh may burn and rot and wither, but bones stay around
almost forever.

THE LONE STAR COWBOY

— or

Don't Fence Me In

STELLA GARRISON stared at skeleton trees lining the road. A chill wind raised gooseflesh on her arms, but she didn't move to close the cracked-open car windows. It was April 1957. Moving day. She and her husband, Wayne, had lived in Richmond for years, but he'd gotten himself the foreman's job at the power plant in Lima, his hometown. He drove their Oldsmobile with a smile on his stubbly face, his brawny arms and solid hands gripping the steering wheel. In the backseat, their twin sons brawled—again. Stella wondered if they'd spend their lives locked in that embrace, the one they'd once shared inside her.

"Wait until you see it, honey," Wayne said, taking the turns too wide.

"Slow down," she said. "The house isn't going anywhere."

In the backseat, Ray and Ricky yelled, "Faster, Dad." They turned pretend steering wheels and made *vroom-vroom* noises, and Stella turned to shush them. They were nine-years-old and identical physically—blond hair shaved into crew cuts, blue-eyed and thin limbed—but their dispositions were night and day. Ray was the oldest by three minutes, strong and bossy. Ricky was quiet, easily hurt, quick to cry.

Ray made a skidding sound, and Ricky spit out a make-believe car crash. Stella turned again to tell them to be quiet while their dad was driving, but she knew there was no point. She was just as excited to see the new house as they were. They'd been in the car all morning. "How much farther?" she asked her husband.

"Not far." Wayne glanced over his shoulder. "Settle down," he said in a low growl. And the boys did.

Stella fiddled with her hands, wishing for something to do—sew or needlepoint—even though she knew it would make her carsick. She hated the idle time of long drives. Nothing to do but sit there. Her mind did funny things when it had time to spare. When she drove or cooked or did housework, her imagination often veered toward tragedy, deaths of both the sudden and the expected variety. *What if I died? What if Wayne died? What if one of the boys died?* From these games of "what if," Stella had discovered much. If she died, Wayne would remarry quickly, within a year or two. If he died, the thought of widowhood did not displease her. If one of the boys died, losing Ricky felt slightly more unthinkable, more catastrophic, than losing Ray. Stella played her cards close to the vest, this last one especially, her preference for Ricky. The glossy ladies' magazines she bought in the checkout line at the market teemed with articles on parenting. They all said that good mothers should love their children equally. But sometimes she pictured love as electricity flowing from her heart to her hand, and Stella wondered if her husband and sons could feel the difference in her touch, a force that manifested itself subtly, invisible to the naked eye.

When they got to Lima, Wayne drove them past the power plant where he'd start work in a few days, then crossed the Winnesaw River. He smiled. "Nice town, eh?"

Stella looked back at the brick storefronts of downtown. It looked like Richmond, like Wabash, like Logansport, like any other town. But she said, "Nice. Yes." In her mind's eye, she pictured another Lima, the one from Wayne's stories about the circus that once wintered there. Stella saw elephants pausing at stop signs, clowns buying sugar at the market, and midgets drinking mugs of beer with their legs dangling from barstools.

She blinked the past away and turned back to the gray asphalt ahead. Their road, "River Road," Wayne called it, was a two-lane highway that shadowed the Winnesaw. The river looked high from the spring melt. Half-drowned trees stood in the water like ladies holding up their skirts. Then the highway turned away from the river, and for a long stretch, there was nothing on either side of the road but newly tilled cornfields. "I'll bet this drifts shut here every time it snows," she observed. "It'll be hard to get into town. Too bad."

Wayne clenched his jaw. "Stop it," he said.

"What?"

"You know what. Please, just let it go."

Stella pretended to be miffed, but Wayne had caught her subtle jab, her scab picking of a weeklong argument. Since they only had the Oldsmobile, she'd wanted to live in town, or at least in one of the new ranch houses in River

Hills, a new subdivision sprawling across south Lima, but Wayne had chosen a lonely, isolated farmhouse outside town on the lot of the old circus winter quarters.

He'd bought the house on his own, without her ever seeing it. Frantic, he'd called from the realtor's office. "This one is too good to let go. There's another couple here in the office right now, getting ready to write a check."

"What's it like?" she asked him.

"Two stories. Big, beautiful. I'd have given anything to grow up in this place."

"Can I walk into town?"

There'd been a pause. "Maybe," he'd said. "On a good day."

He'd driven through the city limits long ago, and for the first time, Stella saw the truth: they were miles from town. Every curve in the road, every barn that flashed by, filled her with dread. "I'll be trapped out here," she whispered so the boys wouldn't hear.

"Only five miles, Stell. And once you see this place," Wayne said, "you won't want to leave."

He rounded another curve and she saw a house—no, a mansion with pillars and stained glass—looming on top of a hill like an ancestral castle, overlooking the river and miles of farm fields.

"Is that it?" she asked, shaking her head in disbelief.

From the backseat, Ray and Ricky said, "Wow" in unison.

"No, no," Wayne laughed. "We're not moving that far up in the world."

He drove past the mansion, and then past barns, paint chipped to the bare wood. CAT HOUSE and ELEPHANT BARN were written above the giant doors. "What are these?" Stella asked.

"I told you about the circus quarters, back in the old days? Well, this is it." He pointed to a yellow barn. "That one is ours."

A barn, Stella thought. They'd never even had a garage.

"The rest of them belong to some farmer up the road. Keeps his tractors there." He stopped the car. "Boys, you have to see the barn. The real estate guy told me Tony Colorado kept his horse Bullet in there winters."

"Who's Tony Colorado?" Ricky asked.

Wayne laughed. "He was like the Lone Ranger, only he wasn't on TV. He was a movie star and traveled around with the circus." Stella remembered him from a silent film she'd seen as a girl—a clean-shaven man in a white hat riding a black horse. When silent movies became talkies, he'd faded from the screen; she'd read in one of her Hollywood magazines that Tony Colorado, the Lone Star Cowboy, was cursed with a high, squeaky voice unsuitable for speaking parts. Wayne turned in his seat to where the boys sat transfixed, staring at the barn. "I met Tony Colorado once, in town at the old Robertson Hotel. Went up and shook his hand." Wayne sighed, waving the memory away with his hand.

He drove through an ornate wrought iron gate. "The guy who owned the circus, Wallace Porter, lived up there," he said, pointing again to the mansion on top of the hill. "Some rich family owns it now, but they're traveling in Europe or something for a year. Can you beat that?" He rounded a bend in the drive and stopped in front of a clapboard farmhouse. Ray and Ricky tumbled out of the car before it even stopped and ran back to explore the barn. The two-story house was painted a peeling white with emerald green shutters hanging crookedly from every window. Ivy clung to the sides of the house like jungle vines, and over-grown bushes blocked the first-floor windows.

"The Realtor told me this used to be Porter's house, be-fore he built the mansion." Wayne helped Stella out of the car.

"Needs work." Stella shaded her eyes from the sun.

Wayne nodded.

"How bad's the inside?"

"Not so bad," Wayne said.

He opened the front door, and Stella stepped inside her new house. She'd pictured sunny rooms with tall windows, but instead of white walls or patterned wallpaper, every wall was a mural, gaudy and bright as a circus sideshow banner line. She walked down the walls, trying to take it all in. Elephants in the study, camels and zebras in the living room. In the dining room, horses grazed in a winter field, colored ribbons and plumes twined into their manes. "This is crazy," she said.

"I wanted to surprise you." Wayne stood with his arms folded proudly across his chest, rocking on his heels and toes. "The Realtor said the workers, the guys that painted those big...what you call them...tableau wagons. They must have practiced in here."

Stella said nothing. An old upright piano stood along the wall, the only piece of furniture in the house. She pressed a few keys. Out of tune, of course. Stella shut the piano hard, and the muffled notes echoed. "Why would someone do this?"

"Must have been too big to move," Wayne said.

"I mean these walls!"

"Well, it's sure . . . different." There was a note of apology in his voice.

"I hate that word," Stella said, touching the walls. "It's just a nice way of saying something's bad." She noticed that over the years, the murals' colors had become muted and dull, and in the places where the painter daubed too thickly, cracks and fissures worked their way through the paint like tiny spiderwebs.

Wayne shrugged his shoulders and frowned. "What's the matter?"

"I can't believe you bought this place without telling me about these walls."

"I thought you'd think it was interesting."

"It's ugly, Wayne," she said, trying not to yell. "And I hate the circus."

"Who hates the circus?" Wayne snorted.

"I do. You know that." She felt guilty, blasphemous. She'd told him years ago, and he'd stared at her in openmouthed shock, like she'd just said, "There is no God," or "Communism is a pretty good idea."

Wayne stomped toward the front door. "Well, it's ours now."

She followed him to the barn, a graveyard of abandoned circus equipment. Harnesses, juggling pins, clown props, spangled and fringed costumes, and steamer trunks marked PROPERTY OF THE GREAT PORTER CIRCUS. A steam calliope from the Coleman Bros. Circus, a whip with WARREN BARKER'S WILD ANIMAL ODYSSEY burned into the leather handle. In the corner, an old Overland stagecoach

with a missing wheel sat propped up on hay bales, TONY
COLORADO'S LONE STAR COWBOY SHOW painted gold on the
side. Ray and Ricky had clambered inside to shoot their toy
guns out the windows. They fired at imaginary Cherokees
threatening to overtake the stage.

Wayne called. "Stella, come over here. You've got to see
this." He pointed at the weathered sign hanging over an
empty horse stall, which read: BULLET, FASTEST HORSE IN
THE WEST. "They kept him right here. Can you beat that?"
Wayne said. His eyes were almost misty.

Stella knew it was useless to complain. She was out-
numbered. She was home.

WHEN STELLA WAS eight, her father took her to a ragbag circus struggling to stay afloat during the Depression. "You'll
love it, sweetheart," he told her as they sat down in the
blue star-back seats, waiting for the show to start. "When I
was a kid, I couldn't wait for the circus to come to town."
The opening spec began—a tribute to "Yankee Doodle
Dandy." Her father sang along, so Stella did, too.

The clowns emerged, and everyone laughed. But to
Stella, they were white-faced ghosts with bloody smiles,
chasing each other through the sawdust with hatchets and
guns and saws. Her father tried to explain it was all pretend,
but Stella cried anyway. Carrying her out of the tent like a
sack of potatoes, he made his way to the ten-in-one, the
carnival midway show: ten freaks displayed in pits under
one tent. Stella looked into the first pit and saw Lobster
Man, a freak with flipper legs and deformed, clawlike hands,
which he shook in her face. She wailed louder than before.
To calm her down, Stella's father bought her an ice-cream

bar and then paid fifty cents so she could ride on an elephant, a baby one lumbering around a never-ending ring.
But Stella refused to get on, and the ticket seller refused to
give them a refund. Wasting money, now that her father
couldn't abide. A spanking followed, a very public one.

Stella's parents spoke to her schoolteacher. Was she
like this in school? No, Miss Yardley said, but Stella was a
moody child who kept to herself a lot, reading books
while the other kids played. The teacher advised fewer
books, more chores. "Give her something to do with her
hands or she might turn out melancholy. You know, different," Miss Yardley said with a tight smile. Her parents
boxed up her books, hid her library card. Her mother
taught her to needlepoint. Her father taught her to play
"Amazing Grace" and "Nearer My God to Thee" on the
piano. When she was big enough, Stella took over the
henhouse, feeding chickens and collecting eggs. The cure
seemed to work—Stella stopped asking for books and
made more friends at school. But her dreams never went
away. For years, she was plagued with circus nightmares:
Ax-wielding clowns chased her down long hallways, Lobster Man grabbed her with his claws, and a slow, sad parade of elephants marched in chains into a big top from
which they never emerged.

THE MOVERS arrived that afternoon. For the rest of the day,
Stella let the boxes sit and studied the walls, tracing the
murals with her fingertips as if she were reading braille.
Wayne knew enough to narrate one of them: the mural in
the study. An elephant grasped a small man in its trunk.

"Is that what I think it is?" Stella asked. "Is the elephant killing that little man in the red shirt?"

Wayne nodded. "I think so. The skull's down at the county museum."

"Whose?"

"The elephant's."

She took her hand away from the wall. "How awful."

But the murals upstairs were a gaudy mystery, startling portraits done in red, yellow, orange, and aquamarine. In the boys' room, big-bosomed women burst from their spangled corsets, their hair done up in white pompadours and red circles of rouge dotting their cheeks. They stood aloft flashy white horses with golden manes. In other rooms, Japanese acrobats tumbled, men walked silver wires, and a man on a flying trapeze blew a kiss across the room to the opposite wall, to a tiny slip of a woman hanging by a bloody wrist.

The house reminded her of pictures from her social studies books—ancient caves and Egyptian tombs. Dark, close places. Walls etched with strange figures and symbols. They told stories in a language she couldn't decipher, and so she was forced to make up her own. The trapeze man and wrist-hanging woman were tragic lovers—he missed a catch and sent her plummeting into the sawdust. The Japanese acrobats saved their money to buy a restaurant in California that made them rich. The family of tightrope walkers perfected the seven-man pyramid, setting world records, but lost their patriarch on a windy day in New York City, forty stories up.

One room, thank god, was blessedly white. Stella

guessed the painter ran out of steam before he finished, and she told Wayne it would be their bedroom, the only room in the house where she could put her mind to rest.

STELLA MET WAYNE her senior year at Richmond High School—at a Moose Lodge Halloween party. He was a denim-clad cowboy in a black hat with a gun slung over his hip. She came as Pocahontas, her long dark hair woven into a thick braid that swung behind her like a tail. Wayne was a good catch, a twenty-three-year-old man in steel-toed boots who worked down at Richmond utilities. Her friends were still dating boys with pimples and letterman jackets.

Her parents invited Wayne to Sunday dinner. After the meal, Wayne and her father went outside to smoke. From the kitchen sink, Stella's mother gestured out the window. "Now, he's got a good head on his shoulders," she said in such a way that made it clear she thought her daughter didn't. Stella nodded and continued scrubbing the casserole dish.

By Valentine's Day of her senior year, they were engaged. Even though she was a good student, Stella had never considered college—and no one thought to encourage her to consider it, either. By June, they were married. By the next Halloween (they went as Roy Rogers and Dale Evans), she was pregnant with the twins.

FROM THE WINDOW above her own kitchen sink, Stella watched her boys play cowboys and Indians. Ray yelled, "A fiery horse with the speed of light, a cloud of dust, and a hearty Hi Yo Silver!"

Ricky waved his hat in the air. "Hi Yo Silver, away!" The boys whooped and hollered, firing their toy guns in the air.

She liked for them to play close by. If they didn't, Stella saw them in the back of her mind, drowning in a pond, walking down the middle of a busy road, taking candy from a convict escaped from Pendleton. When they were babies, she'd slept in the nursery so that every few hours she could make sure they were still breathing. Wayne indulged her at first, but then insisted she stop. "You'll make them nervous with your worry. They'll be fine." He was right, Stella knew, but that didn't stop her from imagining the worst. She did the same thing whenever she left the house. By force of will, she kept herself from going back into the house to check the pilot light on the stove or to make sure she'd unplugged the old lamp. Worry was like a fire inside her that required constant tending to keep it from flaring out of control.

Stella was making a new recipe for dinner: lasagna. Assembling the layers took most of her attention. Then, from outside, she heard a faint moaning. She ran to the window and saw Ricky writhing in pretend anguish in the grass, holding his belly wound as Ray stood over him and continued firing, sounding out each shot between his lips.

Stella yelled out the window, "Ray! You've killed him. Let him die in peace."

It occurred to her then that Ray always played the hero (Red Ryder, the Lone Ranger, the Cisco Kid) leaving Ricky the role of trusty sidekick (Little Beaver, Tonto, Pancho). *Always a pecking order,* she thought. She wondered if this was why she preferred Ricky, because she always rooted for the underdog. Stella handed them two cookies out the window. "You know, the cowboys didn't always win."

Ray munched. "How do you know, Mom?"

She smiled. "I learned it in school. Indians got the better of cowboys sometimes."

"Really?" Ricky asked.

"Sure," Stella said. "They just don't show that on TV."

Ricky ran toward the barn, Ray following close behind. She yelled for them to come back, but they ignored her. She returned to the lasagna—she'd check on them in a while.

Lately, they spent all their time in the barn. Even Wayne. He joined them in there after work and became a boy again, surrounded by Western props and circus costumes. Wayne and her boys thought the barn was a magic portal to Arizona circa 1890, but Stella knew Tony Colorado wasn't a real cowboy, just a slicked-up imitation, a counterfeit gunslinger who died, not from bullets or arrows, but from choking on the toothpick in his martini. She'd read that in her magazines, too.

Stella put the lasagna in the oven, humming along to Glenn Miller on the radio to keep her mind off the boys, but finally, she couldn't take it anymore. Inside the barn, she saw Ricky sitting on a hay bale with Ray behind him, a flash of silver in his hand. Moving closer, Stella noticed Ricky's face—wet with tears and a bit of blood dripping from a cut at his hairline.

"What are you doing?"

"Playing cowboys and Indians," Ray said. "I'm the Indian."

"He's scalping me," Ricky said quietly, staring at his shoes.

"What?" Stella cried, then took a breath. "Give me the knife, Ray." He placed his pocket knife in her hand, and she held her apron against Ricky's forehead.

That night in bed, Stella told Wayne, "I want you to talk to them. They think it's all make believe, but it's not."

Wayne rubbed her back. "Don't worry, Stell. They're just boys."

"Boys with knives."

"It was just a little cut. You're overreacting."

Stella turned to face him. "No. I'm not."

Wayne didn't like it when she raised her voice to him. "I'll talk to them. No more scalping. Stop worrying so much. You know how you get."

"What if I'd come a few minutes later?" Stella whispered, but Wayne didn't answer. In her mind, she saw Ricky's face, his eyes, his chest, all covered in blood.

Then from outside her sleep, Stella heard wailing. A she-cat, she dreamed, sore with heat. The cat's crying reminded her of the years she'd spent listening for Ray and Ricky's cries, and then suddenly the sound was not a cat, or a memory, but a real cry—loud as a late-night phone call, stopping her heart cold. The boys never cried out like that, not anymore, so she rushed down the hall, inching along blindly in the dark. Reaching the boys' room, she found Ricky sitting up in his bed. He'd dreamed something, something he wouldn't talk about, so Stella rocked him in her arms, staring at the equestrienne tarts on the walls, wondering how they rode horses with their bosoms hanging out like that.

Ray woke up finally. "What's wrong," he mumbled.

Stella said, "Nothing. Go back to sleep."

"Did the baby have a bad dream?" Ray's voice was
sneering.

Ricky pulled away from Stella, embarrassed.

"Don't talk like that to your brother."

"I only asked if he had a bad dream," Ray said. "Geesh."

Ricky crawled back under the covers, and Stella considered picking him up and carrying him back to her bed. But
then Ray would want to come, too, and there wasn't room
anymore for all four of them, so Stella left the room, pausing outside the door to listen. In a few moments, she heard
them struggling with each other in the dark, skin scraping
sheet, fists pummeling flesh and pillow. It reminded Stella
of the last weeks of her pregnancy. She could barely
breathe, barely sleep. The baby in her womb struggled,
tumbling and turning within her. At night, it kicked her
ribs, her lungs, her back. She tried singing, stroking her
belly, warm baths, anything to calm the child down so she
could get a moment's peace. When she delivered twins, the
doctor joked, "Two nations were in thy womb."

She wanted to stop her sons' quiet war immediately,
but made herself wait to see if they'd end it on their own.
I'll count to ten, Stella thought. *Then I'll go in and turn on the
light and they'll stop.* She stood in the dark hallway, counting
slowly to herself. Stella remembered the Bible verse she'd
memorized in church long ago: *Two manner of people shall be
separated from your bowels and the one people will be stronger
than the other people.*

THE BOYS STARTED school in the fall, and for the first time,
Stella faced the house alone. One afternoon she decided to

walk into Lima, just to see if she could. But she'd started too late. By the time she got there, the sun was going down, and she had to call Wayne to come get her. She cried all the way home. "I need something to do," she told him. Stella begged him to let her paint over the murals, but he refused, saying they needed the money for real improvements: the roof, the boiler, new shutters. "Maybe you just need a hobby," he suggested.

"What?" Stella asked, unable to think of anything she'd want to add to her day.

"What about the piano?" Wayne said. "I'll get a tuner to come out. Would you like that?"

She sighed. "I don't know."

"Well then, what do you want?"

Stella paused. "I have absolutely no idea," she said quietly.

The next day, the tuner arrived, an elderly gentleman in overalls. "Ephraim Miller, at your service, ma'am," he said, tipping the hat he wasn't wearing. While he worked, the house filled with notes straining to find their correct pitch. Stella served him lemonade, and his eyes scanned the walls. "I've heard about this place," Mr. Miller said.

"Yes, it's..." Stella tried to find her own word, but couldn't. "Different," she said flatly.

"It is indeed," he said with a laugh. "Mind if I check out the barn?"

"You must be a Tony Colorado fan, too."

In the barn, Mr. Miller stood with Stella in front of Bullet's old stall. "Back in the day, I used to drink with him, you know."

"From a trough?" Stella joked, surprised at her quip. Normally she didn't have much of an edge, but lately, it popped up when she least expected it.

But Mr. Miller, a stranger, simply thought she was being funny. "Yep, me and Bullet put back a few." He laughed. "No, I mean me and the cowboy. I had a room at Robertson's Hotel. Played piano in the bar there some nights. He was quite a fella."

Stella looked at Mr. Miller's big knuckles and thick fingers, trying to imagine them spanning the keys. They looked like the hands of a farmer. "Is it true that he had a high-pitched voice? That's why he couldn't break into talkies?"

"Yep, that's right. Poor guy." Mr. Miller took a drink of his lemonade. "Ladies still buzzed around him like june bugs, though. Didn't have no trouble there."

"Really?" She remembered his photograph from the magazine. The Lone Star Cowboy hadn't struck her as particularly handsome. "How so?"

Mr. Miller looked around, as if someone was watching. "Well, I shouldn't speak of things like this to a lady, but in his room, he kept track of 'em. Said he made a tally mark for each one on the wall behind his bed. When he checked out for good, I went in there and saw 'em all."

Stella paused, considering. "Twenty?" she asked.

"More like a hundred."

She laughed through her nose. "Where'd he find a hundred women in a little town like Lima?"

Mr. Miller couldn't look her straight in the eye. "This town used to be hoppin', Mrs. Garrison. All sorts of women come through here at one time or another."

That night, Stella played the piano for hours. She'd

found the sheet music to some Cole Porter songs in the abandoned piano bench, and the boys requested "Don't Fence Me In" over and over. They knew all the words, and pointed to the walls—the winter fields and trees and horses and giraffes—as if the murals had been painted just for them, just to provide a backdrop to their song. After a while, Stella knew the notes well enough to play by heart. Although her eyes remained fixed on the sheet music, she wasn't in her living room anymore, not even in the landscape of the murals. She was walking down the streets of the old Lima alongside the aerialist painted on the wall upstairs, Miss Bloody Wrist, who wore a red feather boa. Stella kept her eyes on the plank sidewalk, feeling hard and plain in her wash dress. Every time they passed a man, Stella could feel his eyes following Miss Bloody Wrist. They paused outside the old Robertson Hotel to watch Ephraim Miller bent over the piano, playing ragtime. Tony Colorado sat at a table surrounded by stockinged legs and red lips. Miss Bloody Wrist sauntered up to Tony Colorado, who rose from his chair and kissed her hand. The other women faded away, but Stella stayed, watching the two of them walk upstairs together.

In bed that night, Stella didn't wait for Wayne to touch her first. She kissed him deeply, running her hand down the length of his chest. Afterward, Wayne lay quietly. "What's gotten into you, Stell?" He sounded a little scared.

"Nothing," Stella said, staring at the blank walls of her bedroom glowing blue with moonlight.

THE MURALS, Stella decided, must have been painted in winter. The windows and walls showed almost the same picture, as if she wasn't even inside her house at all. The stark landscape around her hadn't changed much in fifty years. Same yellow and white animal barns. Same snow-stubbled fields. Same dirty river. Same naked trees. Only the circus animals were gone, replaced by simple milk cows, horses, and the occasional deer. She wondered who painted the walls, a man or a woman. Sometimes Stella imagined a woman, someone with an empty heart and long winter hours that needed filling. But what woman would let such ugliness into her house? Stella decided the artist was most certainly a man, one with too much time and, like her, too many dark thoughts.

That winter, once Wayne had driven into Lima for work and the boys were at school, Stella played Cole Porter songs. She remembered her father's piano lessons as a child, and her mother's warnings after. "A woman plays piano for her family," she'd said. "A happy home is filled with pretty things. Good smells. Nice music. Doilies under every lamp." Sitting on the piano bench by herself, filling the empty house with music, was a guilty pleasure. Stella never played "Don't Fence Me In" when she was alone. She preferred the plaintive songs like "Night and Day," "Ev'ry Time We Say Goodbye," and "Miss Otis Regrets." Underneath the words and the notes, Stella felt a great sadness that made her heart hurt. Stella sang the same songs over and over, as if they were written in a code she needed to break.

When she tired of playing piano, Stella knit. Actually, she watched a great deal of television, which seemed less wasteful and wanton when it produced an abundance of sweaters, blankets, and scarves. Always, Stella flicked the television off fifteen minutes before the boys got home, and always, the first thing they did was turn it back on.

"Why don't you guys play in the barn today?" She almost hated herself for suggesting it.

"Too cold," they said in unison.

That winter, Ray and Ricky fought constantly. She found them locked in closets, tied to their bedposts. They rose each morning for school with hollow eyes and fresh bruises. Stella tried separating them, putting Ricky's bed in the Japanese acrobat room, but in the morning, she found him curled up next to Ray in the narrow bed, bandannas tied over their mouths like bank robbers.

Her worry for them flamed a bit higher, but Wayne didn't want to talk about it. He'd started working extra shifts, and even when he was home, he delayed going to bed as long as possible, watching television or listening to the radio alone with his cigarettes. In the mornings, he rose before sunup and walked the fields hunting rabbits in the underbrush. Stella's only proof that they occupied the same bed was the smell of aftershave and cigarettes on the pillows. He said it was work, the new house, and new bills to pay. "And it's winter, Stell," he said. "You know I hate winter."

Stella told herself that was their problem—another long Indiana winter. Like the sky and snow, people turned gray inside and out.

FINALLY, IT WAS APRIL. Winter had clung to March like a desperate bird, but one Saturday, its grip loosened. Stella threw open all the windows even though it was still too chilly. She felt as though she'd been breathing stale air for

that whole year, as if she'd just woken up from a long, dark
sleep. Ray and Ricky were in the barn—finally, it was
warm enough to play in, and Stella was glad to have them
out of the house. In the kitchen, she made sandwiches and
cookies. Wayne was still in town, getting a haircut at
Smithy's Barber Shop, running errands. When he returned,
they were going back into town for a picnic at the park. To
pass the time, she sat down to play "In the Still of the
Night," and Stella realized during the second verse that she
felt happy. She couldn't remember the last time she'd felt
anything so close to joy.

Stella saw herself walking down the streets of old Lima,
alone this time. She entered the Robertson Hotel and took
a seat at the bar. Again she wore the wash dress, but this
time proudly, like a black eye or a brave scar. A small suitcase sat at her feet, and a train ticket to Chicago peeked out
of her purse. Stella barely recognized herself, this woman
drinking a cool beer, staring at Tony Colorado. He left the
flashy women at his table, crossing the room with a swag-
ger, and took the bar stool next to her. Later, when they
stood to go upstairs, young Ephraim Miller gave them a
wink. In bed, Tony Colorado moved above her, still wearing his white cowboy hat. She woke before dawn, dressed
quietly, and with a hotel pen, added herself to the Lone
Star Cowboy's tally. Number seventy-two.

And then she was on the train to Chicago, which
stopped at little towns where more people in wash dresses
and cheap suits would board the train. Stella studied their
hard, hungry eyes, which were her eyes, full of light. She
saw it all so clearly that at first, she didn't think much of
the noise: a slightly muffled crack. Both Stellas heard it, the

one sitting in her house, playing "In the Still of the Night,"
and the one sitting on a train bound for Chicago, watching
the moon grow dim on the rim of a hill. The sound worked
its way inside her head. A barn door slamming in the wind.
A tree limb breaking. A neighbor shooting bottles lined up
on a fence. Her boys playing trick shooters, Ray aiming for
the quarter between Ricky's fingers or the tin can balanced
on his head.

The train disappeared, and very calmly, Stella stood up
from the piano. She threw on a shawl she'd knitted that
winter, forcing herself not to run. When she reached the
barn doors, she heard screaming, and inside, she saw the
boys. One lay prone, a circle of blood widening on his
T-shirt. The other boy stood over him, holding Wayne's .38.

Which one? she thought, ashamed of herself, both for
thinking it and for not already knowing.

She bent over the bleeding boy, listened for breath, felt
his chest, but there was nothing, nothing but blood on her
hand. The other boy tried to jam the .38 into his toy hol-
ster. Stella's voice shook. "Give Mommy the gun, sweetie.
Careful."

"We were playing," he said, crying now.

"I know."

"'Cause you said cowboys don't always win."

Stella paused, remembering, and then knowing. "Ricky,
please give Mommy the gun."

"I didn't mean to." He set the gun heavily in her hand.

"I know," Stella said. "Now, I want you to listen to me.
You didn't do this. You did *not* do this. Say it, sweetie."

Ricky nudged his brother with the toe of his shoe. "I
didn't do this."

"You didn't."

"I didn't."

Stella wrapped the gun in her shawl. "Now, run up to the house and call the ambulance. Like I showed you."

Alone then, Stella lifted her son's body and held him. He was cold, and his blood filled her lap.

THE CORONER SAID that death had been instantaneous. "I know it's not much, but it's something, something to ease your mind," he said to Stella on the phone. She thanked him and hung up. The police called to inform her they were calling Ray's death an accident, even though Ricky said he couldn't remember anything. Stella thanked the officer and hung up. Their family doctor said that in cases like this, Ricky would probably never remember that day in the barn. "Actually, it's probably for the best that he doesn't," he said to Stella on the phone. She thanked him and hung up. Then she unplugged the phone.

Stella knew Wayne blamed himself. Because he forgot to unload his gun after his morning hunt through the brush. Because he'd told the boys about the big scene in Tony Colorado's movie *Saguaro Showdown* where the Lone Star Cowboy shoots a knife out of the villain's hand. The day after the funeral, Wayne hauled all the Western props out of the barn and burned them. A newly hired reporter from the *Lima Journal* was driving by and took a picture of Tony Colorado's stagecoach consumed by flames, buckling like a falling horse. The reporter asked Wayne, "How does it feel to burn a piece of circus history, Mr. Garrison?" Wayne belted him good and told him exactly how it felt. The reporter apologized profusely for not putting two and two together, and Wayne offered to sell him his gun collection for fifty dollars. The reporter accepted, even though he'd never shot a gun in his life.

The piano went next. Stella couldn't stand to see it sitting there in the living room. Ephraim Miller came to the house with a truck and two movers. "I'm sorry about your boy, Mrs. Garrison."

"I was playing it," she said. "When it happened."

Mr. Miller nodded. "I see."

"It's like..." Stella paused, knowing the word she wanted to say, but not wanting to say it. "I feel like I'm playing a coffin."

"Yes, ma'am."

When they took the piano away, Stella felt no better. The music still hung in the silent house like fog, and she started leaving the television on all the time, filling the house with canned laughter and commercial jingles. A month went by. One morning, Stella walked into the now half-empty barn. She remembered the day they'd first seen Bullet's sign over the stall. She remembered the near scalping in the barn. The day Mr. Miller came to tune the piano. The Robertson Hotel and the Lone Star Cowboy's bed. She wanted to blame the murals, the barn, the piano, even Wayne, but Stella knew that the accident had been all her fault. She couldn't tell real from imagined any more than the boys could, and perhaps she'd cursed them with her dark fancying. Or maybe her responsibility went back even farther than that, to that split second in her womb when they had been one boy, when she'd failed to hold them together.

Stella went into the house, got her purse, and started walking down River Road. It was early this time, not yet nine. At Parson's Hardware, she bought two buckets of white paint and started the long walk home, swinging the buckets in long arcs to keep up her momentum. Halfway home she remembered the toaster was still plugged in. Despite her vow to start fresh, to keep her mind as white as the walls she'd have soon enough, Stella couldn't help but see the house and the barns all burning, paint melting, everything turning to ash. She saw the three of them in the Oldsmobile, and she was ashamed at how quickly they'd become three, not four, in her heart. Wayne was driving on a highway, and they were all singing. *"I want to ride to the ridge where the West commences; gaze at the moon till I lose my senses."* Mountains formed on the horizon. They were going to a new home, a house of her choosing; its walls would be painted the buttercream of fancy paper, waiting for the ink of a happier story.

But when Stella rounded the curve, she saw the house standing there just as she'd left it. She felt surprised and disappointed, like she did on winter mornings when she woke up sensing snow, anticipating a new, white world, only to rise and find everything just as brown as the day before.

THE JUNGLE GOOLAH BOY

Preface
So Many Stories Begin Just Like This,
on a Ship Sailing to a Place That's Not Yet America

Carolina Gazetteer, May 9, 1725

Just imported in *The Empress,* Capt. Carron, directly
from the Sierra Leonne region, a cargo of SLAVES,
healthy men, women, and children, to be sold to
the highest bidder on *Monday, May 16.* Credit will
be extended till the first of December with proper
Security. By Reese & Andrews, Charles-Town.

Chapter the First
The Jungle Goolah Boy's Family Tree,
According to the Tree's Proprietors

Journal & Ledger of Curtis Grimm,
Eastwater Plantation, May 17, 1725

Weather remarcably pleasant. Doctor Wrigley arrived
by Ferry to see Mrs. G. who apeers better today.

House neerly compleat & clearing 40 more aceres for
Rice. Yesterday I perchased 4 Men, 1 Woman (with
child) & 2 Children. Names & ages (aprox): Cassius—
30; Luther—25; Nero—20; Marcus—17; Cordelia—
19; August—10; Helen—13. Paid 350 pounds. For the
Journy from Charles-Town, Mister Plane administerr'd
Spirits to induse Dosility.

Grimm Family Papers (Section A: 1715–1754)

July 7, 1726

TO: Mister Curtis Grimm, Charles Town
FROM: Arnold Plane, overseer, Eastwater

Dear Sir—

*I hope this lettre finds you well and the Climate of
Charles Town more agree-able to Mrs. Grimm than the
malarial aires of Eastwater. The Slaves perchased by you
May last are performing theyre Dutys well, only August still
requires leg irrons and the threat of the lash to keep him to
his task. He may be Angolan which would account for his
stubbornness. The other Males are good at irigation and
pounding with morter and pessle. Cordelia and Helen make
fine fanner baskets from sweetgrass for winnowing the
chaff. My 23 years xperience taught me that one should not
buy Slaves of the same species—when able to talk amung
themselves, they take longer to learn theyre tasks and are
apt to Revolt. But the choice to perchase Slaves ready
equipped to grow and harvest Rice will prove both Wise and
Proffitable. While in Charles Town, perchase more Slaves
from Sierra Leonne or Gambia, if Opportunity arises. The*

Hausas are worth the price as the Males are of keen
inteligence & the Females are handsome & merry. Avoyd
if possible the Ibo, as they are prone to suicide and
meloncolie.

> Faithfully,
> Arnold Plane

Carolina Gazetteer, October 8, 1727

ESCAPED

Run away from my plantation, Eastwater, in St.
Augustine parish. A New Negro male named AU-
GUST. Wearing negro cloth jacket and breeches.
August is a tall young fellow with scars on back
and legs & speaks good English. Whosoever shall
deliver said negro to me in Charles-Town or at my
plantation to Mister Arnold Plane shall receive a re-
ward of Ten Pounds, currency or goods. CURTIS
GRIMM.

Journal & Ledger of Curtis Grimm,
Eastwater, October 12, 1727

Clowds today. Paid Dolly one yd. Indigo cloth for her
fine Tobacco. Mister Plane returns with August who
got to Cooper River before he was fownd. This being
his 2nd escape, Gus receiv'd a branding of a "R" on
his cheek, as new Law dictates. He seems at last
resined.

Grimm Family Papers (Section B: 1755–1804)

August 15, 1773

To Robert Vine, overseeer of Eastwater

Sir,

In Anticipation of my family's return from Charles Town week the next, please direct Berty to ready the house. Last year she was still preparring the house when we arrived, so I ask that this year she have any help neaded. With all speed please issue this seasons alotment of Shoes, Negro Cloth, Blankets, and Provisions. Also I instruct you to select whichsoever wench and buck you think most suitable for sale, as my brother in law in Beaufort is curently in need of more hands. I had thought of Rainie's girl, the mullatoe Pearl, and Berty's Caesar, the Hostler, both Trustworthy & Strong, but whose sale would surly provoke many Lamentations. Therefore upon further Reflection I instruct you to select those whose sale will least effect the Harmony we enjoy with the Negroes.

Sincerely,

Curtis Grimm II

Last Will & Testament of Curtis Archibald Grimm II, 1804

SECTION IV: Property, Servants (Children)

MALE: Aaron, Valentine, Ace, Jupe, Ned, Tom, Chance, Gus, Fortune, Apollo, Bo, Sweet, Collis, Luke, George, October, Damon, Victor, Walt, Virgil, Peter, Simon, Prince, Enoch.

FEMALE: Rea, Alice, Alatea, Little Ellie, Marta, Corrine,
    Little Zosie, June, Loyal, Vangy, Delia, Athena,
    Spring, Sida, Polly, Bodie, Sibby.

Journal & Ledger of Curtis Grimm III,
Eastwater, July 16, 1810

Weather hot & humid. Was forced to sell George
yestiddy as he took one of my pigs. Kenneth found
the bones behind his quarters & flog'd all in house.
Caesar tried to confess to his son's crime, but I new he
was not the culprit. Rice & Peaches both doing well &
if continues to harvest will allow me to buy 50 acres
from Mr. Yardley.

Grimm Family Papers (Section C: 1804–1840)

December 25, 1864

My Dearest Caroline,

*I trust that you and the children are safe and enjoying a
happy Christmas. The provisions you sent along with Festus
have brought a small measure of cheer to us here on James
Island. Please reassure Maum Ellie that Festus is out of
harm's way. She'd be proud of the job her son's been doing
as my valet.*

*I feel we will be together again soon, as it seems certain
that we will soon lose Charleston. These are dark days
indeed. The Yankees will no doubt reach Eastwater within
the next month or two, so it would be best to distribute
whatever provisions you have stored to prevent them from*

*filling the enemy's belly. They will most likely destroy
whatever they find, so please hide or bury what you cannot
bear to lose. Be sure to secure my family papers as I would
rather die than see 150 years of meticulous recordkeeping
thrown on a Yankee cook fire. Do what you can to protect
your womanhood from the Yankees and Negroes, for there
is no telling what wretched acts they may perpetrate upon
us. The Lord was not with us in our glorious fight, but
may He at least protect and keep you safe until we are
reunited.*

All my love,
Curtis

Grimm Family Papers (Section D: 1841–1908)

October 14, 1888

My Dear Friend James,
    *It is with a heavy heart that I write to you. The house
at Eastwater, where as boys we spent so many carefree days
playing under the palmettos, has fallen into decay since
The War, and the grounds have lost their lustre as I can no
longer pay to keep them up. Most of our niggers have left,
so the land's gone to waste, even that which I sold for
shares. I've had some whites try to make a go of growing
rice, but one season standing in the muck does them in,
I'm afraid.*
    *As you suggested, I've turned to reading, the Good Book
and Scott of course, but also the latest by Page, Harris, and
Kennedy. Their words stir my memories of those blissful days*

*of not-so-long ago, and so moved have I been that I decided
to take pen to paper myself. To my mind, no writer has yet
captured the sound of the Gullah spoken by the Low Country
nigger. I have been paying close attention to the peculiar
speech of my drivers Marvin and Sugar (they are the sons of
my valet Festus, whom I think you will remember well). I've
captured fragments of Gullah. For example, "We glade fa see
onah" means "We are glad to see you," and "Uh nee'
sumptin tas'e 'e mout" means "I need something good to
eat." I find it easier to approximate this dialect on the page
than in speech, but it flows quite easily from their thick lips.
It seems to me to be for the most part a careless manner of
speaking, a broken English wrapped around their clumsy
tongues. Some of the phrases are completely incomprehensible
to me, as they are most likely their jungle language secretly
maintained.*

*I am currently working on a tale told in the same
manner as Page's "Marse Chan." A Yankee comes across
an old nigger who tells with pride the story of the brave
Cavalier who was his master. To tell my story, I need
only think of Festus, who passed to a sweet repose last
year. I felt his loss most keenly and remember with
affection his devotion to me on the Field of Battle. He
was like a father to me, since my own passed on when I
was so young.*

*Should you and Paulina desire to venture out, you are
always most welcome, although Caroline and I can no
longer offer you the comforts once at our disposal.*

Most sincerely,
Curtis Grimm IV

Chapter the Second
The Jungle Goolah Boy's Circus Career,
According to the Circus's Proprietors

—The Grand Pacific Hotel—
San Francisco, California

December 29, 1900

Colonel Ford, General Agent
Great Porter Circus & Menagerie
Winterquarters
Lima, Indiana

Dear Colonel:
    I hope this letter finds you in good health & that
you found sufficient Yuletide spirit. My purchase of the
Diamond Show has been completed at long last. Two
28-car sections loaded with property should reach Lima
in the coming days; they are being shipped from the
Diamond winterquarters in Old Mexico. I have inspected
all stock and property and found them to be in good
condition; if they should reach you otherwise, please inform
me immediately. When the train arrives, take precautions
that the animals not catch cold on their pull to the winter
quarters. Hofstadter, superintendent of the Diamond
menagerie, says feeding the elephants bran soaked in
gallons of whiskey prevents them from taking cold. The
big beasts go after the stuff like a child to candy. The
Diamond menagerie includes the biggest bull elephant
I've ever seen named Caesar, and a fine specimen of a
hippopotamus, Helen. The new animals will add greatly

*to the menagerie, and Hofstadter's act with the elephants is
not to be missed.*

*If you have any questions about keeping our route
book, please inform me. I encourage you to include as much
information as possible, as you never know what may prove
useful.*

Best Regards,
Wallace Porter

Route Book of the Great Porter Circus, Season 1898

Portland, Oregon, Thursday, August 1—Population
78,000. Lot corner Twenty-second and U Streets.
Weather fine. City officials raised the license fee to an
extortionate figure, but we succeeded in getting a
concession. Caesar the elephant went on a wild tear
this morning in the parade. A young negro in our
employ seems to be the only one who can handle the
ugly brute, so he was summoned from honey bucket
duty in the Pullmans, a foul task from which he was
quite happy to be liberated. Within the hour, young
Sugar had the situation controlled, and was then
promoted to the menagerie department, where
Hofstadter will no doubt teach the boy a thing or two.
Hereafter Caesar will have the pleasure of wearing
chains for his bad conduct. Oregon Railway &
Navigation Co., 88 miles.

May 15, 1900

Dear Wife,
    *Yuma, Arizona. Population 1,700. The hottest spot on
the American continent, a dry heat much different from our*

beloved Virginia. Reached town at noon. Cloudless sky, blazing sun, and the temperature 120 degrees in the shade. If this keeps up, don't know how the polar bears will fare. At yesterday's stand in Riverside, California, a boy got his hand nipped by that cantankerous camel. Got the croaker away from his bottle long enough to come bandage up the finger, which was bleeding rather badly. Mr. Ryce, our fixer, was quick on the scene with a sucker, a free ticket, and the legal release form, which the lad signed with no fuss, thankfully.

An incident of some humor occurred last week when Mr. Porter decided to make Sugar Church, a very capable Negro handler, part of Hans Hofstadter's act. (I am sure you can imagine how old Hans took the news!) Barnum & Bailey trouped with a Zulu Chief last season, one of their biggest draws. Porter decided we needed a Zulu Chief too, and asked me to come up with a good name. Sugar Church is Gullah—I recognized it in his voice, the same queer nigger speech I heard in Charleston during the War. So I said, "Why not name him the Jungle Gullah Boy." I know I said it right, GULL-ah, but Porter misheard me and wrote it down as "Jungle Goolah Boy." Sounds like Jungle Goulash Boy! I almost corrected him, but Porter is a Yankee, after all, and sometimes one must give Yankees a wide berth.

Overall, show going well. Will write more later.

With Kindest Affection,
The Colonel

Programme of Displays of
The Great Porter Circus Season of 1900

DISPLAY NO. 1
Rings No. 1, 2, & 3: Opening Spectacular—a

Kaleidoscopic Panorama of Regal Magnificence
completely filling the immense Hippodrome course.
Illustrating the grandeur of the Greatest Love Story of
All Time. KING SOLOMON AND THE QUEEN OF
SHEBA. 1,000 characters, 200 chorus members, 300
dancing girls, elephants, camels, and horse-drawn
chariots. A Superb Series of Animated Triumph in
which Imitation surpasses Reality.

DISPLAY NO. 2

Ring No. 1: Thrilling display of Contortion by the
Oriental Wonders from the Land of the
Chrysanthemum. THE FUKINO IMPERIAL JAPANESE
ACROBATIC TROUPE.

Ring No. 2: Mirth-provoking Clowns in Amusing
Antics.

Ring No. 3: Pageant of Pachyderms. Caesar,
Largest Elephant in America. Sambo, Found in
Deepest Africa. And Ying Ying, the Dancing Elephant.
Led by HANS HOFSTADTER, World-Famous Elephant
Trainer. Assisted by his JUNGLE GOOLAH BOY.

The Western Union Telegraph Company
—Incorporated—
23,000 Offices in America.
Cable Service to all the World
Robert C. Clowry, President & General Manager

RECEIVED at   via Chicago, Illinois
Lima, Indiana   June 22, 1903
Wallace Porter
    Winter Quarters, the Great Porter Circus

tragedy   while halted on tracks struck from rear
outside St Charles Ill   cars hit burst into flames
61 men dead   most roustabouts   no records or
identification   must bury in unmarked graves
10 elephants buried where fell   your presence
urgently needed
 Col. Ford, Gen'l Agent 435AM
Paid: to the account of the Great Porter Circus

Route Book of the Great Porter Circus, Season 1905

Hagerstown, Md., Monday, August 28—Population,
18,000. Lot in Fair Grounds. Rain all night. Lot very
soft. Irene Hobzini met with a very painful accident
during her teeth slide. In this act, she slides down an
incline wire while suspended on a pulley by her teeth.
The man who regularly breaks her fall was indisposed
after a long night with the bottle, so Sugar was called
from the sideshow tent. Unfortunately, his duties were
not properly explained to him, and Miss Hobzini
crashed into a pole. The blow knocked out many of
her teeth, the bridge of her upper jaw was split, and all
her remaining teeth were loosened. A dentist was
summoned who did what he could, but we are afraid
she will never be able to perform this exciting act
again. Transfer to Western Maryland Ry., 39 miles.

Route Book of the Great Porter Circus, Season 1907

Wheeling, W. Va., Tuesday, May 9—Population
40,000. Lot on the Island. Rain up to 10 A.M., fine
balance of day. Ed Garland visits from Pittsburgh

where he is performing in the vaudeville "Uncle Tom's Cabin." Ed trouped with us last season in our blackface act, The Black Hussar Band, and since leaving has been sorely missed. Brutus the riding bear nearly caused a panic by rushing up into the seats after his act. Sugarchurch was sent to collect the animal. Chesapeake & Ohio Railroad, 12 miles.

Route Book of the Great Porter Circus, **Season 1910**

Greenville, N.C. Friday, September 29—Population 3,500. Lot four blocks from depot. Weather clear. Promoted Sugar Church from the animal stalls to the sideshow where he makes a good Zumi the Monkey Boy. A negro woman of this town murdered her husband last month and her trial was set for 11 o'clock this morning. The judge and jury all wanted to attend the circus. They discussed and decided if they hurried a little they could finish in half the time and still do their duty. The case was presented in one hour and it took the jury of twelve good men eight minutes to bring in a verdict of not guilty. The afternoon show was attended by all and pronounced superior. Atlantic Coast Line, 28 miles.

Deed of Sale, November 15, 1939

Herewith all property of the Great Porter Circus & Menagerie is transferred to the Coleman Bros. Circus of New York, New York. This includes: 57 railcars (Pullman, stock, and flatcars); all canvas tops (total 575 feet); 12 tableau wagons; 3 steam calliopes; 39 animal cages; concession equipment; hitches; poles; star-back seats; rope; rigging; all draft stock (43 horses) and menagerie stock (7 elephants, 8 Liberty horses, 1 hippopotamus, 9 camels, 4 yaks, 3 llamas, 2 sacred cattle, 3 zebras). All officers, doormen, ticket sellers, ushers, musicians, candy butchers, canvas men, property men, wardrobe attendants, drivers, porters, cooks, performers, and attractions may continue service under new ownership; however, if they choose not to continue, must forfeit any materials used in performance of their duties. Signed this day, the Fifteenth of November in the Year of Our Lord, Nineteen hundred and thirty nine.

X Wallace Porter

Owner and Manager, the Great Porter Circus

X Edgar Coleman

President, Coleman Bros. Circus

Chapter the Third
The Jungle Goolah Boy's Story,
According to *Life* Magazine

Cook, Roger. "May All Your Days Be Circus Days," *Life*. July 30, 1940.

The big top provides many opportunities to the American Negro. For example, "Sugarchurch" (he did not divulge his real name) was a struggling sharecropper in South Carolina until he joined the circus at age 16. He started as a Pullman porter, worked his way up to animal handler, and eventually found himself working for various circuses in a number of different incarnations as "The Wild Man." Currently, he is trouping with Warren Barker's Wild Animal Odyssey as "King Kungo," but over the years, he's worked for the now-defunct Great Porter Circus, the Coleman Bros. Circus, and others, where he was billed under a variety of names: "Zumi the Monkey Boy," "Zootar the Missing Link," and "Jungle Goolah Boy." On average, he earns $30 a week, a sum he says far exceeds that which he can make elsewhere.

According to Mr. Sugarchurch: "They keep me in a cage most times in hardly no clothes, and I'm not to talk to folks, just grunt and look mean. When the people come to look, they throw me raw meat. I poke at it and smell it and worry over it, but I just pretend to eat it because it's horse meat mostly." When his sideshow duties were over, he donned a clean pair of dungarees and went directly to the cook tent to enjoy his real dinner: pork chops and mashed potatoes.

Advance departments often circulate bogus stories in small-town newspapers the week before the circus is scheduled to arrive to increase ticket sales. A common promotional tactic is to report that the wild man has escaped. The advance man for Warren Barker planted such a story in Sioux Falls, South Dakota. The day before the show arrived, the local paper announced that, after a weeklong manhunt, "King Kungo" had been captured by Canadian Mounties and was safely chained for his visit to Sioux Falls. Mr. Sugarchurch claims that in the many years he's worked as a wild man, he's "escaped" thousands of times.

Chapter the Last
How Sugar Church became the Jungle Goolah Boy— According to his Brother—According to the WPA

Federal Writer's Project, WPA Life Histories
South Carolina Worker's Project

NAME OF WORKER: Florence Place, Murrell's Inlet, S.C.
DATE: September 10, 1938

FORM A: Circumstances of Interview
1. Subject: Negro Folklore and Migration.
2. Name and Address of Informant: Marvin Church, Edisto Island.
3. Place of interview: his home.
4. Description of room, surroundings, etc.: Kitchen in three-room pole house, clay chimney. No electricity, meagerly furnished, but clean.

FORM B: Personal History of Informant
1. Ancestry: Negro.
2. Place and date of birth: Eastwater plantation, March 10, 1882.
3. Family: Married, eight children, five living.
4. Occupations: drove a carriage until 1908, when Eastwater's owner died; moved to Edisto in 1908, makes living as ferryman.
5. Special skills and interests: Mr. Church is a "sticker" with

the Edisto Island Shouters. NOTE: "Shouts" are a remnant of the slave-song tradition incorporating call and response singing to the beat of a broom or stick on a wooden floor. Recorded by John A. Lomax. Songs, spirituals, hymns, including a narrative on the storm of 1893 spoken by Mrs. Ursula Brown. Recorded in Murrells Inlet, SC, August 1936. (See AFS 829–877. Two discs. Tape copy on LWO 4872 reels 59; 62–63.)

6. Description of Informant: medium/slightly built, weight about 155, skin heavily lined, the color of coffee with cream.

7. Other points gained in interview: The subject spoke in a Negro dialect that was sometimes difficult to understand. I have translated somewhat for ease of reading.

FORM C: Text of Interview

I was born after slavery time. You can always tell those that come before. The blue hands for one, from tending the indigo pots. The "G" brand on the foot. The web on the back. That's what my brother and me called the whipping scars, spiderwebs. We wasn't to watch my daddy and uncles when they washed or changed shirts or shoes, but we always snuck a look when we could. I never saw my mama's bare back till she died, and she had the webs too, come to find out.

My daddy went to war with Master Grimm and cleaned his clothes and fed his horse. Got a minié ball in his calf and limped all his life. Master Grimm was thankful for all my daddy done and buried him with a nice headstone. It was hard times after the war, so he must had powerful feelings for my daddy to spend that kind of money.

Daddy wouldn't never tell me what he really thought of Master Grimm, so that's a secret he took to the grave. I got treated good because I was my daddy's son, but I wasn't sad when Master Grimm passed.

After Emancipation, they open up the Penn School for teaching the old slaves to read and write, but my mama didn't make us kids go because she teach us. She had stories pass down to her from oldest times, when the first come over the sea. My daddy's line the oldest at Eastwater, go back five generations to a slave boy name Gus. My daddy made me memorize our line all the way back, and I knows it still. My daddy was Festus, who was the son of Maum Ellie, who was the daughter of George, who was the father of Ceasar, who was the son of Berty, who was the daughter of Gus, who come to Charleston and got bought by the first Master Grimm. I teach it to my kids, but they don't wanna remember it. Just like my brother.

See, my folks, they knew the words those old slaves say and the songs they sing. But my brother, he didn't want none of that. He said we all need to go North and get civilized, but my mama say she never leave Eastwater because to see the ocean was to see the bridge from here to there and we be lost if we let it go out of sight. My brother go to find a job up North. His name was Sugar because my mama say he was the sweetest baby ever live.

I drove the carriage when Master and Missus went out, so I got to see a little of the world that way. One time, they go to Charlotte to visit some friends and had me drive them. Got to stay a whole week. While we was there the circus come to town and we go down to see it. I was sitting there in the colored section when I seen the elephants

come out, and sitting on top of one is my brother Sugar,
but I don't hardly recognize him because he got paint
stripes on his face. He was wearing leather britches and a
necklace of bones and was shaking some kind of stick at
folks, looking mean and yelling some talk I never heard.
The circus man say they found him naked in the African
jungle living with a bunch of gorillas. All the white people
looked real scared, one little white boy was crying, but all
the colored folks was laughing and pointing at my brother
and saying, "What kind of fool is that?" I didn't know what
to do. Sugar hadn't wrote us much since he left except to
say he was working and not to worry. Sitting there watching him, I know why he don't write more. He was shamed,
and so was I, so I didn't let him see me. On the way home,
Master Grimm asked me, "Wasn't that jungle boy your
brother that run off North?" and I said, "No sir, it wasn't
him."

A long time ago. After that, we stopped hearing from
Sugar. My folks died, and when I got my own family, I just
never told them about my brother. Didn't seem much
point. Fact, I ain't never told nobody this story but you.

THE KING AND HIS COURT

— or

Boy Meets Girl,
Boy Marries Girl,
The End

IN 1967, Hoosier sportswriters agreed on one thing: Ethan Perdido of Lima, Indiana, was the best baseball player in the state. The sports editor for the *Lima Journal* penned an editorial on Ethan's behalf: "Indiana has a Mr. Basketball. Why not a Mr. Baseball?" It didn't happen, but this revolutionary idea did bear some fruit: Ethan received a full scholarship to play ball at Purdue University. In an interview, Ethan thanked God, his parents, his coaches, and his girlfriend for believing in him. The reporter gleefully noted that Ethan's teammates had dubbed him "The Undertaker," not only for his prowess on the field, but also because he was heir to Lima's oldest mortuary, the Perdido Funeral Home. "I love baseball," Ethan said in the article, "but I'll probably wind up back in Lima eventually to take over the family business."

To keep himself in shape the summer before he started school, Ethan joined a fast-pitch softball league and played first base for the B&B Grocery Roustabouts. He thought the transition would be easy, since the ball was bigger. Quickly, Ethan discovered fast-pitch was tougher than it looked. The distance from home plate to the pitcher's mound was much shorter, for one thing, which threw off his hitting, and since the ball moved differently, his fielding suffered. But by July, Ethan had his game back, just in time for a match up between the Roustabouts and the King and His Court, the Harlem Globetrotters of fast-pitch softball.

The King and His Court was born on an afternoon in 1946. A gifted pitcher named Eddie Feigner threw a 33–0 shutout. When the disgruntled losers taunted him, Eddie claimed he could whip them again with just a catcher. "But you'd probably just walk us both," he mocked, "and then where'd we be?" So he drafted a first baseman and a short-stop and the four-man team still won, 7–0. Eddie declared himself "The King" and took his court on the road like a barnstorming softball circus. The King's fast ball came in at over 100 miles an hour, his curve dropped like an elevator, and he had trick pitches, too: blindfolded, behind the back, between the legs. He threw strikes from second base. His troupe traveled from town to town, taking on all comers. Most nights, the King and His Court went home victorious, and at three bucks a head, a lot richer as well.

But this story isn't about the King and His Court. It's not about the difference between baseball and the dying tradition of men's fast-pitch softball. It's not about Ethan Perdido and his *It's a Wonderful Life*-ish choice between duty to family and personal dreams. This story is about the girl sitting on a wooden-bleacher throne: Ethan's girl-friend, Laura Hofstadter.

Laura attended every game her boyfriend played, but not because she especially loved baseball. She went because it was something to do, and because she loved Ethan, or thought she did. She liked it when people looked at her

when Ethan got a hit or made a great play. It made her feel
like somebody. The summer he played for the Roustabouts,
she became a temporary member of the Softball Wives, the
husband-cheering women who dotted the stands of Winnesaw Park. The Softball Wives didn't care much for Laura.
They thought her standoffish, and they resented the way
their husbands stared at the browned belly revealed by her
knotted shirts. Laura felt the resentment in their smiles and
polite waves, but when Ethan asked her why she wouldn't
sit with the other women, she couldn't find the words to
explain.

But the night that the King and His Court played the
Roustabouts, Laura was forced to join the Softball Wives in
the bleachers. The game had brought out half the town,
after all. That day's edition of the *Lima Journal* claimed
Eddie Feigner was the most underrated athlete of his time.
Earlier that month, in an exhibition game with major-
league all-stars, Eddie had struck out Willie Mays, Willie
McCovey, Brooks Robinson, Maury Wills, Harmon Kille-
brew, and Roberto Clemente. In a row. K-K-K-K-K-K.

The stands were packed with sweating bodies. Laura
tried hard to keep herself contained, but she couldn't help
but touch the women on either side of her, couldn't help
but wonder how many years away she was from becoming
them. Betty Pollard, who worked down at the Lima Savings Bank with her, had thighs that spread like dough, and
Carol Winters bore a whole river system of varicose veins
on her legs. Both women had children, two or three each,
although Laura could never count them because they were
always racing around chasing foul balls.

The two teams were finishing their warm-up. The King

and His Court played catch, two pills slapping leather mitts, one exclamation mark after the other, punctuating the night. Ethan stood at home plate, hitting balls to his team- mates. Laura didn't care much for baseball, but she loved its sounds, the notes Ethan played on his bat; the long flies for the outfielders hit the bat's sweet spot with a deep, woody thwack, and the skittering ground balls he ham- mered out for the infielders cracked like gunshots. She liked baseball because you could feel it humming inside you every time something good happened.

A woman with a bad vibrato sang "The Star-Spangled Banner," and then the King got on the P.A. Laura saw him up in the scorekeeper's box, a stocky man with a flattop and a big grin.

"LADIES AND GENTLEMAN, I'M EDDIE FEIGNER, AND WELCOME TO TONIGHT'S GAME BETWEEN THE B&B GROCERY ROUSTABOUTS..."

He paused, letting the crowd cheer for their native sons.

"AND THE ORIGINAL FOUR-MAN SOFTBALL TEAM, THE KING AND HIS COURT!"

Everyone clapped politely.

"WE'RE PARTICULARLY HONORED TO PLAY IN LIMA, BECAUSE OF YOUR HISTORY AS A CIR- CUS TOWN!"

The clapping was a little louder this time, and Laura looked around to see who was hooting. She saw Mrs. Hobzini, a former trick-horse rider who owned the local bakery, and then the hooter: Rowdy Rubens, a human cannonball turned farmer. Rowdy stood up, waving his hat, whistling. Laura's dad used to troupe as a clown with the Great Porter Circus, and he said Rowdy came by his name for a good reason.

"YOU PEOPLE KNOW WHAT SHOWMANSHIP REALLY MEANS, AND I'M SURE YOU'LL APPRE-CIATE WHAT WE'VE GOT IN STORE FOR YOU! LET'S PLAY BALL!"

The King's cleats clinked down the metal staircase and across the cement walkway to the field.

During the game, Betty and Carol kept up a steady stream of chatter, and Laura wished she hadn't sat between them. Every once in a while, they stopped gossiping about other people's lives long enough to pry into Laura's.

"You must be so proud of Ethan," Betty said, lighting a cigarette. "Going off to college and all." Laura almost asked to bum one, but decided against it. Ethan didn't like it when she smoked in public.

Carol nodded. "You going off to school, honey?"

Laura blushed. "No, not right now. I'm going to stay on at the bank."

"Oh, that's what I did, too, before I got married," Carol said. "Had to give it up when the babies started coming."

Betty sighed. "Wish I could give it up, but we need the money." Laura knew Harvey Pollard worked at a variety of jobs, none of them for very long.

Laura stared at the field. "Well, I don't think I want kids for a while yet." She wanted to say, "not at all," but it wasn't something you said in Lima in 1967.

Carol touched Laura's knee. "Honey, sometimes they come whether you want 'em to or not."

The Softball Wives stopped chattering only when they heard the crack of bat meeting ball, and just then, a member of the King and His Court sent a line drive up the first-base line. Ethan dove and caught the ball easily, as if it was the most normal thing in the world to hit the dirt with your chest. Betty and Carol clapped, then turned the discussion to Tupperware. Laura excused herself to get a Coke.

HERE'S SOMETHING you need to know about Laura Hofstadter: She was not a nice girl. Oh, on the outside, sure, she looked just fine, but on the inside, Laura was all bad, and she knew it. Laura was a chronic stealer of lipsticks, always red, which she never wore. She liked to drive too fast with the radio too loud. She drank and smoked when she could get away with it. She enjoyed sex, but sometimes just pretended to, and she couldn't decide which was worse. Laura felt bad that she didn't like women much; they prattled on about nothing, which always turned out to be something. Men, on the other hand, said what they meant. She liked when men looked at her; she felt it deep inside, like needing to pee, but later, when she thought about what their eyes had said, Laura felt frightened and small.

Sometimes Laura thought she was a little insane, as if she might fly apart at any second. When those moments came, she looked at the people around her and did whatever they were doing, or whatever she thought they wanted her to be doing. Sometimes Laura thought she wasn't alive at all, only sleepwalking. When she looked back on her life, she could remember what people had said to her, never what she'd said back. Every day, Laura's mouth opened, but the words always seemed to come from somewhere else, like she was a character in a story—a stupid boy-meets-girl-story someone else was writing.

IT WAS THE bottom of the fourth. Dust hung in the fecund air from a stolen base two batters ago—it was that kind of summer night, the kind that hovers like a hot fog. Ethan Perdido stepped up to the plate. The King had been pitching blindfolded for a while, fanning Roustabouts one after the other, but when Ethan—the only batter who had managed to get any wood on his pitches—stepped up, the King removed the handkerchief from his eyes and settled in to hurl for real, without gimmicks. The King windmilled his arm when he pitched, picking up velocity, and then shot the ball from his hip so it zinged toward the batter. No arc whatsoever, no lofting the ball toward the plate like a red-stitched gift. With a count of one and one, Ethan swung at a pitch that came in at his thighs, sending a long pop-up toward left field. The shortstop for the King and His Court took off at a dead run and caught the ball midfield. Everyone had stood up to watch the ball's flight, as if standing would help them see it better, but now they settled back down, waiting for the next sound that would bring them to their feet.

Ethan was the only person at Winnesaw Park who didn't watch that ball. He'd already rounded second and was almost to third when he heard the crowd groan and the third-base coach told him to hold up. Ethan was quick, on the field at least. Quick bat, quick feet, quick hands. Laura liked having a boyfriend who always did well, who never needed consoling after a poorly played game. Harvey Pollard played right field for the Roustabouts, struck out more often than not, and committed at least two errors every game. Betty always kept a smile on her face, but Laura could feel her shame. She wondered what it felt like to love a man like that, and how often Harvey Pollard dropped the ball elsewhere: in the car, at work, in bed. What did Betty say to him when he cursed his performance? Laura knew what a woman was supposed to say in moments like that, but she also knew she didn't have it in her to speak those words. She'd tell Harvey to get a job. She'd tell him to let her drive. She'd tell him to take up bowling or golf. She'd tell Harvey practice makes perfect. Laura knew she was lucky; Ethan always came through, in every way, and she knew that was a rare, rare thing. Ethan was like a very pretty, dependable car, one that always started and never needed oil, the kind you can drive forever.

THE FIRST TIME Ethan and Laura had sex was after the Christmas Dance their junior year. Laura knew it was the night. She wasn't scared, but she wasn't excited, either. She felt like she had a dentist's appointment, something to be gotten through. They cut out early, and Ethan headed west of town, toward his family's cabin. It wasn't a cabin at all, actually, but rather a two-story lakefront home with a pier and two boats—a fishing boat and a motorboat for skiing. The first time she saw the place, she marveled that the Perdidos had enough money to fill not one, but two, houses. The Perdidos spent their summers at Yellow Lake, but rarely used the place during the rest of the year, which is why Ethan forgot it had no electricity or heat. Laura stood with him, shivering in the kitchen as they drank half a bottle of vodka from the liquor cabinet. They were still in their winter coats when Ethan carried her upstairs, although Laura had asked why they didn't just do it in the running car, where it was warmer.

"I love you," he said. "I want this to be special. I want to do it right."

He carried her to the queen-size bed in his parents' room, which had a picture window overlooking the frozen lake. The full moon lit the room a glowing blue, and they undressed in its light, shedding their heavy coats, then the formal skin of tuxedo and red satin gown.

"What's this," Ethan asked when she'd removed her dress. "You look like Scarlett O'Hara."

Laura stepped out of the crinoline, but it remained standing at attention on the floor. "It makes the dress stick out, silly."

"We could take it camping. Use it for a tent."

"Very funny." She tried to kiss him, but her teeth were chattering.

"Come here," Ethan said, taking her hand and leading her to the bed. Getting in was like sliding between slabs of ice, and they moved together quickly, looking for the warmth inside each other. Until that night, they'd done pretty much everything but what they were about to do, and Laura feared Ethan would forego it all. But bless his heart, Ethan took his time and went to every base: first, then second, then third. When he rummaged for his wallet, she wanted to ask when he'd bought them and where.

He turned on the transistor radio beside the bed, and she heard a faint, big-band ballad. Sitting with his back to her, Ethan put it on, and Laura wished she could see this part, but instead she felt herself and discovered that she was hardly even wet, which scared her a little, and then he was on top of her, and the radio turned to static, and then it was happening.

The bases probably helped a little, but Ethan couldn't get inside, so she put her hands on his buttocks and brought him into her. She felt the tearing, then the give, then the movement in and out of her. It felt horrible, like being cut slowly with a serrated knife. His head was down in the crook of her shoulder and he never saw the way she looked, only heard the sharp intake of breath, which made him moan and move faster. She put her hands on him again, pushing him, thinking it would make things go more quickly. But there was all that vodka, and it took a long time. Afterward, they lay quietly for a few minutes, and Laura felt something inside she thought was love, but wasn't. It was the astonishment you feel after you sleep with someone for the first time, like you've just survived some small danger together.

Ethan found a flashlight in his father's bedside table and shone it under the sheets, like a child playing a game. That's when he saw the blood streaking the bedsheets and her inner thighs. "Jesus. Are you okay?" In the cold, he'd shrunk back into himself, but Laura could see the red on him and in his dark, curly hairs. The water was turned off to keep the pipes from freezing, so they stood shivering in the bathroom, cleaning themselves with toilet paper. "What'll we do with the sheets?" he asked.

She sat on the icy toilet. "Take them home and wash them. Make sure it's cold water. Not hot."

"How do you know that?" he asked.

Laura gave him a withering look. "My dad owns a laundry. Plus, I'm a girl."

"Oh, right."

She watched Ethan stride into the bedroom, strip the bed, and remake it without sheets. Maybe seeing this, her naked boyfriend bent over the bed, should have filled Laura with warm, domestic thoughts, but it didn't. She made a sanitary pad out of toilet paper and laid it in the crotch of her underwear. If she asked, would Ethan give her his handkerchief for this purpose? Yes, he probably would, and it made her feel sorry for him.

They dressed, and with each step, Laura felt the knife again. As they drove down the snow-blown highway, she groaned every time they hit a bump. Ethan said, "I'm sorry about the radio. Now we don't have a song to remember this by." Laura didn't tell him that the whole time, she'd been playing "Take Me Out to the Ball Game" in her head. Already, Laura knew there were some things about what happened between two people in bed that you just can't ever say.

THE SCORE WAS one to nothing. The King had tripled in the fifth, driving in the only run scored. It was the bottom of the last inning, two outs, the Roustabouts' last chance to get something going. Ethan dug in, his foot at least six inches behind the now-blurry batter's box, but nobody said anything. More than likely, he was the last out anyway. The King threw his first pitch, a sinking curveball. Ethan had guessed a heater, and so he swung at the spot where the ball would have been. The crowd groaned, and Laura felt her heart tighten a little. The King's next pitch came from between his legs, a perfect strike, but Ethan missed that one, too. The crowd oohed and ahhed a little, and Ethan stepped out of the box to knock the dirt from his cleats and take a few mean swings. Laura could tell he was mad, and she sent a thought out to him: *Knock his block off.* Ethan stepped back in, down 0 and 2, and the King wound up like a spring. The bleachers were silent, so everyone heard the King's "*Unnnhh!*" as he whipped the ball from behind his back.

Ethan got ahold of it, of course. A drive up the middle, over the King's outstretched mitt, into the stubbled grass of center field. The first baseman got to the ball quickly, and Ethan pulled up with a double.

Harvey Pollard stepped to the plate.

Betty and Carol yelled in unison, "Bring him in, Harvey!"

Laura hoped he would, but doubted it.

Harvey swung at the first two pitches, the second one so hard he almost fell down. A chuckle rippled up and down the stands.

The King wound up and threw. Laura heard the ball's slap and saw the catcher rise from his crouch and toss the ball back to the King. All of this—the pitch, the catch, the throw—happened seamlessly, like still images you finger flip into a moving cartoon. Harvey's bat never moved. The umpire paused, then said, "Strike three!"

Harvey whirled around. "You call that a strike! It was high! It was way high!"

Laura whispered to Carol, "He must have thrown that awful hard. I didn't even see it."

The King stood on the pitcher's mound, grinning and tossing the ball up and down. Ethan came trotting in from second base, pulled Harvey away from the ump, then whispered something. Harvey's face turned red, and he shook his fist at the King. That's when Laura got it.

"He never threw the ball," she said to the people sitting around them. "The catcher just held another ball."

"That's not fair!" Betty yelled. "He gets another turn!"

Laura heard the King yell back at the crowd. "The ump called it strike three, folks. Never argue with the ump." The King and his Court trotted to their dugout, threw their red, white, and blue mitts on the bench, then came back out to shake hands. The game was over, but it took a few minutes for everyone in the crowd to understand what had just happened. Laura heard weak laughter, followed by applause. During the hand slapping and good game–ing, Harvey Pollard stayed on the bench, pouting, with his arms folded across his chest. Laura stood behind the dugout's chain-link fence and heard the Roustabouts' teasing.

"So how high was that one, Harv?"

"Myself, I like 'em a little lower."

"Harvey, had your eyes checked lately?"

"Shut up," Harvey told them. "Just shut the hell up."

"I still don't think it's fair," Betty said to Laura and Carol while they waited for the team. "He didn't have to make an example out of Harvey like that."

Laura looked her in the eye. "It's just a game, Betty."

Carol giggled.

"Well, I bet if it had happened to Ethan, or to Bob,"

Betty said, putting her hands on her hips and staring at
Carol, "you'd both be saying the same thing!" Then she
stomped away.

Carol patted Laura's shoulder. "Never mind her. She'll
get over it."

"I hope so," Laura said. "I have to work with her tomorrow." They worked adjoining windows at the bank,
and Laura hated it when their breaks overlapped. In the
employee lounge, Betty liked to sit at the table and talk
about what the women around her were eating. "You're so
lucky you can eat like that," she'd say to the thinner tellers.
"Everything goes straight here on me." Betty would slap
her thighs and light another cigarette. Once, Laura caught
her in the restroom, stuffing a cupcake into her mouth.
"Don't tell Ethan," she mumbled. "Harvey thinks I'm on a
diet."

Ethan emerged from the dugout, and the couple walked
past the King's red, white, and blue Winnebago. The King
was sitting on a lawn chair, signing autographs, but he saw
Ethan and called out, "Hold up there forty-two."

Ethan and Laura had been holding hands, but for some
reason, they dropped them.

The King walked over, hitching up his pants. "You
really got ahold of a couple of them. Another couple of
feet, one way or another, and this could have turned out a
whole lot different."

Ethan smiled. "Well, I got lucky. You threw 'em by me
pretty fast there."

"What's your average, son?" The King rubbed his hand
over his flattop.

".625."

Laura stood, smiling politely.

"My first baseman's taking a coaching job in Washington. I've been on the lookout for fresh blood."

Ethan said nothing, but Laura placed her hand in the belt loop of his pants.

"Come down tomorrow afternoon and we'll give you a little tryout. I seen a couple guys already, but you never know what might happen." Finally the King looked at Laura. "What do you think about that, little lady? Think your husband could be a member of the court?"

Laura was startled. "I'm not his wife."

Ethan stared at her for a second. "Sorry. This is my girlfriend, Laura," Ethan said. "I'm supposed to be playing for Purdue in the fall," he added quietly.

"Is that so? Well, you two think on it and come back tomorrow. Plenty of time for college." With that, the King went back to his lawn chair and continued signing autographs for the gathering crowd.

AFTER GAMES, Ethan liked to drive up to Yellow Lake to cool off in the water and make love. Since the Christmas Dance, Ethan had avoided taking her to his parents' room, although there was no longer anything to worry about, bloodwise at least.

On the drive up, Laura kept the dome light on and read from the game program. "It says here they drive all over the country. And Canada, too. Fifty thousand miles a year."

"That's a ways," Ethan said. Nothing else.

While they swam and dried off and drank beers on the dock, Laura kept talking. She described their life, a year from then. They were driving down a highway, following the King's Winnebago. Every day, they passed through new towns, waving to kids on bicycles. Every night after the game, they'd camp somewhere and drink by the fire and go inside and make love and sleep all night together, listening to crickets. "Wouldn't it be wonderful, Ethan?"

"I don't know," he said. "It sort of scares me, actually." He opened another beer and took a long swig.

"What part?"

"The driving actually. I don't like not knowing where I'm going."

She repeated the names of towns from the program's schedule: Cincinnati, St. Louis, Kansas City, Grand Forks, Omaha, Missoula, Tucson, Bakersfield. It reminded her of her father's circus route books. As a child, Laura read them like children's stories full of adventure. Her father rarely spoke of his clowning years, but when he did, he always smiled in a secret way.   ·

The list of towns didn't calm Ethan down. "Now, how does the King know where the ball fields are in all those towns? And the roads to take to get there?"

Laura just looked at him. "He's been there before. We'd just follow him."

"I suppose I'm just being stupid."

"It's not stupid," Laura said, choosing her words carefully. She did think it was a little stupid. "Look, Ethan, it'll be fine. We could see the country!"

"We?" Ethan said, smiling.

Laura punched his arm. "You know what I mean."

Ethan rubbed his bicep. "Easy. Did you hear Eddie tonight? He thought we *were* married." He looked down at his feet dangling off the dock in the dark water.

Laura said nothing, and a moment later, Ethan got to his feet and held out his hand for her. They went to his parents' room, and Laura knew that meant something. They did it on top of the bedspread, too eager to pull it down. Since the Christmas Dance, things had greatly improved. Sometimes when Laura came, it felt like a rock tossed with a plunk into a lake, sending out circled waves, gentle ripples. But once in a while, they were bigger and brighter, like atom bombs—a bright light and then a roar and then plumes rising into her head. Laura didn't like comparing them to something that killed people, but tonight she didn't care. Tonight was Hiroshima, Nagasaki, the Bikini Atoll.

ETHAN DIDN'T GET her home until nearly one. From the driveway, Laura saw the blue light of the television blinking in the front window. It was her mother, who would pretend to have fallen asleep watching the news. This was how Mildred Hofstadter spoke, in the language of the Not Said, and Laura had learned to speak this language fluently.

Laura walked in the door, and her mother shook awake, saying, "Oh, you startled me!"

Don't you feel bad, coming in like a cat in heat and waking up your poor mother?

"I'm sorry, Ma. Why don't you go to bed now?"

Please get out of here so I can take a bath and wash the smell of lake and beer and smoke and sex off of me.

"How was Ethan's game? It must have gone into extra innings."

You've been up to something.

"They lost, but it was a really good game. We went over to the Pollards' for a cookout after."

Of course I've been up to something, but I'm not going to tell you about it.

"Oh, Harvey and Betty. Isn't she the one who smokes?" *I don't like them.*

"Yeah." Laura yawned, then exaggerated it. "I'm real tired, Ma. Good night."

Boy, I just had sex three times.

"Laura, I really don't like you getting in this late. What will people think?"

You're dating the best catch in town, but you're acting like a tramp.

"Nobody cares when I get home, Ma. Don't you want me to spend time with Ethan before he goes to school?"

What a pickle you're in! If you tell me to stop seeing him, he might break up with me. And then what would happen to your plan to marry me off?

"Of course I want you two to spend time together. Did you know that his mother actually spoke to me today down at the market? Never given me the time of day before. Probably felt like she had to. Now."

Don't you remember the night after the Christmas Dance, how you came home with blood in your underwear and I helped you get the stains out? He has to marry you. He has to.

"Ma, Mrs. Perdido just didn't know you before we started dating."

I remember. I told you it was my period, but I knew that you knew the truth. You started planning my wedding that night.

Mildred held out her arms. "Come here and give your mother a kiss."

I want to smell your breath, your hair.

"Oh, can't it wait until tomorrow?"

I squirted toothpaste in my mouth, and I've got my bra in my purse. Laura leaned down and kissed her mother's papery cheek.

"You smell different," Mildred said.

You smell like a whore.

"Well, you know, it was hot tonight."

If I'm a whore, then you're my pimp.

ETHAN TRIED OUT for the King and His Court the next day, and after an hour of snaring throws and hitting dingers to the fence, he'd made the team. The King shook his hand. "Okay, Perdido. My guy's got about a month left before he takes off. Meet us August twentieth in Cleveland."

For practice, Ethan kept playing with the Roustabouts, but Laura stopped going to the games. "I think I've got some kind of summer cold," she told him. "I'm sure it'll pass."

Something was happening. Her insides felt warm and full, and her limbs seemed imperceptibly heavier. She stopped eating desserts and candy, thinking she was just putting on weight, but the sensations persisted. Then, one day at work, she threw up her lunch in the employee restroom. "I must have a bug," she told her boss, who let her go home early. Betty Pollard waved good-bye, and as soon as Laura was out the door, the tellers all looked at each other and smiled.

That night in bed, Laura did some math in her head. She remembered the night at the lake, after the King and His Court game. She remembered the atomic bombs, the first, the second, but for the third, Ethan hadn't gotten up to get his wallet, and she'd been too busy to notice. Vaguely, she remembered him pulling out early, how she

helped him finish on her stomach. But maybe. Oh, surely
not. They'd done that so many times before and nothing
ever happened. It was a virus, or something.

But a week later, something else happened. She was at
work, again. She saw her hands counting out singles to a
customer, but then the edges of the picture went dark, like
those pinhole shots in old movies, and then she was looking up at Betty Pollard. Her ears roared, and the other
tellers had to help her stand up because her legs had
turned to marshmallows.

"Do you want me to call your mother?" Betty asked.

"Oh no. I'll be fine," Laura said evenly. "I just need to
catch my breath."

Betty brought her a glass of water and crouched down
beside her. "You need to see a doctor, Laura. You need to
get this checked out."

"I don't think that's necessary," Laura said, but she
knew she didn't sound as sure this time.

Betty stood up, her knees popping. "I'll just go get our
purses."

A few minutes later, they were driving down Main
Street. "I called Dr. Spencer's office," Betty said, lighting a
cigarette. "They said they can work us in right away."

"Could I borrow one of those?" Laura asked.

Betty looked at her for a second. "I didn't know you
smoked."

Laura lit the cigarette and it shook a little between her
fingers. "I think I just need a nap."

"Well, you tossed your cookies last week. Remember?"

They rode in silence, then passed Clown Alley Cleaners, her father's business. He was there a lot, even at night,

and a long time ago, Laura had figured out he wasn't a hard worker, just a henpecked husband. She could hardly blame him; she didn't spend much time at home, either. Laura saw her father for a split second, talking to a customer over a pile of shirts, and then she started crying.

"You aren't going to call my parents, are you, Betty?"

Betty paused. "We don't need to worry them."

"Thank you."

Well, you probably know what happened to Laura at the doctor's office. Betty was reading *Reader's Digest* in the waiting room when Laura emerged, her eyes puffy, her face pale. Without saying a word, they walked to Betty's car.

"So, what's the verdict?" Betty said.

Laura was stony. "They aren't sure. It might be mono."

"Oh come on, honey. You don't have to lie. I know." Betty took a cigarette out of her purse and handed one to Laura.

"I don't want Ethan to know," Laura said.

"Why the hell not?"

"Well, the King and His Court want him. He's leaving in a week."

Betty turned to look at Laura. "Is that so? He hasn't said anything about it to anyone. I'd know. Harvey tells me everything."

"We didn't want to tell anyone until he told his folks."

"Just Ethan, huh? Well, that's great for him."

Laura threw her cigarette out the window. They were coming into downtown, and she didn't want anyone to see her smoking.

"What are you going to do?" Betty asked.

"I don't know," Laura said, but she did know. She'd always known, in a way.

THREE MONTHS EARLIER, Laura had turned eighteen. Ethan told her they were going to a fancy French restaurant in Indianapolis, and her mother went crazy making her a new dress of pink eyelet. "If this doesn't make him pop the question," her mother said, fluffing the skirt, "I don't know what will."

"Maybe," Laura said. She stood on a stool while her mother pinned the hem. "We haven't even graduated yet." Until this moment, she hadn't even considered that he might propose that night.

Her moony friends had their nuptials perfectly planned, everything from the dress right down to the music and centerpieces. When they asked her what kind of wedding she wanted, Laura just waved her hand and said, "Oh, something small and tasteful." But the truth was Laura never dreamed of tuxedos and white cakes. What kept her up at night was the transistor radio under her pillow, tuned to Chicago radio stations. Long after the radio was off, long after she'd gone to sleep, a song played in her head, very very softly, and one day, Laura knew she'd walk into a bar in some far-off city and hear a sad piano playing her song, and then she would know she was home.

Laura held the tomato pincushion and tried to imagine herself married to Ethan. He'd play ball for a while, and that would be fine, every night encountering a diamond made of dust and chalk. But eventually, they'd end up back in Lima at the Perdido Funeral Home. How would she spend her days in that big house? Mrs. Perdido greeted people at the door, baked casseroles and chickens for griev-ing families, and played "Amazing Grace" on the organ. Laura couldn't picture herself doing any of that. She prac-ticed in her head what she'd say if a ring box appeared on the table. *I love you, but I don't want to hold you back.* This was partly the truth, but more to the point, she knew she should say, *I love you, but not like a wife should love a husband. I want something else, but I don't know what it is yet.* Laura didn't yet know the real truth: *I don't love you; I love what my body does when I'm with you.*

As they drove into Indianapolis, Laura stared at the swanky cars purring alongside them. She wondered who the drivers were, these men in dark suits with lipsticked women, their faces empty but determined. Where were they going? Laura wondered; in Lima, she sometimes knew which way cars would turn before their blinkers came on. No one in Indianapolis knew that this was her birthday and she was on her way to a restaurant with her boyfriend who might propose. They couldn't care less, and instead of making her feel small and alone, this sudden anonymity made Laura so happy she scooted over next to Ethan and rubbed his thigh, not stopping until they reached the restaurant.

After dinner, Ethan placed a long jewelry case on the table, and she cried in happiness and relief when she saw the silver necklace inside. None of her prepared speeches would be necessary now. After dinner, they spent an hour in the Starbright Motel, a neon-lit room reeking of beer. Her mother waited up for her, of course, and when Laura showed her the necklace, Mildred sighed and said, "Well,

I'm sure his mother helped him pick it out. The Perdidos
don't like to show off their money, now do they?"

BETTY DROVE HER back to the bank. She finished the day
without looking a single person in the eye. After work,
Laura went to the drug store and bought travel-size toothpaste, shampoo, and soap. "Going somewhere?" the cashier
asked. Laura didn't recognize her, an elderly lady in a wash
dress, and so she said, "Yes."

"Where you going then?"

Laura hadn't thought about it, but then she said,
"Chicago."

The woman smiled and handed her the change. "The
Windy City. I been there once. The World's Fair back in '33.
It's a big, big place. Watch your purse, though. Mine got
snatched."

"I sure will." She walked out, palming a tube of Very
Cherry lipstick.

That night, Laura packed a small suitcase and snuck it
out to the car. Then she wrote her parents a note. "By the
time you read this, I'll be gone," it read, and the words
came easily, as if she'd already written them before. She
put the note in the book next to her father's chair. Tomorrow, she'd swipe a few bills from the till, and at five
o'clock, she'd get in her car and start driving.

What would happen next? She ran through all the sce-
narios in her head. If she told Ethan about the baby, he'd
ask her to marry him, and if she said yes, well, she knew
that story. If she left now, before Ethan knew, she'd go to
Chicago and get a job, an apartment. Then there was the
baby, keep it or not, and having to think about this made

her want to scream and cry. Instead, Laura tried to invent her new name, because surely Ethan and her parents would come looking for her. She saw Ethan crying, calling hospitals and morgues, but eventually, he'd give up and his life would go on just as it was supposed to. My god, Laura thought, so many things could go wrong, problems she could anticipate and name, and invisible ones buried like booby traps. Thinking about it all made her temples throb like timpani drums, so she stopped thinking. Laura sat herself down in the chair across the room and watched the body in the bed sleeping all night. A new moon rose outside her window, and she watched it hover in the air like God's thumbnail. The night hummed with crickets and cicadas, and her body hummed, too, electrical and alive, and the girl in the chair wished the girl in the bed would wake up and see her eyes glowing hot in the dark room.

AT FOUR O'CLOCK the next afternoon, before she took the money, before the story Laura had half written in her head could begin, Ethan Perdido walked into the Lima Savings Bank. He got in Laura's line, and said, "I'd like to make a deposit," pushing a velvet ring box toward her. Then he jumped over the counter and got down on one knee. "Laura, will you marry me?"

The customers applauded and laughed, but she just stood there.

Betty said, "Why don't you two go in the break room?"

Laura led him there, shut the door, and took a deep breath, inhaling hairspray and ashtray and Ethan's Old Spice cologne.

"You look nice," she said, pointing to his chinos and white Oxford shirt.

He smiled. "I know about the baby, honey."

She felt like curling into a ball on the floor. "Betty told you, didn't she? She promised me she wouldn't."

He touched her stomach. "Betty? No, your mother called me this morning."

"My mother?"

"How far along are you?"

"I don't know," Laura said, then remembered the laminated diagram the doctor had shown her, the square containing a pink and red blob. "Over a month. Two."

"What do you say," Ethan said. "Will you marry me?"

Laura thought about the speeches she'd planned three months earlier, about the suitcase in her car, about the map she'd bought that morning at the gas station. She could get to Chicago, yes, but then there was everything after that, and it was just too hard, too much. And since the road to Chicago was closed, she turned around in her mind and headed for Cleveland, where the King and His Court were waiting. She saw Ethan driving a red, white, and blue Winnebago, the baby sleeping in her lap, the road unfolding over the Earth's curve

"Yes," Laura said, thinking, *It can still work out. We'll still get away.*

THIS IS WHAT happened instead.

When Laura got home that night, her good-bye note had vanished. Her mother crept up the stairs to Laura's bedroom. "I found this suitcase in the car. Thought I'd

bring it in so it doesn't get wet or anything." Mildred unpacked it and smiled. "We'll have to go down to the lingerie
shop and get you a little trousseau. Some real nice things."

When Laura returned to work the next day, Betty Pollard told her everything. "Sweetie, Mr. Vaughn at the bank
called your mother to check and see how you were, and
you were out somewhere, so she called me. I tried not to
say anything, but she just kept at me. But you know, it's
better this way. You can keep on at the bank until you start
to show, and I've got a whole bunch of cute maternity
clothes." She pinched Laura's arm. "It'll be fun, won't it?"

When they went out to dinner with both sets of parents to celebrate the engagement, Ethan told Laura he'd
called Eddie Feigner. "I'm going to mortuary school instead, starting next month," he said on the way to the
restaurant. "Gotta start thinking about my family." Laura
cried, and Ethan said, "I know, I know. It's all happening so
fast." At dinner, many toasts were made, and then the Perdidos and the Hofstadters fought over who should pick up
the check.

When Laura went wedding-dress shopping, her
mother said how grateful she was to Betty Pollard for con-
fessing everything. "I called Ethan straight off and told
him. He told me about that foolish idea about playing for
those clowns that call themselves a baseball team. I said no
daughter of mine is going to go traipsing all over the place
towing a baby." Her mother touched her arm. "I just want
you to have a nice life, dear. You're so lucky. You'll live in
the nicest house in town."

The night before Laura's wedding, Ethan's mother,
Mrs. Perdido, said, "I'm so glad your mother called me after

she spoke with Ethan. We told him he could have the business right away. We've been wanting to retire early anyway. Got a nice little place picked out down in Florida." Then she whispered in Laura's ear. "My husband doesn't know about...you know...and your mother says she's not going to tell your father, either. This is a little secret between us girls." Mrs. Perdido squeezed Laura's hand. "After all, women make the world go round."

ETHAN PERDIDO and Laura Hofstadter were married in a small ceremony at the Church of the Brethren in 1967. The bride wore a floor-length gown of antique white with an empire waist—a good choice since she was just starting to show. Ethan looked a little stunned amid the popping flashcubes, like a prom-night boy in a tux. Laura was the calm one, moving with grace and purpose, as if she'd been waiting for this day all her life. Throughout the ceremony and the reception, the opening of gifts and throwing of rice, she did everything by the book. But on the inside, she was flipping through another story, full of color and Chicago skyline. Laura saw a silver cigarette case and red lipstick on a cocktail napkin. She smelled coffee in an all-night diner. She heard heels clicking down a sidewalk, cars whooshing down a highway, and music tinkling from a piano bar. She saw the dark doorway, and Laura knew that someday—when she was ready—she would walk through it.

BOSS MAN

— or

The Gypsies Appear and *Poof!* They're Gone

EVEN WHEN IT was all over—the money counted, the caravan disappeared, the carcasses rotted, the blacktop washed away in the rain—Earl Richards never spoke ill of the gypsies. He had been warned, after all, the day he'd gone out to sign the papers that made him the new manager of the KOA Kampgrounds in Lima. The owner, name of Altman, had run the place for twenty years and was more than ready to pass the torch. Altman showed Earl around in a campground golf cart, driving one-handed, pointing out what all needed to be looked after. The pinball machines and pool tables. The pH level of the pool. The warped and flaking picnic tables. The massive griddle for the Sunday pancake breakfasts. The goop on the maple syrup dispensers. The Frisbee golf course. The restrooms and showers. The coin-operated washers and dryers. Earl wrote down the list on the only paper handy—his pay stub from the railroad. Altman was still talking, still going strong, and Earl was running out of paycheck.

Finally, Altman turned the cart back toward his house (soon to be Earl's house), a two-story split-level a hundred yards from the KOA A-frame. "Oh. Almost forgot," Altman

said, pulling his Titleist hat over his eyes. "There's the gypsies, too."

Earl nodded, clicked his ballpoint, and wrote "Gypsies"
without thinking. Then he thought about it. "Gypsies?" he
asked.

"There's a band of them show up every year in late
summer, about a hundred of them or more. They pay cash.
Tell me they travel around blacktopping and roofing. You
gotta keep your eye on them, especially when they come
in the store," he said, "or they'll take everything in sight."
Earl's pen wavered over his check, but Altman clapped him
on the back. "Don't worry about it. They pretty much take
over while they're here, but they're good people, mostly.
They just don't see things our way."

Earl knew the railroad paycheck in his hand wouldn't
always be there. Altman's deal meant he'd be able to give
his wife, Peggy, and their fourteen-year-old son, Joey,
more than they'd ever had or even dreamed of having: a
two-story house in the country with a fireplace, more bedrooms than they needed, an in-ground swimming pool,
pinball machines, a pool table, foosball, even a Frisbee golf
course. Earl figured if he saved every penny he earned over
the next two or three years, he could buy Altman out. The
idea of owning a franchise, of owning land, amazed him.
Earl was descended from a long line of milkmen, firemen,
and factory workers who'd never owned their houses out-
right, let alone the acreage they sat on.

The contract was waiting on Altman's dining-room
table. Earl signed it, shook Altman's hand, and accepted the
beer offered. They clinked cans.

———

EARL WAS nineteen years old when he hired out as a clerk on the Chesapeake & Ohio Railroad. A good job, back then. Every year, the head office in West Virginia sent boxes of C&O windbreakers and baseball hats to its yard office in Lima, one for each man, and no one, not even Earl, took more than his share. Then came the so-called prosperous 1980s. The C&O merged with the ailing Baltimore & Ohio and became the Chessie System, and from the new head office in Baltimore came boxes of coffee mugs and plastic pens. Earl stared at these gifts and knew, somehow, that hard times were at hand. He took eight mugs and stuffed thirty pens in his coat pockets.

Five years later, VTX Transportation bought the Chessie System, and all that came from the new HQ in Jacksonville were key rings and College Boys, business majors who didn't know dick about trains. For one, they didn't know that on the railroad, you call a man by his last name, not his first. College Boys wore Dockers and polo shirts, slicked their hair with styling gel, and, worst of all, drove foreign cars and never even bothered to explain why. Their job was to lay off any man with fewer than fifteen years seniority.

That's when the men at the yard office started stealing, openly and earnestly, taking whatever could be smuggled out without the College Boys noticing. Typewriters. Chairs. Lanterns. Coffeepots. Flashlights and batteries. The old C&O logo, Chessie the Sleeping Cat, became a collector's item, and some of Earl's friends swiped Chessie calendars and clocks and sold them to nostalgic railroad buffs for a tidy profit. A memo appeared on the bulletin board: "VTX RECOGNIZES THE NOSTALGIA FELT BY EMPLOYEES OF ACQUIRED

SYSTEMS, BUT URGES SAID EMPLOYEES TO DESIST FROM PILFER-
ING MEMORABILIA."

Underneath, someone had written, *"Translation: Quit
stealing our shit. Signed, VTX."*

A disgruntled brakeman named Ellis rerouted three
covered grain hoppers to an abandoned siding and hired
semis to come unload the corn. A pissed-off clerk by the
name of Warren fixed the waybills and entered the cars into
the computer as empties, a somewhat complicated scam
that made them $30,000 each. That is, until VTX figured it
out and brought criminal charges against them, state and
federal. Afterward, Earl realized that if one of those men
had come to *him*, he'd be the one in prison, and it scared
him more than a little to think how easy a man can be
driven to lawlessness. Earl didn't hate VTX. He simply felt
no loyalty to it. Whatsoever. VTX was just three letters that
sounded good together and didn't stand for anything.

But he loved the railroad itself, the idea of it, at least.
As a boy, Earl loved to play down at the siding, where old
cars sat abandoned, like mammoths waiting to die. His favorites were once owned by Wallace Porter, red Pullmans
and yellow animal cars beaten gray by half a century of Indiana winters. He liked to go down there and imagine
rocking in his sleep with the beat of the train, waking up
each morning in a different town. After high school, after
he married Peggy, he was offered jobs at the phone company and the railroad—he didn't even think twice.

But perhaps he should have. Sooner or later, VTX would
give him the same choice put to the men who were already
gone: move to Cincinnati or Jacksonville to keep your job or
take a payoff and find some other way to make a living. It

was only a matter of time before VTX closed the yard office. The signs were clear. The cinder block building on Canal Street needed paint and new windows; the panes broken by vandals had been covered by VTX with pieces of cardboard. Broken glass, garbage, and cigarette butts were scattered along the tracks snaking along the Winnesaw River.

Leaving Lima. The idea began to take on the distinct, inevitable edges of fact. His mother started inviting him over for lunch on Fridays and made Earl's favorites. "Don't know how long I'll be able to make beef and noodles and rhubarb pie for my baby," she'd say, start crying, and run into the bathroom, leaving Earl in the kitchen with his food and his father who said, "Now look what you done." Peggy put the pressure on him, too. Her folks lived in a nursing home nearby in Kokomo, and she visited them often. If Peggy skipped three or four days, her parents told horrible stories about the patients who didn't have family or friends stopping by. "They get bedsores, Earl. What good things they have come up missing. They cry and no one's there to hold their hand." Her worry kept them up half the night sometimes.

Peggy started putting brochures for correspondence courses and technical schools next to his La-Z-Boy. If he fixed the toaster, she told him he'd make a fine small-appliance repairman. Earl went from a pack a day to two. Sometimes on the way to school, Joey would point to the few businesses left in Lima—convenience stores, used car lots, quick-lube garages. "There, Dad," he said. "Why don't you work there?" and Earl tried to imagine himself punching a cash register, hustling cars, changing somebody's oil. He was forty-four years old.

In the end, Peggy saved them. She was the receptionist at the hospital, which was where she overheard one of the nurses, Altman's wife, say that she and her husband were looking for someone to manage their KOA. They were moving to Fort Wayne to open a Dairy Queen. Peggy acted quickly, and a week later, Earl sat with Altman in a golf cart, writing down the old man's warnings on the back of his VTX paycheck. Pool. Frisbee golf. Bathrooms. Gypsies.

THE GYPSIES appeared five months later, on a muggy August morning as Earl was getting ready for work. He looked out his bedroom window, and through the wet mist, he saw it glittering in the distance, just like Altman had said. A train of Airstreams, Winnebagos, Chieftains, Avions, and Prowlers, thirty of them at least, coming down the road. One by one, they turned in the driveway and headed for the KOA A-frame. Peggy had just left to open the store, and Joey had gone with her to clean the pool. By the time Earl called in sick to the railroad, changed into tennis shoes, and ran down to the A-frame, the situation was already out of hand. Women in colorful skirts pulled children into the bathrooms, and teenage boys swam in the pool fully clothed. The game room was crowded with dark-skinned men pumping quarters into the pool table and humping the pinball machines. Joey was in the camp store behind the cash register, ringing up candy and cheap KOA T-shirts like crazy. Peggy had her hand around the wrist of a little boy who had tried to walk out with a Frisbee, and a gypsy woman, the mother probably, was yelling at Peggy in a language Earl couldn't understand. He thought the gypsies would speak Spanish, like the migrant workers who came through town around harvesttime. But this wasn't Spanish.

He tapped Peggy on the shoulder. "Thank god," she said, giving up on the boy, who walked out of the store with the woman and the Frisbee. "There," she said, pointing to a fat man chalking up a cue stick in the game room. "That's him. The king or whatever. I'd better go check the bathrooms." She stuck ten rolls of toilet paper down her mop handle and marched out the door.

Earl walked into the smoke-filled game room, stuck out his hand, and introduced himself.

"Are you new Boss Man?" The king ignored Earl's hand.

Earl put his hand in his back pocket. "I guess so. I'm the manager."

"I only talk to Boss Man." The king leaned his pool cue against the wall. "We stay for three days, okay?"

"That's fine. How many sites do you need?"

"Over there. We stay over there." The king pointed out the window to the campsites by the Frisbee golf course. They were closest to the woods, the most secluded, and, on the weekends, the most popular. But this was Tuesday, and the sites were empty.

"How many sites do you need?" Earl asked, trying to count the number of campers outside the pane-glass window.

"I don't know. Other Boss Man figure it out."

Earl got a map of the campgrounds and circled off a large area. "This is twenty-five sites. Sewer, water, and electric.

How many vehicles do you have?" Outside the window, a few kids zipped around on quad runners, spraying gravel from the fat tires. "And those."

"Oh, many of those."

"I need license numbers. And you can only have one vehicle per site, or you have to pay an extra five dollars each."

From his back pocket, the king took out a roll of hundreds as thick as Earl's arm, held together by a rubber band. The king wet his fingers and laid ten bills on the counter. "This how much last Boss Man charge us. When we go, I to give you ten more. Is this okay, Boss Man?"

Earl stared at the bills on the counter. Technically, the king only owed him $900. Twelve bucks each for twenty-five sites for three nights. The rates were posted right over the counter, but Earl thought maybe the king couldn't read the sign. Instead, the king was offering him more than he'd made during the entire month of July, counting the Fourth. So far, Earl hadn't saved one dime toward buying the KOA; Altman's monthly profit estimates had been grossly exaggerated. At the moment, they had only one site filled, the Ramseys, an elderly couple on their way up to the Wisconsin Dells. Earl took the money.

Joey punched a one and three zeroes on the cash register, and Earl placed the bills inside, trying to be nonchalant. "Checkout's Friday at noon. No later. We're full up for the weekend." Earl pointed to the stack of registration cards, every site booked in advance for Labor Day, the last big weekend of the summer. "I just need you to sign here," he said, making an X on the registration card with his pen. The king made another X right next to it. "No," Earl said, "I need your name."

The king was walking out the door, but he turned and said, "You write John Smith." Outside, he held up his arm and whistled. Instantly, the game room, bathrooms, and pool emptied themselves of gypsies. The caravan headed back to the campsites, and Earl wondered where all they'd been over the years. Part of him wished he could be like the gypsies, but who lived like that anymore except for retirees and thieves? Earl hadn't even seen a hobo around for at least a decade. When he walked back to give them their three-day supply of garbage bags, Earl found the gypsies completely unhitched and unpacked, campfires ablaze, like magic.

THE NIGHT THE gypsies arrived, Earl opened the *G* volume of the *Encyclopedia Americana*. He'd bought the encyclopedias for Joey, although it was clear his son had hardly used them. When Earl opened the book, the spine made a pained, cracking noise. Earl read the entry for "Gypsies" at the dinner table. Periodically, he'd look up at Joey and Peggy. "They're from India originally," he said, his mouth full of hamburger. "They speak Romany. Hitler gassed a bunch of them."

Peggy nodded her head and said, "Really? That's interesting, honey."

Earl ran his finger down the page. "It's this diaspora thing. They call us *gaje*, like gentile to Jews."

Raising her eyebrows, Peggy said, "Oh. They're Jewish?"

"No, they're not Jewish," Earl said, shutting the encyclopedia. "They're just trying to get by, you know?" Peggy and Joey nodded and kept eating.

In bed, Earl heard the gypsies singing and clapping into the small hours of night. Their voices blew in his windows, open to catch the night breeze. Earl got out of bed and pulled back the curtains. His own camper sat below him in the backyard, dark and abandoned, the wheels braced by two-by-fours. It was a Skamper with a small kitchenette, an oven, sink, refrigerator, bunk beds, and a bathroom stall. It smelled of cigarette smoke, mildew, and fish. When he bought it off a guy at work years ago, he told Peggy, "We can go anywhere now." He'd never seen the country. All he ever saw was the inside of the yard office and the trains passing by the window, bound for somewhere else. Once, Earl had taken them to Michigan, but that was as far as they ever got. When his vacation time rolled around for the next few years, either money was short, or something needed fixing. So instead, they'd camped locally—at the KOA. At night, Earl would sit by the campfire with a beer, trying to imagine that he was somewhere else—a New Mexico desert, a Colorado mountain, a redwood forest— anywhere but where he was, which was five miles from his house in town.

Ever since they'd moved to the KOA, Peggy had been after Earl to sell the Skamper. "We live at a campgrounds, for godsake. What do we need with a camper?" she said. Earl knew she was right, but he said, "I like the idea of keeping it around, just in case we get a chance to go somewhere."

Across the field, the gypsies' campfires flickered, and he imagined them moving north in the summer, south in the winter. In his dreams that night, he was in the king's Chevy Silverado, headed west with the windows down, moun-tains on every side.

———

IN THE MORNING, the Ramseys came into the office to complain. "We're missing our lawn chairs and an Igloo cooler," Mr. Ramsey said. "I think we both know where they're at."

Earl remembered what Altman had said: *They pretty much take over while they're here.* Finally, Earl understood the deal struck between Altman and the king: Altman made a much-needed profit, and the gypsies got free rein of the place. Earl shrugged his shoulders at the Ramseys. "I'm sorry. There's not much I can do. I doubt they'd cough up your stuff anyway." He punched a key on the cash register, and the money drawer flew open. "Look, why don't I refund the two days you paid up for. Maybe you could head up to the Dells a little early?" Earl smiled, but he felt bad, buying them off this way. The Ramseys took the money, packed up their Winnebago, and headed for the highway.

After they left, Earl called the yard office to take a couple personal-leave days. He half listened to the "This isn't good teamwork" tongue-lashing from his supervisor, a College Boy named Jones—Travis or Trent or something like that. A few weeks earlier, College Boy had spotted boxes of VTX urinal cakes, toilet paper, and industrial cleaning supplies in the back of Earl's truck. He'd been saving on expenses this way, and College Boy knew it. "This is the last break you get, Earl," he said, and hung up.

Sitting at the camp-store counter, drinking his morning coffee, Earl tallied the numbers from the night before. The gypsy's $1,000. A bucket of quarters from the games. Sales in the camp store had doubled. Sure, a lot of merchandise walked out the door unpaid for, but the markup was high enough that he'd still come out ahead. As a sign of this blessing, a string of cars and trucks led by the king's

Silverado passed by the window, shining in the pink morning light.

A few hours later, some of the trucks returned. The king, dressed in a suit and tie, walked into the office escorted by five young men in jeans and short-sleeved dress shirts, smelling of incense and cologne. "Boss Man," the king said, "where we find a pig and a sheep?"

Joey stopped refilling the candy jars, and Earl looked up from the T-shirt racks, losing his count. "Excuse me?" Earl asked.

"We christen new babies this morning. These the fathers," he said, gesturing to the men. "Every year, we come here, and then we have a feast."

Earl pointed out the store window. "There's grocery stores in town."

"We want big ones."

"You mean *alive*?" Joey said, his eyes wide.

Earl set his clipboard down on the counter. "There's farms all around here. You can ask. We just moved and I don't know any of them right well yet."

The king straightened his tie. "I understand. We be back later." He started to walk out of the store, but turned at the door. "Boss Man, you need paved driveway here. We do good job."

"Thanks, but I think everything's okay," Earl said, waving his hand.

The king shrugged and walked out the door. Children streamed into the camp store clutching quarters in their hands, clamoring for candy and pop. Earl's father usually only came out to help on Sundays with the pancake breakfasts (he was a navy cook during WWII and could prepare a meal for fifty more easily than for two). But today, Earl had assigned his father to stand guard in the middle of the store. He frowned, folded his arms sternly over his chest, and asked, "What do you want?" in a gruff voice anytime a child wandered toward the merchandise. The gypsy children fled to the game room, where Joey waited with his arms folded, trying to look as imposing as his grandfather. Peggy was on hold with the phone company. The pay phone outside the camp store was full; since the moment the gypsies had arrived, the booth had been occupied by a steady stream of gypsy women, gesturing and yelling into the silence of the enclosed glass, dropping coin after coin into the slot.

A skinny young boy ran up to Earl, who was wrapping rolls of quarters, dimes, nickels, and pennies. "Boss Man, your machine took my quarter."

The pinball machines were unreliable and acted cranky every so often; the rental company had promised to send out a serviceman who'd never showed. "There you are," Earl said, handing over a quarter from his stack. "What's your name, son?"

"Macho," the boy said, smiling a smile without many teeth.

Earl laughed. "What's his name?" he asked, pointing to another boy standing nearby.

"Fuzz. My sister is Peaches." The boy closed his hand around the quarter. "Thank you, Boss Man," he said and ran back into the game room.

His father grunted. "Who the hell would name a boy Fuzz."

Earl shrugged. "They keep their real names secret, for protection." Earl's father grunted again.

Thirty seconds later, Earl found himself surrounded by ten children, all of whom said the machines had taken their quarters. "Trust me for a quarter," a little girl said. "My daddy beat me if I ask for another."

Shit, Earl thought. "Joey!" he yelled, "Get in here!" The children stood with their hands out, palms up, their eyes enormously brown. "No more free games," Earl said, trying to sound stern and in charge.

"But you gave him a free game," a pudgy girl said, "and he lies. I no lie, Boss Man."

Joey stepped into the camp store, his eyes small slits, his face red. "Whaddaya mean, you don't lie. I saw you in there playing just a second ago, and it was working fine."

A teenage boy in a blue T-shirt stepped up. "My sister is no liar."

Peggy hung up the phone and stood beside Earl. "If you want to play the games, you have to take the risk."

"Yeah," Joey said, looking right at the gypsy boy.

Earl raised his hands. "Okay, Joey, why don't you go on out and get the garbage. Pop," Earl said, "would you check the pool for me?" The children gave up asking for quarters and ran back into the game room. Looking out the window, Earl watched the blue-shirted gypsy boy peel out of the driveway on his quad runner. Joey followed, humming along at a fast clip in the golf cart.

Earl wanted to make sure Joey wasn't getting himself into any trouble, but his father called to him from outside. "Earl, you'd better come take a look at this." Walking around the A-frame, Earl saw the problem. The pool was packed with bobbing gypsies. A man pulled himself out of the water, his clothes shining wet and clinging to his dark skin. He yelled and did a cannonball that sent a spray of water all over the cement. The water level was down a couple of inches already. "Guess I need to put more water in the pool," Earl said.

Earl's father shook his head. "Why don't they wear bathing suits for godssake."

"Something about it being against their religion. Unclean. That's why they don't touch us, either."

"They're sure making the pool unclean, damn dirty wops."

"Dad, they aren't Italian. They're from India. By way of Europe." Earl knew he'd only corrected half of what was wrong with his father's statement, but he'd given up trying to correct the other part. Earl counted himself lucky that at least he'd gotten his father to stop saying "nigger" around Joey. He said "negro" instead.

"What's the word for somebody from India, then?"

Earl sighed. "Indian, I guess."

"If I was you, I'd tell them to hit the road. We're missing two buckets of pancake batter." In the distance, they heard a crashing sound and the whine of a motor revving too fast. "The golf cart," Earl said, already running toward the Frisbee golf course. Behind him, Earl heard the keys and change in his father's pockets jangling as he tried to keep up. When Earl trotted up to the first hole, Joey was climbing out of a ditch. Down below, the mangled golf cart sat smoking.

"Are you okay," Earl asked, bending over, breathing hard.

"Goddammit," Joey said, "he ran me right into the woods!" A cut over Joey's eye dripped blood down his face and onto his T-shirt. Earl handed him a handkerchief from his back pocket. "The big mouth from the store. On the quad runner. He ran me into the ditch." Then Joey looked down at the ground. "I'm sorry, Dad. I think I totaled the cart, but it wasn't my fault."

"Don't give me that shit, Joey. You were racing him."

Earl's father arrived, pale and breathing hard. "It wasn't his fault," he said. "The gypsy kid didn't have to get so rough."

"He still shouldn't have been fooling around," Earl said. "Get on up to the house and have your mother look at that cut. We'll talk about this later." Holding the handkerchief to his head, Joey dragged his feet in the gravel. Earl walked to the edge of the ditch where his father now stood. "Probably should just leave it down there for the time being. Don't know how to fix it even if I do get it out of there."

Earl's father threw a rock into the ditch. "How much one of them things run?"

"I don't know, but I'll bet they're not cheap."

"You should make them gypsies pay for part of it at least."

In silence, Earl and his father turned and walked toward the A-frame, past the gypsy section. The campers were arranged in rings, facing into the campfires. Clotheslines, strung from every tree, sagged with wet towels and clothes. The smell of cooked meat hung in the air. The king got up from his lawn chair. "What happen, Boss Man?" the king called out.

Earl kicked the gravel. "My son ran our cart into a ditch."

"One of yours ran him into the ditch," his father said, "if the truth be told."

The king shook his head. "Oh, no. I know this boy. He good boy."

"Like hell," Earl's father said. "That golf cart was an important piece of equipment. I think you owe my son for the damage. It's only fair."

"I don't think so, Boss Man."

Earl's father stepped forward, his chest inches from the king. "I *do* think so, or do we have to call the police to come out here and have a look-see?" He spoke right into the king's face. "Understand, Cochise?"

The king lit a cigarette and reached into his back pocket. He looked at Earl's father, then at Earl. "Okay, Boss Man. You right. We pay." He peeled two hundreds from the roll and held them out.

Earl knew his earlobes were red. "Thanks," he said, taking the bills and walking away. They felt damp in his hand, and he stuffed them in his back pocket. Earl felt queasy and sluggish, as if something inside was squeezing his stomach and heart.

His dad followed. "That gypsy kid deserves a good ass whupping, if you ask me. Joey wouldn't be getting in so much trouble if you tanned his hide once in a while." Earl remembered well how handy his father had been with a yardstick and belt. His father stopped walking and touched his arm. "Son, these people are no good. This is probably one of the only places that'll take them, and you're being more than fair just by letting them stay here. But hell, they're taking everything they can off you."

"Don't you think I know that, Dad?" Earl tried to keep his voice level. "But we're making more money this week than we would have in a whole month. We need that money, or we're going to have to move." Earl pulled out his cigarettes and lit one. Twenty years of smoking, and he still didn't like to do it in front of his father, but he needed one bad. "Just let me handle things the way I think's best." Earl knew his tone sounded disrespectful and ungrateful, but he couldn't help it.

"Maybe your mom and I should go on home."

"Maybe you should," Earl said.

"Fine. You're the boss," his father said, turning his back and walking away. A few minutes later, Earl heard his parents' Oldsmobile hustling down the driveway, rocks pinging, spraying gravel from the tires.

THE NEXT MORNING, Peggy and Earl got up at daybreak to clean the game room. Earl found a cigarette burn on the green felt of the pool table. A june bug buzzed around the fluorescent lights. Joey was filling the pool and dumping gallons of chlorine into the water. He walked in to tell them that the levels were way off. "It's probably not safe to swim. Should we close the pool?" he asked.

"If we did, they'd probably swim anyway," Peggy said, dropping beer bottles into the garbage with a clank. "Just make sure it's filled up and keep dumping in chlorine."

A cloud of gravel dust hung over the driveway; the gypsies came and went day and night, but through the haze, Earl saw his parents' Oldsmobile coming toward them, even though he'd expected his dad to stay home and pout all day. His mom got out with an armful of the baskets she wove in her art and crafts class. "It's going to be a hot one today," she said, walking into the store. "These people will buy anything just to be buying. Thought I'd bring out my baskets and make me a little mad money." She covered a card table with a red and white gingham tablecloth. Off the edge of the table, she hung a sign, HANDMADE BASKETS, $20 EACH.

"Don't you think that's a little pricey, Mom?" Earl asked.

His mom winked. "We'll see." And sure enough, when the store opened, the gypsy women hovered over her table. They tried haggling, but Earl's mom stood firm by her price. In an hour, she'd sold every one.

Later that morning, the king came into the office and asked how much Earl wanted for the Skamper. Earl's knees popped as he stood up from his crouch behind the Coke dispenser. "It's not for sale," he said.

"The sign say it for sale." The king pointed toward the Skamper parked in Earl's backyard. From a distance, he could make out the orange and black FOR SALE sign.

"It's a mistake," Earl said.

"I give you good money for it."

Peggy walked in with a large box, ignoring Earl's glare.

"I'm sorry," Earl said, his voice rising. "I'm not selling the camper." The king shrugged his shoulders and walked out of the store.

Peggy set the box on the candy counter and began tearing off bits of masking tape. The box was marked FOR GARAGE SALE. Peggy kept it in their closet.

"Don't you think this has gone far enough?" Earl asked.

"Some of those boys running around are the same size as Joey."

"When did you buy the sign? That's what I'd like to know." Earl could no longer keep his voice from rising.

Peggy kept tearing tape. "Your mom had such good luck with those baskets, Earl."

"I'm going to get the garbage," Earl said. He'd risen early enough to need a jacket that morning, so he took off his C&O windbreaker and laid it over the box. "I'm coming back for that. Don't sell it while I'm gone."

Peggy finally looked Earl in the eye. "Yes, Boss Man." He pushed the front door open with a hard shove that sent the bells ringing and shook the glass in the panes.

Earl collected garbage in the lone golf cart, slamming the lids down on the trash cans. At the gypsies' camp, he saw two animal carcasses skewered on spits, turning over an open fire. The gypsy men sat in lawn chairs gathered around a small color TV placed on a picnic table. A Cubs game. Earl recognized Harry Carey's voice. The king walked up to Earl carrying an aluminum roasting pan full of steaming meat. "Boss Man, you take this. We always give to Boss Man for let us stay. Not so many are nice as you." The king gave a small bow. "You good man. You take."

"Thank you," Earl said, taking the pan from his hands. He drove slowly back to the store, trying not to spill the meat threatening to avalanche all over the inside of the golf cart. Earl set the pan on the counter. "What the hell is that?" Earl's father asked.

"Meat," Earl said. "A gift from the king."

"I wonder what they put in it?" his mom asked. Earl looked at her. "For flavor," she added.

ON FRIDAY MORNING at eleven thirty, Earl told the king, "You know checkout's noon, right?"

"We be gone by noon. Yes."

Earl looked around. Boys on quad runners raced around the field. Women hung laundry on the lines, and men lounged in lawn chairs, smoking and drinking beer. "But you haven't started packing up yet. Breaking camp takes a long time. I know," Earl said.

The king laughed. "When we go, we go like that," the king said, waving his hands with a magician's flourish.

Earl remembered how quickly they'd set up camp and figured the king was telling the truth. "I'll give you until one. We've got a lot of people coming in this afternoon who already booked these sites."

The king nodded. "Okay, Boss Man. We be gone by one."

At one thirty, Earl walked back to the gypsies' camp. The king said, "We fixing trucks. Have problems."

Earl noticed that the hoods of the trucks weren't open, and the gypsy women were serving lunch. "I don't see anybody working on trucks."

"My nephew go to town for parts. Can't go until he get back. Then we fix trucks."

From inside one of the campers, Earl heard a man laugh and speak a word. More laughter. Lighting a cigarette, he thought about calling the police. He knew a few guys on the force, knew they'd come out quick if he called, knew they'd laugh at him, too. He looked at the king. "Well, in any case, I guess you owe me some money."

"I was to bring you this when we go, but we not go yet." The king handed Earl a roll of bills, wrapped by a rubber band. He weighed it in his hand, thick and heavier than the first payment.

Earl said, "I've been good to you, right?"

"This Boss Man best one we have."

Earl ground out his cigarette. "You know, I know something about you people. How you've been treated and such. You might even say I'm a bit sympathetic." Earl thought the king might appreciate this, but he didn't see any reaction on the man's face. "But enough is enough. I don't want to call the police."

"Oh, you not do that. You good man, I know. How much you want for us stay longer?"

"I don't want anything else from you people. I just want you to stick by our agreement and be on your way." Earl looked the king straight in the eye. After a few seconds, an urge to look away came over him, but he fought it and kept on staring. Finally, the king nodded his head, turned, and whistled. The gypsies left as swiftly as they'd come. In ten minutes, the campers filed down the driveway, the king's Silverado in the lead. And then they were gone.

Earl walked to the A-frame. Ringing another one and three zeroes into the cash register, he took the bills from his back pocket. "I'll be goddamned," he said, fanning out the bills.

A hundred dollar bill wrapped around fifteen singles.

PEGGY WORKED graveyard shift that night, and Joey, freed from gypsy duty, escaped to a friend's house, leaving Earl alone to check in the Labor Day campers. He welcomed them with a smile and a firm handshake, glad to have the gypsies out of his hair. But near sundown, he found the animal carcasses, tiny pieces of meat still hanging on the bones, thrown near the start of the first hole of the Frisbee golf course. Flies buzzed and clung to the skeletons. In the dim twilight, Earl picked up the carcasses with his bare hands and threw them into the bed of the truck. The stink of rotten meat was all over him. He scratched his nose, smelled the carrion wedged under his fingernails. His stomach turned, but he kept it all down. After dumping the bones into the green garbage Dumpster, he walked back to the house, took a hot shower, and threw his clothes away.

At nightfall, he set up a lawn chair next to the Skamper in the backyard and opened a beer. In his mind, he saw the king in his Silverado, leading his family in that long caravan. He knew where they were going. South down I-65. Indianapolis. Louisville. Bowling Green. Nashville. Birmingham. Montgomery. Mobile. The Gulf of Mexico. Sometimes at night as Peggy read her Danielle Steels and Janet Daileys, Earl read the Rand McNally, skimming the highways with the tip of his finger, making up the plot as he traveled from town to town. But all the roads, all of his stories brought him back to the place he started. He didn't know how else to finish. The gypsies were their own home. Earl saw their secret, and that was why they were going on to the next thing, and he, Earl Richards, was sitting in the backyard of his two-story house, watching the flicker of campfires not his own.

EARL DECIDED never to tell Peggy or Joey or his parents about the carcasses. They would take the carcasses personally, a confirmation of gypsy lowliness. Earl knew he'd never be able to explain to them that the carcasses were just part of the deal, and certainly no different than the cases of VTX toilet paper sitting in the campground storeroom. For weeks, neighbors came by to complain that the blacktop sealer the gypsies had spread over their driveways had melted and run in the first rain. The mailman delivered bills for tires, truck repairs, portable video games and televisions, and car stereos—all addressed to "John Smith c/o KOA Kampgrounds." Earl returned the bills, "Not at this address." Angry merchants called, trying to hold Earl accountable, but he hung up on them.

In the spring, Altman called. The Dairy Queen hadn't done well, and they were thinking about moving back to Lima, back to the KOA. He asked Earl if he was ready to buy, two years before he was even supposed to ask. Earl told him, "We've been having second thoughts. Not enough cash flow. Too far from the highway."

"It's a shame you have to move again," Altman said smoothly. "You barely just got there."

"A man's gotta be mobile," Earl said.

As it turned out, it was a good thing Earl never got rid of the Skamper. They had to move in with his parents, and since the house only had two bedrooms, Joey slept in the Skamper parked in the driveway. Then, in the fall, VTX closed the yard office and Earl, Peggy, and Joey were gone, following the rails to the next biggest railroad town, Cincinnati, the Queen City.

At the Queensgate Yards, Earl asked, "Is there somewhere I can work so I can at least *see* a train?" His boss, another College Boy, rolled his eyes at Earl's request, as if trains were quite beside the point. He led Earl to a small room containing a TV, VCR, and boxes of videotapes, hours and hours of passing trains. Eight hours a day, Earl rewound and fast-forwarded, writing down the numbers painted on the sides. When he tired of that, Earl was assigned to the stockroom, where he pointed a laser gun at computer barcodes so every box was inventoried and accounted for. When Peggy asked him to bring home a case of toilet paper, he had to tell her that it was no longer possible.

Earl says there's no honor in railroading anymore. He works to pay the bills, secure his retirement, and send Joey to college. On summer nights, he likes to buy a six-pack and sit on a picnic table down at the city park and watch the barges moving up and down the Ohio River. He thinks about the quarter of a million he'll get when he retires at sixty-five, about how he and Peggy will finally see the West. They'll take the Skamper over the prairies, the desert, the mountains, all the way to the Pacific. They'll sit on the beach with beers and watch the blue ocean until the sun goes down.

THE BULLHOOK

The Blizzard of 1900

THE STORM HOWLED across Illinois, hovered over Lake Michigan, then swooped down into northern Indiana, dumping over three feet of snow onto Lima. Outside town, at the winter quarters of the Great Porter Circus, animal handlers fed the big cats, which were pacing nervous circles, spoke soothing words to the liberty horses fretting in their stalls. Nettie Hofstadter woke up alone in a cold bunkhouse and touched the empty space beside her. Her husband, Hans, was superintendent of the menagerie, responsible for keeping the animals calm. Over the roaring wind, Nettie thought she heard the elephants screaming. Still, Nettie cursed Hans and his absence from under her mountain of quilts. In the night, she'd told him she felt sure the baby was coming. He'd touched her taut belly and laughed. She'd been saying the same thing every day for a week.

For hours, Nettie lay completely still, watching her smoky plumes of breath and the angry white cloud outside the window. Her water broke at nightfall, and she shouted for help. No one came. Perhaps the storm drowned her cries, but more likely, the neighbors had become all-too accustomed to the shrieking that accompanied Hans and Nettie Hofstadter's nightly spats. Afraid to deliver her first child alone, she considered walking to the nearest bunkhouse, but it belonged to a reclusive acrobat, a woman Nettie strongly suspected of witchcraft. A labor pain sent a sharp knife into her back, and finally, she decided to head for the elephant barn.

Nettie pulled on her coat, but it wouldn't button over her belly. Swaddling herself in the bed quilt, she stuck her swollen feet in a pair of Hans's boots. Outside, she staggered toward the elephant barn, trying not to waver. She'd forgotten to pick up the blizzard rope—if she missed the barn and wandered past the camel paddocks, she'd disappear forever into the winter fields. The falling snow was blowing sideways and slantways and up from the ground. Nettie turned around, saw her footprints disappearing behind her, and trudged forward.

As Nettie made her way to the barn, inside two old gypsy women—sister seamstresses, passing the time with a bottle of spirits—were watching Hans put his herd of elephants through an amusing pachyderm headstand lesson. The class was not going well. When Nettie threw open the barn doors, she let inside a tornado of cold and snow. Hans scolded her, raising his metal bullhook over his head. She might have sent the elephants into a panic. The gypsies came upon them, separated man and wife, saying, "Let us take care of this, boss. You go now, and we bring you good news later."

They led Nettie to an empty stall, spread out her quilt, and ordered her to lie down. Hans stoked the nearby stove, listening to Nettie's curses—all in German. He smiled.

Mostly, he and Nettie spoke English now, thickly accented but passable. When they fought, which was often, they did so always in German. Afterward, they had sex in German, an indifferent but necessary joining done in silence. Hans spoke his native tongue when he talked to God, when he talked to his elephants. His mentor back in Hamburg taught Hans that German was the only human language wild beasts could understand and obey.

A half hour later, one of the gypsies handed him a mewling bundle of scarf. She said, "Look here, boss. I bring your son."

"*Hier ist mein Sohn,*" Hans said, holding the baby up to each of his elephants. The biggest, a bull named Caesar, touched the baby's head softly with its trunk.

The gypsy sisters whispered only to Nettie, "A sign. Your son will live a hundred years." Then they turned back to look at the baby in Hans's arms.

Nettie sighed. She wished she'd had a girl, a daughter to keep her company through the long winter days in the bunkhouse, the summer nights in Pullman cars and cheap hotels. Instead, her son would grow up in the elephant barn with a bullhook in his hand.

She almost got it right.

The First Time Ollie
Got His Name in the Paper

The Lima Journal, April 25, 1901

ELEPHANT IS KILLED

CAESAR IS BROUGHT TO JUSTICE

Pays the Penalty for the Murder
of Hans Hofstadter with his Life
Elephant Jack Pursues the Beast
to the Fields and Shoots Him

A short time after dinner yesterday afternoon, Keeper Hofstadter and his assistant Elephant Jack took the elephant to the Winnesaw River for water, as the pump for the Elephant House was not working. On the way down to the river, Caesar showed a disposition to be unruly and was given a couple of jabs by Hofstadter. Down in the water, Caesar took the idea of revenge and caught Hofstadter in his trunk. He threw him in the air about 25 feet and Hofstadter came down flat in the water. He was able to get up and return to his former position and was trying to control the beast again when Caesar caught the man once more and this time threw him into the water and drowned and crushed him to death by holding him at the bottom of the stream with his tusks and feet.

An order was quickly put out by Wallace Porter to put down the elephant, and he was disposed of with a combination of rifle shots and apples filled with strychnine. People crowded around the remains and viewed them until dark. The tusks, four feet and two inches in length, were sawed off and taken in for safekeeping, as they are of great value. The remains will be skinned and the hide sent to a tanner. Caesar weighed about 9,500 pounds and was the largest animal in captivity. He was worth

$6,000. The act Hofstadter went through with him at the circus was worth $100 a week to the circus. It has been reported that he was vicious and had killed three men before coming to this circus, but this is denied. Hofstadter had him in charge for eight years or more. He was first with the Washburn Show, then with the Diamond Show, and when Mr. Porter bought the Diamond stock, Caesar and Hofstadter came along. He showed no specially mean traits at the farm here, though yesterday morning he made a swipe at Hofstadter who had been sick of late.

Mr. Hofstadter was about thirty-five years of age and leaves a wife, Nettie, and son, Ollie. His skull was fractured and his arm broken by the beast's awful treatment.

Childhood

OLLIE SAW his father's dark, featureless face almost every night. Always, he woke from this dream feeling melancholy, a few notes of a sad song stuck in his head. But no matter how hard he tried, Ollie could remember neither the words nor the melody. Sometimes his mother looked at him strangely, as if at any moment she might start singing the song, but she never did. Instead, she'd look away, pressing her lips into a firm and final line. When he asked her, "What was my father like?" she said nothing. She said, "Look at that funny dog." She said, "Are you done with chores?" She said, "Don't ever ask me that again."

And so Ollie's father became not a memory or even a

ghost, but rather a pocket of absence with distinct shape and form. It slept on the side of the bed his mother never touched, even in her sleep. It sat in the empty chair when they ate. It stared out from the wall where his father's framed picture should have hung, but didn't. It floated in his mother's clipped-off words, like soap bubbles that disappeared with a silent pop. It was the book his mother never read from, the story she never told.

Art Appreciation Class

OLLIE FOUND his father on a wall.

His mother worked as a maid for Colonel Ford, the show's general agent. Mrs. Colonel had hired a painter to cover the walls of her house with murals of circus life, and one day, Ollie wandered into the study, the one room his mother had forbidden him to enter. The mural depicted a tiny man in a red shirt held aloft in an elephant's trunk. The man on the wall had no face, but Ollie knew it was his father even before Mrs. Colonel slipped up behind him, even before she told him everything she knew.

She let him look at the wall whenever his mother wasn't around. After, she gave him cookies. "Our little secret," Mrs. Colonel said. "A boy needs a father, even if it's only like this."

The Spanish Flu Epidemic of 1918

THE DISEASE did its work quickly—one morning over breakfast, Nettie complained of a headache, and by nightfall, she had a fever of 105. Blood and fluid filled her lungs, leaving her gasping for breath. The doctor quarantined her, so Ollie waited outside, entering every couple of hours to check. The bunkhouse reeked with the stench of death, and he could hardly wait to escape outside, to fill his lungs with the wet, earthy smell of early spring. Smoking his cigar, he listened to Nettie moan and scream, all in German, a language she hadn't spoken in years and which Ollie had never learned. Stubbing out the cigar, he set it on the windowsill, realizing that the next time he came outside to smoke, his mother would be dead.

It was late afternoon on the third day since she'd been stricken. Ollie walked through the shadowed bunkhouse—no fire, no candles, no lamp, only the dying winter's light guiding him to his mother's bed. Perhaps it was the unique quality of this light—a deep, shimmery, underwater radiance. Perhaps it was the unknowable epithets spoken in that foreign tongue. Or maybe it was the sound of water rushing into lungs, or possibly the wide eyes of fear. Likely, it was the combination of these things that made Ollie believe he was being made privy to two deaths—his mother's and his father's. He watched them drown, struggling for enough air to plead for their lives. They were looking up, not at him, but rather past and through him. Ollie turned and looked over his shoulder, wanting to see what they were seeing—a mad elephant or an impatient angel leaning against the wall—whatever it was that filled their eyes and hearts with such horror, such surprise.

Then it was over. He stripped the bed linens, collected all the dish towels and washcloths and blood-spotted handkerchiefs. But he couldn't bring himself to take off his mother's nightdress. It was dark by then, and a new moon hung thinly in the sky. He threw the windows open and went outside to finish the cigar. When the draw became too hot, he held a piece of newspaper to the stub, and then lit the mound of contaminated cloth. Ollie watched the windows of neighboring bunkhouses grow bright with lamplight. The circus people were rising from warm beds, pulling on their shoes and coats, and soon they would come into the bunkhouse and take his mother's body away. Ollie ducked inside and went straight to the Saratoga trunk at the foot of his mother's bed—his parents' old trouping trunk. Kneeling before it, Ollie jimmied the lock. On top, he found his mother's wedding gown of yellowed lace. He left it on the foot of the bed. Someone else would dress her.

Inheritance

AS OLLIE RUMMAGED around, he let himself hope that the trunk contained the words his mother had never spoken about his father. If Nettie *had* written down all her musings and memories, Ollie would have found a million tiny slips of white paper—every passing thought and long-winded anecdote, accumulated inside the trunk like a pile of snowflakes.

Your father and I met at church.

Sometimes at night, I can see him sleeping in you, in your face and your hands.

The gypsies told me you would live one hundred years, but I don't believe a word they say.

But of course, Nettie didn't write these things down. This is what Ollie Hofstadter found in the trunk:

His father's entire wardrobe of three black suits, starched white shirts, two hats, three pairs of shoes, a pair of mud-stained boots, a graying nightdress, and socks.

A sliver of ivory as slender as a new moon resting inside a leather drawstring pouch. Caesar's, he assumed.

Two photographs. In one, his father standing next to Caesar. A loin-clothed Negro sitting on Caesar's neck. Written on the back: *"Iowa 1900 Hans Hofstadter and his Jungle Goolah Boy."* Ollie calculated in his head. His mother is somewhere outside the frame of the picture. And he himself is inside her, waiting to be born. The other photograph was very dark. A flower-draped casket resting between two chairs. A picture placed on the casket. Ollie squinted. The other photograph, the one he's holding in his hand. His mother is somewhere outside the frame of the picture, and he is in her arms, just over a year old.

The last thing Ollie found was his father's metal bullhook, bent into a C-shape, handle tarnished, prongs blunted. Holding it in his hand, he imagined the struggle, the force that bent it. *My father fought for his life with this, the last thing he touched.* A cold shiver tingled up his arm. Anyone holding the bullhook might have felt this, but to Ollie, its faint, almost electrical impulse seemed like a telegram that had waited eighteen years to be delivered.

The Roaring Twenties

OLLIE EARNED his keep at the Great Porter Circus trouping as a clown with his best friend Joe Price. Ollie, the smaller of the two, was Mr. Ollie, an Auguste clown in flesh-toned makeup and a giant nose. Joe became Jo-Jo the Clown, a tall white-face clown who teased, harassed, and tortured Mr. Ollie until the blow off, when the tables always turned. They were drunk most of the time, even in the ring. At night, while the roustabouts dropped canvas, they'd stumble around laughing, holding each other up. They found that evening's lineup joint, which was an empty wagon taken over by industrious local prostitutes. Wallace Porter liked to keep a Sunday School show, so he often broke up the lines—they generated too much heat from the cops. So Ollie and Joe sometimes resorted to lonely dancers from the girl shows. Most nights, Ollie and Jo-Jo found what they were looking for, and they always managed to get on the train before they passed out in their bunks.

Ollie spent his twenties this way and thought he was the luckiest fellow in the world.

The Cowboy and Indian Act When Soused on Canned Heat

JO-JO, BEING THE BIG MAN, played the Cowboy to Mr. Ollie's Indian. It went as so: Cowboy terrorizes Indian. Tables turn. Indian sinks hatchet into the head of Cowboy, who wears a wooden wig. Audience laughs. Simple, so simple they did it blind drunk most of the time.

But one day in Mankato, Minnesota, it went as so: Cowboy terrorizes Indian. Tables turn. Indian sinks hatchet into the head of Cowboy, who has forgotten to wear wooden wig. Audience laughs. Cowboy is just as surprised as Indian at this new end to the gag. Blood running down the Cowboy's head fills his eyes. Then they fill with nothing.

Someone to Settle Down With

OLLIE WENT ON clowning solo for a couple more years. He fashioned a skeleton out of papier-mâché and rigged its arms and legs to shadow behind him, mimicking his every move. He tried to make the act funny—running in circles to elude the skeleton, hanging a PLEASE FEED ME sign from its ribcage. Wallace Porter shook his head. "Please come up with something else," he begged. "You're scaring the kids." But it was no use—all the gags Ollie came up with were just as maudlin. *I just can't be funny anymore,* Ollie realized. *I might as well get married.*

That winter back in Lima, he saw a pretty young woman standing with Wallace Porter at the elephant paddock. Normally, Ollie avoided elephants at all costs, but he wanted to meet the girl. When he approached, Wallace Porter clapped Ollie on the back and made their introduction. "This is Ollie Hofstadter," Porter said, "world-famous clown. Born right here in this elephant barn, isn't that right, Ollie?"

"Right," Ollie said, embarrassed. This was his favorite story, gleaned from various sources (not including his mother, of course). Over the years, he'd polished the scene until it sparkled like a beatific Nativity scene—his mother's dangerous journey to the elephant barn, his proud father presenting him to the assembled animals. But as much as he loved the story, Ollie would never tell it to a pretty girl he was trying to impress.

Wallace Porter turned to her. "Meet Mildred. Harrison. Her folks are Charles and Grace. Live just down the road. You've probably seen her dad around here. Best carpenter in Lima if you ask me."

"I think. Maybe." Ollie nodded, even though he couldn't remember meeting the man.

Porter touched Mildred's shoulder. "Can't believe you're almost sixteen. Doesn't seem possible." Turning to Ollie, he said, "Speaking of curious births, Mildred was born during the flood. Had to rescue the whole family." Porter's voice went soft and faraway, as it always did when he spoke of the Flood of 1913, when he'd lost almost everything. After a long pause, he wiped the memory away like a cobweb. "Mildred here wouldn't stop crying, so her dad gave her apple brandy to calm her down. Showed up at my house one week old and drunker than a sailor."

Mildred went a mortified white. "Please," she begged. "Don't tell him that!"

Porter laughed and bid them good day.

Ollie fancied himself good with the ladies, but he had absolutely no idea what to say after an introduction like that. So he rambled about the weather. Mildred kept her eyes on the paddock, her hands inside a fur muff. An elephant ambled over, and Mildred reached out to stroke its hide. The animal wrapped its trunk around her muff, snatching it away. "Oh!" Mildred cried. "Please get it back for me."

But instead, Ollie stepped away. "Oh," he said.

The elephant put the muff in its mouth, and finding it not too tasty, dropped it into the mud. One of the handlers retrieved it. Ollie was red-faced. "Sorry," he said. "It's just that I can't. Um."

Mildred laid her hand on his arm. "You don't have to explain. I know who you are."

The Second Time Ollie
Got His Name in the Paper

MILDRED REFUSED to marry a clown. "I have nothing against the circus, mind you," she said. "Uncle Wallace is a great man. But I want a normal life." Ollie didn't put up a fight about it—he'd already decided to leave the show anyway. So he bought a dry cleaners in town with the money he'd saved trouping (minus what he'd spent on liquor and lineups). If a different kind of business had been for sale, he might have become a baker or a grocer. But a dry cleaners it was, and he named it Clown Alley Cleaners. Ollie painted clowns all over the plate-glass window, and he lined the walls out front with photographs: clowning with Jo-Jo; posing with Annie Oakley and Buffalo Bill; his arm around Wallace Porter. He called the *Lima Journal* to see if they'd do a story for the grand opening, a little free publicity. Mildred said it was tacky. "My mother always said that good people should only have their names in the paper three times—when they're born, when they get married, and when they die."

The reporter came anyway and wrote the story: FORMER CLOWN CLEANS UP HIS ACT. Ollie had it framed and hung it behind the cash register.

Honeymoon

OLLIE AND MILDRED drove to Indianapolis and stayed in the Monument Hotel. He remembered that Wallace Porter,

Colonel Ford, and the advance agents always stayed there whenever they traveled to Indy. Ollie had never seen the rooms, but he knew the lobby had red carpet, brass spittoons, and a crystal chandelier. Classy.

After dinner, he drove Mildred outside town to a roadhouse he remembered liking from way-back-when; the beer was cheap and the dancing sweaty. In the parking lot, Mildred took one look at the place and complained, "What kind of girl do you think I am?" Yet she obliged him and went inside. At first, it was like dancing with a mannequin, but after a few beers, Mildred leaned into him. The band played "Stars Fell on Alabama" and Mildred's taffeta dress swished against his legs as soft as a promise.

The Marriage Bed

THE FIRST NIGHT Mildred cried, begging him to hurry and finish. But he was drunk, and it took a long time. They woke to find her blood blooming red on the sheets. Mildred spent the day in the bathroom, moaning on the toilet, bent over the bathtub, scrubbing out the stains. Ollie spoke softly through the door. "Leave them be, Mildred. The maids will give us fresh ones."

"I will not have anyone see these," she said. "No, I won't."

The next night, Mildred flinched when he touched her hip, so Ollie simply held her, rising once she was asleep to relieve his want in the bathroom. On their last night, he tried again.

"Can't you just hold me?" Mildred begged.

"It gets better."

"How do you know?"

"We just have to keep going."

Mildred drew her nightgown over her boyish hips, over her candy-apple breasts, over her head. "Go ahead then," she said through the fabric.

And he did. Mildred never moved. Ollie closed his eyes and pretended the body beneath him belonged to his favorite lineup girl, the one in Kansas City who had let him take her from behind, the one who'd moaned "big boy, big boy," over and over as they rocked the wagon. When he was through, Ollie pulled down her nightgown, wet with tears. They checked out of the Monument Hotel the next morning with the stained bedsheets stuffed in their suitcase.

Ollie thought it was just jitters, or the fact she was only sixteen, but at the end of the week, at the end of the year even, Mildred stayed stiff under him, seething with contempt. After, she always took a bath. She said only animals and circus trash needed it every night. Ollie found himself staring at men on the street, women dropping off their clothes at Clown Alley. What happened in their beds at night? Everyone else seemed to be moving through life smoothly. Ollie saw no torment in their eyes, no lust, nothing like the reflection in the bathroom mirror that haunted him every night. Maybe Mildred was right. Maybe all those years on the road had made him into a pervert, a sex fiend. He pledged to do better, to try only on Saturday nights.

But he slipped a few weeks later, on a Wednesday. He came home with a bottle of wine for dinner, took Mildred into his arms, and sang "Stars Fell on Alabama" in her ear as they danced. That night, Mildred was not Mildred, but

another woman she kept deep inside, the woman he'd felt
in his arms for a few minutes as they'd danced at the roadhouse. For the first time, Ollie didn't have to imagine a
lineup girl or shut his eyes. This was a new Mildred, and
Ollie liked her much better. But in the morning, she became the old Mildred again. "I'm going to church," she
said.

"It's Thursday," Ollie said. "Nobody's there."

"God is there."

Ollie laughed, and she slammed the front door. For a
week after, she slept on the couch and refused to speak to
him.

Birthday: 1935

ON JANUARY THE second, Ollie turned thirty-five. His father
had died at thirty-five. Ollie couldn't imagine his life from
that point on. After thirty-five, his frame of reference disappeared. Not that he had much of one before—just a
couple of pictures, precious few stories. What would he
look like as he aged further? Would he go bald? Would his
heart last? His eyes? He had no idea. He took the afternoon
off, went home, and sat in a chair to think about it.

After a while, Ollie heard a metal clank; the mail
dropped through the slot into the hall closet. He retrieved
the mail and stood there, looking at his father's bullhook
standing crookedly in the corner next to one of Mildred's
coats. Reaching down, Ollie took the bullhook in his
hands—it sent an icy shock through his arm. He put his
coat back on. The next thing he knew, he was in his car,
driving out to the winter quarters.

He pulled off the road and crunched through knee-deep drifts down to the bank of the Winnesaw. The frozen river was topped with a layer of sugar-soft snow, and the skeleton trees swayed in the icy wind. He knew that in a few months the water would turn muddy with spring melt, and in the summer, the branches would form a green canopy over this spot. A good place to fish, to make love on a blanket, to sit alone and think. Ollie shivered, wishing he'd been born in June or July.

He walked onto the ice, bullhook in hand, then lay down. For old time's sake, Ollie made a snow angel, his laugh breaking the still of the afternoon. He looked up at the sky, a cloudless, robin's-egg blue. He waited for the bullhook to send him another message, to quiver like a divining rod, leading him to the place where his questions might be answered: *What was the last thing his father saw? The last thing he thought? What secret picture had he seen behind his eyes?*

But the bullhook was just cold metal in his hand.

As he lay inside his snow angel, Ollie realized: *Someday I'm going to die.* He put his hand over his heart and wondered how many beats he had coming. Maybe, like his father, he'd die young in some unfortunate accident. A car wreck or lightning strike or druggist's mistake—anything was possible, really. Who would have thought that Hans Hofstadter would die in an Indiana river, drowned in the now-frozen water beneath Ollie? Or perhaps what passed from father to son wasn't bad luck, but something else entirely. Maybe, like the bullhook and photographs and ivory, Ollie had inherited his father's unused heartbeats.

Ollie heard a car pass on the road above, and he stood quickly, embarrassed someone might see him. Near the bank, his shoes broke through the ice, and his wet feet ached with cold all the way home. Straightaway, he took a hot bath so he wouldn't catch pneumonia. Mildred walked into the steamy bathroom just as he stood up in the tub. "Oh. I'm sorry," she said, stepping back behind the half-opened door.

Her modesty annoyed, and then saddened him. Ollie sighed. "It's fine, Mildred."

"What are you doing?"

"What's it look like I'm doing?" he said, reaching for his towel.

"In the middle of the day?"

"I was cold." He wrapped the towel around his waist and opened the door, startling her again.

Mildred looked at his navel, down the towel, then flitted over to the stove. "What's that old elephant stick doing out?" she asked, pointing to the kitchen table.

"Nothing." Ollie padded into the living room and put the bullhook back in the hall closet. When he returned to the kitchen, Mildred stood with her hands behind her back.

"Happy birthday, Ollie." She handed him his gift, ten white handkerchiefs with the initials *OH* embroidered in gold. "I did that myself." Ollie kissed her cool cheek. "Why don't you go get dressed. You'll catch your death," Mildred said.

Ollie's Girls

OLLIE KEPT TWO employees: a colored woman named Verna, and a succession of white women. He tended to hire divorcées with children or women whose husbands had run off, leaving them desperate for work. Mildred said he was a good man to hire such hard-luck women, and each week, she sent him to work with casseroles for "his girls." He kept Clown Alley Cleaners open late on Tuesdays, Thursdays, and Saturdays. When he made up the schedule, he made sure Verna worked Mondays, Wednesdays, and Fridays. The other nights, after closing, he sometimes took his girls into his office where he kept his bottle of whiskey and a box of rubbers. Lois and Polly and Constance and Jane and Myrtle and Georgia. Ollie paid them more than he paid Verna.

If instead he'd hired young ones, high school girls, they might have thought it was a love affair, but Lois and Polly and Constance and Jane and Myrtle and Georgia were old enough, smart enough, to know better. "You and me, we're just lonely people with needs." That's what Ollie said, handing over a tuna-noodle casserole. After a polite peck good-night, Ollie went home where he knew Mildred would already be asleep.

In Between Polly and Constance

OLLIE TRIED "Stars Fell" again, hoping to awaken the other Mildred. She did not emerge, but the old Mildred obliged him without much of a fuss. Nine months later, their daughter, Laura, was born.

In Between Constance and Jane

IN HER JOB interview, Constance told Ollie that her estranged husband was in the army, fighting Japs in the

South Pacific. He'd left without a good-bye. "I hope he gets shot," Constance said. A year later, he did—lost a foot and wrote her a long letter from the hospital, begging her to come to California. Ollie spent five months looking for a suitable replacement. "Women willing to work in a hot laundry aren't so easy to come by anymore," Ollie told his wife, "what with the war and all." Mildred offered to help out, but Ollie wouldn't hear of it.

During the prolonged job search, Ollie got desperate. He tried "Stars Fell," and again, Mildred obliged. Confusing her easy acquiescence for ardor, he approached Mildred from the rear. As they rocked together, he thought he heard her saying "*oooohh.*" Finally, he'd found the other Mildred. Afterward, she stayed quiet for a long time, then rose from the bed on shaky legs. "The baby," she said more to herself than to him. Ollie fell into a happy sleep.

Two months later, Mildred miscarried in the bathtub. The doctor said, "Give her time, Ollie. Let her be." So he took Laura with him to Clown Alley, kept her in a laundry basket on the counter while he worked. He told his customers that his wife was ill, "so I'm helping out until she gets on her feet again." Jane, his newest employee, wouldn't join him in the office, not as long as the baby was there. Going to Mildred for release was out of the question—she spent all her time in bed, carrying her baby's ghost to term. At first, Ollie resorted to long bathroom breaks, but eventually during his seven months of full-time fathering and laundering, his well of desire went dry. *Maybe this is what Mildred feels all the time,* he thought, *this nothing.* Ollie had to admit, however, that he appreciated the efficiency, the focus of that nothing.

On the day that her baby would have been born, Mildred rose, went to church, and resumed her life as if nothing had happened. She never spoke of those months. With time and rain, Ollie's well filled again, and he tried "Stars Fell." Mildred said, "You can go to hell, Ollie Hofstadter."

He never bothered touching her that way again.

The Family Library

IN OLLIE AND Mildred's living room, there was a set of shelves filled with Reader's Digest Condensed Books, the complete works of Louis L'Amour, dime-store paperbacks, and subscriptions to popular magazines. Pressed within the pages of these books and magazines were seventy years' worth of letters Mildred and Ollie wrote to each other. They left each other notes stuck in something they thought the other was reading or might read soon. They guessed wrong sometimes, and on more than one occasion, ten years passed between delivery and receipt.

On page 25 of *Riders of the Purple Sage:* "Ollie, you have made my life a misery. If it wasn't for the fact that I believe God punishes those who divorce, I would leave you and take our daughter with me."

On page 210 of *Gone with the Wind:* Advertisement for Dr. Drago's Female Passion Potion. "Guaranteed to increase a woman's libido or your money back!"

On page 39 of *National Geographic:* "You are a perverted man, looking at these pictures of jungle women. Your seed is animal tainted. Our baby was conceived in sin, in the posture of dogs, and that's why we lost the child."

On page 87 of *Good Housekeeping:* "Dear Abby, I love my wife, but I believe she is frigid. We no longer even sleep in the same bed. What can I do to save my marriage? Signed, Frustrated in Fresno."

On page 165 of *The Hound of the Baskervilles:* "Dear Ann Landers, I think my husband is having an affair with his secretary. I don't want to follow him around because it's so unseemly, and I'm not even sure if I want to know. I'm so degraded. What do I do? Signed, A Devoted Wife."

On page 89 of *Love's Wicked Ways:* "Dear Mildred, if I have made your life a misery, you have done the same to mine. You are a cold, cold fish."

The Third Time Ollie
Got His Name in the Paper

WHEN THEIR DAUGHTER, Laura, announced she was going to marry Ethan Perdido, heir to the Perdido Funeral Home, Mildred rejoiced. The Perdidos lived in one of the nicest houses in town. Ollie, on the other hand, wasn't too sure about the match. Laura seemed more bored than in love, as if she were marrying to have something to do. The boy loved her to death—that was clear. When Ethan came to dinner, he followed Laura with his eyes wherever she went, but Laura was aloof and distant, like her mother.

One night in bed, Ollie heard Laura creaking up the steps. He checked the clock—it was after two. Since the engagement, they'd moved her curfew from eleven to midnight, but she broke it regularly. That night, she'd gone to one of Ethan's baseball games, but that was hours ago. Mildred stirred next to him. "Was that Laura?"

"It was nothing," he lied. "She's already in bed."

"She'd better not have been at the Perdido's house on Yellow Lake." Mildred yawned. "Her hair smelled like fish the other morning."

"Well, I hope they *are* going up there. To see if they're suited for each other. Good for them."

"Oh, you would say that." Mildred rolled over. "Well, I'm sure she's a good girl. We raised her right."

Ollie wasn't sure if he'd raised his daughter right or not. He couldn't remember anything specific he'd ever taught her. Truly, Laura mystified him. He looked at her one morning standing at the sink and thought, *Who is this?* He wondered what a father was supposed to do, to feel, but he had no idea. For a while, he made a conscious effort to touch her once a day—her shoulder, her hand—but she always flinched. Ollie stopped that the day she called him a creep and Mildred gave him one of her withering looks.

Now, Laura was grown-up and getting married, and he'd never gotten to know her at all. For this, Ollie was ashamed, so he spent too much on her wedding.

Six months later, Laura gave birth to his grandchild, Jennifer. Mildred tried telling folks the baby was premature, but the *Lima Journal* published birth announcements complete with all the details, including the fact that Jennifer Perdido, daughter of Ethan and Laura Perdido, granddaughter of Ollie and Mildred Hofstadter, weighed in at almost eight pounds. Mildred was mortified—everyone in town would know!—but it amused the hell out of Ollie.

Birthday: 1969

FOR A WHILE, every birthday after Ollie's thirty-fifth had felt like a gift, but now he was tired of presents he hadn't asked for, didn't deserve, and couldn't return. Already, his friends were dying—at least once a month, he recognized someone on the obituary page of the *Lima Journal*. Ollie figured he'd live to see seventy, exactly twice as long as his father had lived, and that would be that. Surely, he'd almost used up his father's unspent heartbeats. Against Mildred's wishes ("You're in perfectly good health," she said), he sold Clown Alley and retired. He would spend his remaining time in peace.

On his birthday, Ollie celebrated by visiting Mount Pleasant Cemetery. He bought a plot and had his headstone engraved, including a quote he remembered from when he trouped with the circus, the last thing the ringmaster said at the end of the show.

OLLIE F. HOFSTADTER

1900–

MAY ALL YOUR DAYS BE CIRCUS DAYS

Then he went home and rummaged around the hall closet for a while until he found it. Despite Mildred's objections, the bullhook stood sentry beside his easy chair while he waited for death to walk in the door to claim him.

Retirement

HE ROSE AT FIVE or six and drank coffee alone in the dim kitchen, waiting for the sun to rise. As soon as he heard

Mildred stirring upstairs, he left the house; in the winter, he went to the garage to smoke a pipe, and in the summer, he walked. By the time he returned, Mildred would be gone. She'd told him she couldn't stand to share the house with him all day long, so she volunteered down at the Lima County Historical Museum four days a week, collecting admission fees and giving tours. "Why don't you donate that old stick to the museum?" she asked, pointing behind his chair. "Round out the collection. We've got a nice display set up with that old elephant's head." Ollie thought that was just about the meanest thing she'd ever said to him, and that was saying a lot.

In the afternoons, he watched soap operas while Mildred went to her meetings: Flower Club and Women's Circle and Circle K and Book Circle and the Ladies' Prayer Auxiliary. At four, Ollie napped and Mildred came home and started dinner. At five, she woke him by letting the oven door slam shut or rattling the pots on the stove. They ate in silence on TV trays in the living room, watching whatever was on.

At nine, Mildred would yawn, run her bath, and go to bed. Ollie would stay up another hour or so, smoking his pipe in the dark room, listening to his house. Finally, he'd slide into bed beside Mildred. Long ago, Mildred had insisted they *not* get separate beds because she didn't want her friends to come over, see the brother-and-sisterish twin set, and start talking about her.

There's not much else to tell, really. Whole days went by just like this. Days. Weeks. Years.

Days of Our Lives

WHEN JENNY WAS in second grade, she came down with a bad ear infection that kept her out of school for a month. Because her parents both worked, she went to her grandpa Ollie's house. They started watching *Days of Our Lives* together. After she went back to school, Jenny came over in the summers to get caught up on all she'd missed in the previous eight months. She said, "I can't believe you can skip so many episodes and still know what's going on. Nothing hardly changes."

"I wouldn't know," Ollie told her. "I watch it every single day."

By the Time You Read This, I Will be Gone

ONE DAY, Laura went missing. She'd gone out for a drive in Ethan's hearse and never came back. They found the hearse in a Chicago parking garage. The police said she had either been abducted or she'd run off, but they couldn't prove one way or the other. Mildred was certain her daughter was dead, and she prayed for a body for Ethan to bury, but none ever turned up.

A few months after her disappearance, Ollie found a letter from Laura in an old *Life* magazine: "*Dear Mom and Dad, by the time you read this, I will be gone.*" He took it to the police, certain it was proof she'd run away and was alive somewhere if they'd just get off their butts and look. The detective asked him, "How's your eyesight, Mr. Hofstadter?" Ollie told him it wasn't too good. "Well, I'm afraid this letter can't help us much, sir." It was dated 1967.

In Sickness and In Health

IN 1995, Ollie fell down and broke his hip. After the surgery, Mildred told the doctors she couldn't care for him at home, and they suggested she find him a bed at Sunset Village, a local nursing home that smelled of urine, mothballs, and talcum. He agreed on two conditions: that Mildred wouldn't sell the house to pay for it, and that he be allowed to take his bullhook with him. Mildred honored one of his wishes.

Once he was settled, Mildred sold their house and most of their furniture and moved into an apartment complex for senior citizens. She didn't tell Ollie this. On her Sunday visits, Mildred sometimes took him for a drive, and he often asked her to go past their house. One day, they went by and there was a little boy digging a hole in the front yard. Mildred told him it was the son of their new next-door neighbors. Ollie said, "Don't let him dig up the hostas. We paid a fortune for those."

The Lord Hears All Prayers

THE NEW PASTOR from Mildred's church came by. Reverend McCanliss or McCormick or something. He'd been pastor for over a year and was finally getting around to visiting the shut-ins. "Your wife tells me you've never been a churchgoing man, but that you might have some things you want to get off your chest," he said, smiling. Ollie laughed and sent the man away. Then he started thinking about all the things he wasn't too proud of. The lineups and the Cowboy and Indian act and the girls in his office. And Laura. Yes, Laura most of all.

Ollie picked up the bullhook next to his bed and held it in the air. A radio transmitter sending his regrets straight to God and to Laura, wherever she was. The bullhook quivered above him, and Ollie let himself believe this meant something. He kept his eyes upward—not seeing, ignoring, his shaking hands.

Apples and Bras and Greasepaint

OLLIE ASKED the nurses at Sunset Village when he was going home. At first, they were nice and said, "Oh, Mr. Ollie. You can't go home now. We like you too much." But he kept asking, every day his voice getting louder, so they lost their patience and told him the truth. "Your wife sold your house, Mr. Hofstadter. You've just forgotten." Maybe he had forgotten. He was forgetting a lot of things, sure, but never a whole house. He told Mildred what the nurses said, and she promised to send a complaint to their supervisor.

Every day was new because every night he forgot the day before. Instead, Ollie started remembering things he hadn't thought about for a long time: the swish of Mildred's taffeta skirt, his mother paring apples for her famous apple strudel, the way his friend Joe snored, his girl Lois hooking her bra in his office at the cleaners on Tuesday nights. Then Ollie began to remember things that he didn't even know he knew: the perfume his wife wore on their wedding day (Chantilly), his mother's strudel recipe (in German, unfortunately), the tune Joe was whistling as he applied his greasepaint the night he died ("Yankee Doodle Dandy"), the size of Lois's bra (36DD).

Then the memories went farther back. He saw his father's wake—not from the photograph in the drawer next to his bed, but a real memory with a minister delivering the eulogy, people moving around the casket, and his mother crying. Then he saw his father's face peering down into his crib. Ollie was certain this was a real memory. In a fantasy, surely he would use the likeness he'd seen in photographs. But instead, this was the dark oval from his dreams, the sound of deep coughing, the smell of cigar on the breath.

The wheelchair-bound residents of Sunset Village formed a metal gauntlet down the hallway, and he made his way among them in his own chair, paddling along like a duck. Ollie tried to tell them about these visions, about the apples and the bra and the greasepaint, but nobody listened. They were too busy talking about socks and radios and Hawaii. Nobody cared that every night the nurses tried to take him to the post office and leave him there. He woke up scared, surrounded by letters and packages addressed to people he didn't know. When he yelled, "Take me home right now," the postman would come in and give him a shot, and by the time he woke up from its effects, they'd have taken him back to Sunset Village. Ollie tried to stay awake, to catch them in the act, but they put drugs in his food to make him sleepy. He tried not to eat, but they found his mother's recipe for apple strudel, and gee, he didn't know when he'd have the chance to eat it again.

The nurses taped gauze around the tip of his bullhook, but he still kept it next to his bed. The bullhook scared the angels away. At night, the light in the walls started out the size of a firefly, but then the light got bigger and brighter so the angels could get through. If he picked up his bullhook, the light always disappeared. The angels wanted to take him away, but he didn't want to wake up at the post office ever again.

The Fourth Time Ollie
Got His Name in the Paper

The Lima Journal, January 1, 2000

ELDERLY MAN ATTACKS EMT

Local EMT Scott Powers, 25, was treated for bruises and contusions today. His patient, Mr. Ollie Hofstadter of Sunset Village, was being transferred to King's Memorial Hospital when the attack occurred.

According to hospital spokesperson Peggy Richards, Hofstadter has been experiencing stroke symptoms, including slurred speech and dementia.

Hofstadter attacked Powers with a metal rod hidden under his blanket. "When I tried to wheel his stretcher into the hospital, he started beating me with this thing," Powers said. "He was obviously confused. He thought I was taking him to the post office."

Hofstadter was unharmed in the incident, but was admitted to King's Memorial Hospital for observation.

Hofstadter's wife, Mildred, said that the rod is an elephant hook, probably used by her husband's father, who worked for the circus. "My husband hasn't been himself," Mrs. Hofstadter said, adding that January 2 will be Hofstadter's one-hundredth birthday. "Plus, he was up late at Sunset Village, ringing in Y2K."

Mr. Hofstadter is a lifelong resident of Lima. He owned and operated Clown Alley Cleaners for thirty years, and for a short time was a clown in the Great Porter Circus.

Birthday: 2000

A FIREFLY FLICKERED on the wall opposite Ollie's hospital bed. He reached for his bullhook, but it was gone. "Where is it?" he moaned.

Mildred rose from her chair. "Where's what, Ollie?" He tried to roll over, but he was tangled in tubes. "Oh that. I've got it somewhere so you can't hurt anyone else with it." She held the *Lima Journal* in front of his face. "We're the laughingstock of town. Thank you very much."

The light on the wall glowed brighter. Ollie pointed— he wanted Mildred to see the angels coming for him. "Look," he said.

Mildred crossed the room to a bouquet of Mylar balloons. "Aren't they pretty? I got them for your birthday. Was just bringing them to you when I got the call that the ambulance had come." Her voice wavered, and she looked away.

The light shone in his eyes now, but Ollie had no way to make it stop. Panicked, he prayed. "My father who art in heaven, hallowed be thy name."

"It's *Our Father,* dear. And you'd know that if you ever spent a day in church."

"Forgive me my trespasses."

"Debts," Mildred said. "Debts."

He saw them now, struggling to get their wings through the opening. "Even though I walk through the valley of the shadow of death, I will fear no evil because you are with me."

"Ollie, are you all right?"

"Please, Mildred. It comforts me."

She looked at him for a long moment, and then touched his arm. This was an old, old Mildred, the kind-eyed girl he'd met out at the winter quarters. Ollie wondered where the hell she'd been all these years. Mildred reached into the large shopping bag at her feet. "Here," she said, handing him the bullhook. "Are you happy?"

He gripped it in both hands. "Amen." He shut his eyes.

"Ollie! Wake up." When he didn't respond, she pushed the call button next to the bed. "No. No. No."

He felt Mildred lean over him. She was saying something in his ear, something that made her cry, but he couldn't hear her over the squeal of his hearing aid.

Then the angels were there, fussing with his tubes. Ollie looked out the window at the scalloped snow clouds, the sun trying to shine. And then he wasn't in the room at all, but standing on the Winnesaw River, brushing away snow until he found his father's frozen face looking back at his own. Ollie lay down over his father's body and flailed his arms and legs. And then Ollie was gone, leaving a perfect angel pressed into the snow.

CIRCUS PEOPLE
— *or*
WLMA, Your Hometown Music Station,
1060 on the AM Dial

A LONG TIME AGO—before French fur traders came to cheat the Miami Indians, before it belonged to anyone or even had a name—Indiana was a vast forest, but the land was scraped bare, first by ancient glaciers, and then by pioneers with axes and mouths to feed. There are hills in southern Indiana, but everything north of Indianapolis is so flat that sometimes, especially in winter, it is difficult to tell the difference between the earth and the sky. My mother once told me that if she had to draw a picture of loneliness and despair, it would be Indiana in winter: a wash of gray, a stand of naked trees, and a line of electric poles disappearing into infinity.

When I left for graduate school, I knew one thing: I needed a horizon that wasn't horizontal. Eventually, I got my wish—a job teaching history at a little college in Pennsylvania. A year later, I bought my first house, a hundred-and-fifty-year-old stone farmhouse in the middle of an apple orchard. Where I live now is a Grandma Moses painting, a rolling valley in the shadows of South Mountain. That's where I am the day after New Year's Day 2000, the day the world didn't end. I'm trying to write a syllabus but staring outside at the snowy hills instead when the phone rings. "Grandpa Ollie just passed, sweetie," my dad says. "The funeral's the day after tomorrow. Can you come home?"

"One hundred," I say. "He made it."

Dad sighs. "Sort of."

It's January, the snowiest month of all in Indiana. Most flights into Indianapolis are canceled, but I manage to get one into Midway, and my dad manages to get there to pick me up. When I hop in the car, Dad sings in his best Jim Nabors. *"Back home again ... in Indiana ... And it seems that I can see ..."* We drive thirty miles an hour on the way down to Lima. Snow blows across the highway, gathering along fence posts like thousands of ghosts. "It's drifting pretty bad," he says, his voice as solemn as the sky.

"Yeah. It is."

He punches at the radio, tuning in a weather report. "How's school, Jenny?"

"Fine," I say. "Classes don't start for another week, so this is a good time. I guess." I clear my throat. "How's Nana?"

"Mildred's more upset than I thought she'd be." He sighs, then touches my hand. "It's good to see you, Jen. How was that conference you went to?"

"Fine. San Francisco was great."

He sings again, his way of telling jokes. *"I left my heart ... in San Francisco."*

I didn't come home for Christmas because I had to go to the conference. Actually, that's a lie. I *could have* come home, but didn't. I flew to California early to visit a grad school friend—and went to the beach every day—then I went to the conference. It was the first time in my life I hadn't woken up on Christmas morning under the same roof as my father, and even though I convinced myself at the time that I deserved the trip, that it wasn't a big deal, I still feel guilty just thinking about it. But I don't let my voice betray that guilt—in fact, my tone sounds a tad exasperated. "You know I'm sorry I couldn't be here for Christmas, Dad."

He sighs. "I just wish I could see you more often, that's all."

"I know I know I know." If I still lived in Lima, would he still complain he didn't see me enough? Probably. I lean down to tune out the static behind a Ray Charles song. "Come Rain or Come Shine," I think. My dad breathes in swiftly, like he's been startled. "What?"

He grips the steering wheel tighter. "Nothing."

"No. What?"

"Well, it's just that... Well, you looked like your mother there for a second."

I hold my breath. I haven't heard my dad talk about my mom for years.

"We were on this same road. Going to Chicago for our honeymoon. And she was stooped over just like that, trying to tune in the radio."

"I didn't know Mom liked Ray Charles."

"She liked any kind of music you couldn't get in Lima." He tells me that back when they were dating, she made him crisscross county roads, looking for the spot where Chicago-born radio signals would come in. He'd make a left, then a right, and the music would arrive. *Stop the car,* she'd yell, and they'd sit there in the middle of nowhere, listening to a black man sing what sounded to him like a funeral hymn, but what she called the blues.

I'm afraid to say anything more, afraid it will spook him and he'll stop.

"On our honeymoon," Dad says, "she just kept saying how strange it was. Sixty miles north of Lima, and it was like a different world. She made me listen to that stuff all the way there."

What he doesn't say is, *Fourteen years later, when she left, she probably listened to the same station all the way to Chicago.*

What I don't say is, *Until she left, she told me over and over, "When you get out of this town, Jenny, make sure you find a city that has good radio stations."*

For the rest of the drive, we let the radio do the talking for us, and somewhere along the way, I drift off. He nudges me awake as we pass the familiar sign that greets us at the city limits: WELCOME TO LIMA, INDIANA, CIRCUS TOWN U.S.A.

NOBODY ASKS YOU where you're from until you leave the place you're from. For me, like most people, it happened when I went to college at Purdue. I had three stories that served as my signature party tricks. One was called "My Dad Is an Undertaker." The title alone was usually all people wanted to hear. Another was called "My Grandpa Was a Circus Clown." This story entailed giving an abbreviated history of Lima's circus past: Wallace Porter, winter quarters, bunkhouses, barns, boom, and bust. My best trick, my best story, was the one called "My Great-Grandpa was Killed by an Elephant" It went like this: "One day, my great-grandpa led his elephants down to the river for a bath, and one of them picked him up with its trunk and threw him in the air"—I flail my arms for effect, sloshing beer—"Then it stepped on him until he drowned. They had to kill the elephant, whose name was Caesar. Its skull sits on a pedestal in the county museum. No, I'm not making this up."

There was one story, however, that I never told. It was called "I Have No Idea Where My Mother Is." It would have gone like this: "When I was fourteen, my mother disappeared. She took the hearse out for one of her so-called long drives, but this time, she didn't return. The police found the hearse abandoned in a Chicago parking garage, and that was the last sign of her. *Poof!* Gone. For a year afterward, the *Lima Journal* kept the story alive. The city dragged the Winnesaw River, just in case. My father hired detectives to find her. The police even investigated *him*. But I always knew what he didn't want to admit: she didn't want to be found."

In Lima, everyone in town knew what happened, but in college no one did. When my friends asked about my parents, I just said they were divorced and I didn't like to talk about it. People understood and didn't press for more. I liked walking around campus knowing that people weren't thinking, "There goes Jenny Perdido whose mother ran off." Instead, maybe they thought, "There goes Jenny Perdido, the undertaker's daughter from that weird circus town." Or maybe they thought, "That girl has a pleasant face." But mostly, I don't think anyone noticed me at all, which is why I went to a big state school. I wanted to disappear like my mother had, melt into the throng, and become whomever I wanted to be.

THE PERDIDO Funeral Home sits on a quiet side street in Lima. The basement is where my dad works, the first floor has two funeral parlors—one mauve, one blue—and the second floor is the family residence. When I walk downstairs the next morning for Grandpa Ollie's viewing, the foyer is already full, a somber crowd gently stomping snow off their boots. They pause from removing their wool coats and look up at me with kind faces. For a brief moment, I feel panic in the pit of my stomach. *What will they say to me? What will I say back?* But they clear a path so that I can stand next to Nana and my father. A line forms. People shake my hand, some even lean in for hugs, and suddenly I feel calm, like I'm exactly where I'm supposed to be and know exactly what to do.

"Your grandma tells us you're a college professor. I go to her church, you know."

"I'm so sorry. I went to school with your dad."

"Do you remember me? My daughter was in Girl Scouts with you."

"Jenny Perdido! I used to cut your hair."

They all know me, I think. What felt claustrophobic at eighteen feels strangely comforting at thirty-two. I count in my head—how many times have I moved since college? Four? No, five. I've become accustomed to my relative anonymity, I suppose. How long has it been since I lived in a place and was *known,* really known? There are fifty-odd people milling around the mauve parlor, and not one of them is a complete stranger to me. As they introduce themselves, almost every single name seems familiar.

Even though I haven't lived in Lima for a long time, I still know what happens there. Nana sends me clippings from the *Lima Journal*, the kind of small-town paper that tells you everything about your neighbors, and then some. I know that someone stole the skull of the elephant that killed my great-grandfather, and that Mr. Barnett, the owner of the B&B Grocery was arrested last month for peddling kiddy porn. My favorite high school teacher, Mr. Flinn, died a year ago—they ran a picture with the obituary, as if anyone could forget his Tweety Bird face. Viola Clark, my softball coach, just published a detective novel, and Shane Stevens, my first boyfriend, fell from a ten-foot ladder and lives in a wheelchair. Nana made sure I knew that Darcy Williams, the girl who stole Shane from me, is on marriage number three.

The next person in the receiving line is Rowdy Rubens, a former human cannonball who worked as the head trainer at the Lima Amateur Circus. Nana sent me the article when he retired a few years ago, about how back in 1965 the Chamber of Commerce asked him to train some local kids to perform, and he did so for thirty years with no pay. Rowdy is shorter than me, and he looks up through Coke-bottle glasses and says, "Your grandpa was a very funny man. Very funny."

I nod and say, "I know," even though I don't remember Grandpa Ollie having any sense of humor whatsoever.

A middle-aged black woman approaches and takes my hand. "I'm Verna Bowles."

Nana leans over. "She worked for your grandpa down at the cleaners."

"That's right. That's right. He was real good to me." Mrs. Bowles turns to Nana. "How you doing, Mildred?"

Nana sighs. "Pretty good, I s'pose."

"Couple weeks ago I went up to the nursing home to see Ollie. He asked me when my daddy was coming to visit." She shakes her head. "Didn't have the heart to tell him." Then she moves into the parlor.

"What?" I ask.

Nana lowers her voice. "Her dad's been dead for a long time. He trouped with your grandpa back in the old days."

"He was a clown?"

This time, Nana whispers in my ear. "Sideshow pinheads. The whole family."

I want to ask what a pinhead is, but before I can, Nana has turned to the next person in line.

WHEN I WAS A little girl, my mother told me stories about the old days when the circus people lived in Lima. She said they had come from lands far away, where the sun had burned their hair a glossy black and warmed their skin to the color of ripe olives. They roamed the dark forests of Europe for centuries in slow-moving caravans, reading crystal balls and outstretched palms, swallowing fire and swords, twisting their bodies into queer shapes, all in trade for the gold coins that tinkled as they walked. I pictured young circus women dancing around fires in purple veils, and the older married ones stooped over, draped in black and black. I saw vagabond men combing the countryside for a lone pig or sheep for their dark feasts, and a few days later, dumping the boiled bones back in the farmer's paddock, as if to tell him, *Thank you.* And, of course, my mother said, the night before they broke camp, the music would begin, pipes and reeds and strings luring bad children who dreamed of big cities and blue oceans into their waiting arms, children who were never seen nor heard from again.

My mother told me that when the old-time circuses traveled in brightly painted railcars across the country, they stopped each night in little places like Middletown, Ohio; Radford, Virginia; Ottumwa, Iowa; Leadville, Colorado. From the railroad siding, the men in the wickey wagon hung kerosene lamps in the trees to lead the rest of the show to the designated lot on the edge of town. For a night or two, the circus people glittered on dangling silver webs and smiled, sitting atop their roaring beasts. When the shows were over, they dropped canvas and, deep in the night, paraded silently back to the waiting train. And always, there was this danger: that in the morning, the towns of Middletown, Radford, Ottumwa, and Leadville would awaken to empty beds, their wayward sons and daughters disappeared.

My mother told me that small towns tolerate the wanderer because wanderers bring them as much of the outside world as they can bear. A night swarming with circus people satisfies this need for upwards of a year. But small towns don't likewise tolerate the wanderers among them, those who leave on midnight trains, moonlit back roads, or in brightly painted railcars. Like a parent, the town takes this leaving as a sign of failure it can hardly face. And so, small towns tell their children the same story, intoning it over and over again to keep them from leaving: *You are lucky to be from a place where nothing bad happens.*

"Don't believe it," she always said. "I want you to leave this place someday. Promise me you will."

Of course, I told her yes.

WHEN I FINALLY work up the nerve to approach the casket, I can see that Dad did a good job on Grandpa Ollie, who looks like he's sleeping, albeit in a brown suit. His face looks like his face, not a slightly off wax sculpture. His skin is as mottled as a leopard's coat with a century of age spots. The last time I saw him up at the nursing home, he kept calling me by my mother's name. "Laura," he said, "I'm so glad you're here. I have so many things to tell you." I tried to correct him—"I'm Jenny, Grandpa! I'm Laura's daughter!"—but it made him agitated, so I let him think what he wanted. I took his hand, which was cold and a little blue, and offered to read *Soap Opera Digest* to him. When I was a kid, we used to watch *Days of our Lives* together. But he didn't seem to hear me. He said, "Laura, one of these days, I'm going to tell your mother off, but good! That woman hasn't let me touch her in years." I told him, "I know, I know," wishing I didn't. Staring outside, he watched a cardinal perched on the birdfeeder Nana had hung outside his window. "There's a lot of funny business goes on in this place when nobody's around," he said, pointing at the bird as if it was proof. "Every night, them nurses take me to the post office." He started crying, and then I did, too, rubbing the tissue-papery skin on his hand. Finally, he fell asleep, so I slipped out the door. An old man stood in the hallway, pissing weakly against the wall. That night, I called Nana and told her what Grandpa had said. "He has good days and bad days," she sighed. "You just never know." I went up to the nursing home two more times while I was home, waiting to see if my old grandpa Ollie would come back, but he never did. I suppose that's why I'm not so sad today, because it feels like he's been gone for a long, long time.

Someone walks up behind me. It's Nana, and she puts her arm around my shoulder. "How you doing, sweetie?" She looks me in the eye, then stares at a flower arrangement, looking anywhere, it seems, except at the casket we're standing in front of.

"I'm fine, Nana." I look down at Grandpa, trying to think of something to say. "What did he look like when he was young? When you met him?"

"Oh, surely you've seen pictures, child."

"He's pretty old in them," I say. "I don't even know how you met."

"Oh Lord." Nana waves her hand, but she still doesn't look down. "I was out at the winter quarters, watching the elephants, and he came right up and introduced himself to me." She tells me she was wearing a fur muff that day to keep her hands warm, and an elephant snatched it off and tried to eat it. "Your grandpa was going to let that elephant do it, too."

"Oh, surely not," I say, glancing down at Grandpa, who can't defend himself.

Nana's face softens just the slightest bit. "Well, I guess he just didn't want to get it back for me. He's always been a scaredy-cat around elephants. Since ... well, you know. His dad."

"I know," I say. I love Nana, but even her apologies come out like put-downs.

She dabs her eyes with a handkerchief and finally turns to the casket. "I'm really gonna miss you, you old coot." Then she walks away just as the organist starts playing "Amazing Grace," the signal to take our seats.

At most funerals, my dad stands respectfully along the wall, hands crossed at his waist. But today he is both funeral home director and son-in-law. Dad takes a seat next to me as the minister from Nana's church begins to speak. "We've gathered this afternoon to mourn the passing of Ollie Hofstadter, a man who saw the sun rise and set on the twentieth century." The minister points out the major landmarks of Grandpa's life: his days with the circus, his marriage, and his business, Clown Alley Cleaners. The minister says, "Mr. Hofstadter was also a proud father and grandfather." He never says my mother's name, but suddenly, the whole room starts fidgeting and coughing behind us. I feel this urge to turn around and catch people staring at us, but Nana, Dad, and I just keep staring straight ahead.

WHEN I WAS fourteen, Dad took us on a camping trip to Tennessee. He borrowed a camper from Earl Richards, a guy he went to high school with. It had a little kitchen, complete with fridge and stove, and a bathroom—thank god. By day, my dad and I fished and swam and hiked while my mother stayed in the camper by herself. We'd come back to her tight smile and find the campfire burning, dinner started, the camper neater than campers are supposed to be. At night, my dad wanted Mom close by—on his lap or at his side—and so I'd yawn and say good night. Trying to fall asleep, I'd hear their voices speaking softly— mostly his. They were doing a lot of talking then, which was certainly better than the yelling that preceded it. When the campfire died, they'd come inside and get in the full-size bed up front (I was in the back, a thin door between us), and then I'd feel the gentle rocking begin, the way the tires bounced, the jacks letting out small squeaks. Then they'd start talking again.

I knew what they were doing but had never seen it done. I lay there in my bunk bed, listening to the hum of cicadas, the wind moving through the trees, my parents making love, trying to save their marriage. I wished they'd just wait until we got home, but I also knew (without really knowing, because I was just fourteen) that something important was happening up there in the front of the camper, that sex is how people really, really talk to each other, that a marriage isn't who people are in the daylight, but rather who they are at night.

That was the year I'd started living in my head. Every Friday night, I walked to the B&B Grocery to check out the latest copies of *Vogue, Spin,* and *Rolling Stone.* I stared at the slick photos of rock stars and movie stars, artists and fashion designers, and imagined myself interviewing them: sipping espressos under umbrellas at sidewalk cafés, drinking martinis in secluded cocktail lounges. Creepy old Mr. Barnett always interrupted my fantasies, saying, "What are you reading that hippie trash for, Jenny?" Then, as a kind of apology, he'd say, "You're looking more like that mother of yours every day," touching my palm as he handed me

the change. Every night after dinner I escaped to my bedroom alone instead of watching television with my parents.
When I couldn't avoid them—in the car, at the dinner
table—I made up stories in my head. Teen romances
mostly, starring me and the boys I loved in secret.

The camping trip, I came to realize, wasn't a family vacation at all, but rather a group second honeymoon, my
dad's attempt to save their marriage. I was there to cinch
the deal (*For Jenny's sake, we have to try, Laura!*), and I resented that. I didn't want to be there, but I was trapped
with them in that cramped camper, and so I escaped into
my own head, lost in a conjured-up world. I don't remember a lot about that week in Tennessee except the camper
rocking with all of that terrible, desperate trying. And I remember the dream.

Our last night in Tennessee, I stayed up late, trying to
decipher my parents' whispers, but I couldn't tell if the trip
had done its intended work or not. Finally about three or
four, I fell asleep and into a dream—and it wasn't about
any of the boys I secretly loved or about me interviewing
Sting for *Rolling Stone*. It was about David Lindsey, an older
boy who went to Nana's church. All the girls in Lima knew
who David Lindsey was, but I'm sure he had no idea who I
was. In the summer during the amateur circus, he was the
catcher in the trapeze act, and in the fall, he quarterbacked
the football team. Only in a place like Lima can a boy wear
a leotard and still retain hunk status. He was a sight to
behold, hanging upside down in his black leotard, his
lats spreading like a bat's wings as he caught flying girls by
the wrist. He was almost a senior, a lithe, blond god in the

spotlight. I was a little girl in the stands, eating a snow cone. And that about sums up how close I was to David Lindsey.

Anyway, in the dream, we go to a party. I'd never been to a party before, but in the dream, this didn't seem to matter. When we get there, we split up immediately, as if that was the plan. David mingles, and I stand at the front door, talking with the parents who've decided to let the party happen at their house. All night, I watch him out of the corner of my eye. When the parents say it's time to go home, David gets very sad. He's drunk and hugging everyone. "Don't go, man! Let's party some more." This, apparently, is my cue. I edge my way into the throng and take David by the elbow. "Time to go," I say, and I steer him toward the front door. He's having trouble walking. Everyone seems to understand this is my job, and they clear a path. The parents tell us to take care, drive safe. We walk out the screen door, and then I woke up to another humid Tennessee morning and the sound of my parents talking over morning coffee.

ALL DAY AT Grandpa Ollie's funeral, I keep thinking I see my mother out of the corner of my eye—a rustle behind the heavy curtains, a flash of shoe leaving the room. The same thing happened when I graduated from high school, from college, from graduate school, and I know it will happen when I get married, if I have a child, when that child graduates from high school, if that child gets married—and so on—for the rest of my life. She's like the blurry smear in a photograph when someone moves too fast for the shutter speed. I wonder if she even knows her father is dead. I wonder if she cares.

The sun is going down by the time we get into the

hearse. The windows are frosted over, and looking out at the pinkish sunset is like peering through a scrim of lace. Dad drives and Nana and I sit in the back for the ride up to Mount Pleasant Cemetery. Very few cars are in the funeral procession, and as we make our way through town, nobody stops on the sidewalks or pauses while getting into their cars to watch us pass. The time and temperature sign at the bank reads twenty degrees. Dad pulls into the cemetery and up to Grandpa Ollie's row. The dark earth is powdered with last night's sugary snow. We climb out and stand there silently, waiting for the pallbearers. I've seen my grandpa's headstone a hundred times; he bought it when he retired from Clown Alley, right around the time I was born. It's been waiting for him up here for more than thirty years—I used to ride my bike past it all the time.

OLLIE F. HOFSTADTER

1900–

MAY ALL YOUR DAYS BE CIRCUS DAYS

On either side of his grave are his parents' headstones, Hans and Nettie Hofstadter, and one waiting for Nana. Walking down the row, I find the Porter family crypt, which I've seen before, but then I notice a small group of graves marked "Bowles": Bascomb, Pearly, Gordon, Mimi. "Verna's family," I say, although Nana isn't within earshot. In the next row, there's a small cross for a Jennie Dixianna—there's no birthdate, only the year she died, 1913. My dad crunches along behind me as I keep walking toward some of the newer graves. Flinn. Burns. Miller. Lockwood. Stringer. Garrison. Ames. Polowski. Krup. Then I see the one marked DAVID LINDSEY, 1965–1982, and I stoop

down to brush away the snow that's blown over the epi-
taph. OUR BELOVED SON, it reads.

"I can't remember if you knew him or not," Dad says.

"No. Not really."

THAT MORNING in Tennessee as we broke camp, I kept thinking about my dream. I was getting ready to start high
school, and maybe something was going to happen between us that year. Why else would I have had a dream
about a guy I'd never really thought about before? During
the long drive back to Lima, I dozed in and out of my new
dream about me and David Lindsey. The beginning of the
story was always the same: David and I go to that party, but
I made it up from there. David and I go see a movie, or we
go eat breadsticks at Pizza Hut and play stupid Air Supply
songs on the jukebox, or we go park down by the Winnesaw River, and then I'd fall asleep with an ache between
my legs.

We got home late that night. Dad pulled the camper
into the funeral home parking lot, and I ran inside to use
the bathroom. That's where I was, sitting on the toilet,
when my mom walked into the bathroom, holding that afternoon's copy of the *Lima Journal*. She looked at me and
asked, "Do you know this David Lindsey?"

I must have had a pronounced reaction, because my
mother said, "You do?"

"No, not really," I finally said.

She laid the newspaper on my bare legs and left the
bathroom. That's when I saw David's senior picture on the
front page, and the headline: LOCAL BOY KILLED IN TRAGIC
CAR ACCIDENT.

The night before, after the circus performance was over, David had gone out to the Winnesaw Reservoir to swim and drink beer with his friends. Around one, he told a girl named Sharon Gregg he'd give her a ride home, but on the way back to town, he fell asleep at the wheel and drove into a tree. Sharon lived, but David died instantly, the paper said.

After he unhitched the camper, my dad drove the hearse to the hospital to pick up David's body. I heard him come home around two in the morning, and for the rest of the night, I kept thinking about David. No, I didn't go downstairs and look at him. Why do people think I spent my childhood sneaking into the embalming room? But you'd be right if you wondered if—just this once—I actually considered it. All my life, dead people slept two floors below me, but this was the first time it was someone almost my own age, someone I had a crush on for about eight hours when I didn't know that he was already dead.

The next day was Saturday, the last day of Circus Week. In the morning, the town put on an old-fashioned circus parade, complete with calliopes and refurbished Great Porter Circus tableau wagons. In the afternoon, the kids put on their final performance, the grand finale, and it was almost always sold out. The paper said that the kids had voted to go on with the show, and my dad pulled two tickets from his wallet. "I bought these before we went camping," he said. "Do you still want to go?" He and I went to the grand finale every year, and this year especially, I wanted to see it. My mom never went to the circus because she said it was too hot.

It's only a couple of blocks from the Perdido Funeral

Home to the circus. The building is Wallace Porter's old livery stable, painted white and red with a big-top roof. We walked down Broadway, transformed for Circus Week into a carnival midway, blocked off with orange cones and yellow sawhorses. We made slow progress toward the circus building; Dad knew so many people in town, and everyone wanted to shake his big hand and talk about David Lindsey. The funeral was the next day, and by the time we got to the circus building, it seemed almost everyone in town had said they would be there.

The inside of the circus building resembles a huge high-ceilinged gym rimmed with bleachers—with three rings instead of free-throw lines. The walls are draped with old sideshow banners—Two-Headed Lady, Dog-Faced Boy, Sword Swallower—each one sponsored by a local merchant. Enormous exhaust fans roared, and a bunch of big-shouldered riggers tinkered with the impossibly intricate web of wires and ropes. Up in the bandstand, the musicians tuned their instruments, and clowns with brooms cleared sawdust from inside the rings. All of these people were volunteers—plus the red-coated ringmaster, concession-stand workers, ushers, wardrobe assistants, makeup artists, nurses, electricians, trainers. We found our seats and bought programs, listening to the buzz around us. Everyone was talking about the accident.

"I was down at the drug store today buying a card and I ran into Mrs. Lindsey's sister Ann, and she told me that David wasn't drunk. They're mad that got into the paper."

"My daughter's in the trapeze act with him. She was supposed to go out to the reservoir, too, but she was tired.

No, they aren't doing the trapeze act tonight. I don't see how they could."

"Our grandson's doing the Roman Ladders this year. He's nine and won't talk about it. I didn't think he should go on today, but his mom said he wouldn't hear none of it."

"My friend Joe is in the band, and he told me about the song they've been playing all week during the trapeze act. They didn't realize it until last night, when they skipped that act. You aren't gonna believe this. It's that song by Billy Joel, 'Only the Good Die Young.' It's so spooky, I get shivers just thinking about it."

"I made them a casserole. They got a fridge full of casseroles."

"It's just so sad. It's just so awful thinking about his folks."

Every year, before the circus started, my dad would always say, "Now *this* is what a town is supposed to be. Everybody working together to make this happen." That year, he didn't say it, but he didn't need to, really. Already, I was sweating, but I knew that the ringmaster would remind the audience that up high, where the performers were, it was much hotter. It was over ninety that day, and the show usually ran for more than three hours.

Finally, the lights dimmed, and the ringmaster (my school superintendent) shouted:

"LADIES AND GENTLEMEN! CHILDREN OF ALL AGES! WELCOME TO LIMA, INDIANA, CIRCUS TOWN, U.S.A.! HOME OF THE GREATEST AMA-TEUR SHOW ON EARTH!"

The band played the national anthem, and then all the performers filed into the building and stood quietly behind the
ringmaster, who said:

"THE KIDS VOTED TO DEDICATE THEIR PER-
FORMANCE TODAY TO THE MEMORY OF DAVID
LINDSEY, WHO PASSED AWAY THURSDAY NIGHT.
WE'RE GOING TO DARKEN CENTER RING NOW
IN HIS MEMORY. LET US PAUSE FOR A MOMENT
OF SILENCE."

The lights went down, and everyone in the building lowered their head—except for me. I couldn't take my eyes off
the performers, who were all holding hands. I couldn't see
their faces, only their backs, which were heaving and shaking. The place echoed with sobs and sniffs underneath all
that silence, and I felt it all gathering in my chest and behind my eyes. My head ached from trying not to cry.

Finally the show began, and for the next three hours,
everyone tried to forget about the one person who wasn't
there. Teeterboards. Kiddie Clowns. Roman Rings. High
Wire. Slide for Life. Rolla Bolla. Unicycles. The aerial ballet
of the Spanish Web was always my favorite, twenty girls
pirouetting on thirty-foot ropes. For the finale, each cinched
a small loop around her wrist and spun while the rigger
below twirled her cable like a jump rope. Looking up, I saw
they'd become twenty human disco balls, their shimmered
costumes flashing in the lights. But this year, all the smiles
were forced, and it seemed like every girl had raccoon eyes
from crying. After the Walk Around, after all the applause
had finally died down, the ringmaster said what he always
said at the end of the show, but that year, he said it more

softly, without his usual bombast: "May all your days be circus days."

Afterward, Dad and I bought elephant ears (pizza-sized servings of fried dough covered in cinnamon and sugar) and walked back home. It was dusk, but the heat hadn't let up yet, and the air was thick with humidity and mosquitoes. Midway rides glowed pink and green in the distance, and the calliope music blew more and more faintly. I thought about telling Dad about my dream, but I was still trying to come up with some kind of explanation. It wasn't false déjà vu, because I remembered the dream long before I knew anything about the accident. It seemed more than a coincidence that I had that particular dream about that particular person at that particular time. I didn't have words yet for what had happened, only a bunch of images that somehow seemed to go together: the rocking camper, a screen door, the center ring, a jean jacket, a trapeze bar, the moon.

AFTER GRANDPA Ollie's funeral, Dad goes straight upstairs to bed, but I linger in the darkened parlor, wondering whether every person in Lima has been inside my house at one time or another—either by the front door or the back. There must have been four hundred people here for David Lindsey's funeral alone. Almost every kid in town came to the viewing; the receiving line stretched around the block. The eulogy was barely audible over all the sobbing and choking. I'd never seen so many people—young and old— crying at one time. One girl started to hyperventilate, and I had to lead her to the bathroom. Once she calmed down, she told me she'd been up to the hospital to visit Sharon

Gregg, who said that the song on the radio when they hit the tree was "Jack and Diane" by John Cougar Mellencamp. That summer, you just couldn't get away from that song, and for years afterward, whenever it came on—at dances or parties—everyone would get really quiet and look at their hands.

I woke up the day after David's funeral feeling groggy. My dad was out "on business," Mom said, so I told her I wanted to go see my friend Michelle. She was supposed to be in the circus, but I hadn't seen her that Saturday for some reason. When I got to her house, Michelle's mom shook her head. "I'm sorry, Jenny. She's been real upset, so I gave her something to help her sleep. I don't want to wake her until she's ready." So I walked home, stopping at the B&B to buy a Coke.

Ever since we'd returned from Tennessee, the camper had been sitting in the funeral home parking lot. When I got home, I saw that the camper was rocking gently. I knew Mom and Dad were inside, playing hooky, looking for what they'd found in Tennessee. Then it was quiet. I went to my bedroom and looked out the window, waiting for my parents to emerge. Instead, I saw Earl Richards step out, looking left and right. He walked over to his blue truck and backed it toward the camper. My mom came out, her shirt tucked in, her hair tied back in a neat ponytail. She guided Earl backward, saying "A little more. To the right. There. Stop." Earl lowered the camper onto the trailer hitch. When he tried to kiss her good-bye, my mother held out her hand. Earl shook it and drove off. I watched her wave, and then she came inside and started making dinner.

I went to the kitchen and stood there.

"Jenny!" she said, "Why aren't you at Michelle's?"

"She was sleeping, so I came home." I paused. "A while ago."

She looked at me for a long moment. Then she looked away. My dad got home around five. That night for dinner, we had meatloaf, sliced tomatoes, and corn on the cob, but all the time, I couldn't look at my mom, and she couldn't look at me. And a few days later she was gone.

Standing in the parlor, I feel like I'm at two funerals at once, the one that happened today, January 2000, and the one that happened in July 1982. I am fourteen, I am thirty-two, and I can't shake this feeling, especially when I crawl into my childhood bed where I know I won't find anything like sleep. I'm thinking about Grandpa and my mother, wondering where they are now, and about David Lindsey. It took me a long time to figure out what my dream meant, but here's my best shot: I didn't have the dream when David was dying, but rather the next morning, when everyone was finding out about it, when everyone in Lima, Indiana, was thinking about one thing simultaneously. When the emotional voltage of a town spikes like that, where does all that sorrow go? What form does it take? Maybe I have an antenna in my brain tuned to WLMA, The Music of Circus Town, U.S.A. Maybe my mother hears this station, too, wherever she is.

When I was little, my mother told me there are basically two kinds of people in the world: town people and circus people. The kind who stay are town people, and the kind who leave are circus people. Dad used to tell me that I'm a lot like my mother, but this worries him, like I'm cursed, like he somehow failed to give me more of himself.

And I have to admit, the part of me that's my mother scares me more than a little. It's a fire that burns hot and bright, and I know if I let it get out of control, I'll turn into flecks of scorched paper and blow away. But that fire also gave me the courage to leave Lima and make the life I wanted, for which I'm thankful.

At the college where I teach, I'm surrounded by circus people. We aren't tightrope walkers or acrobats. We don't breathe fire or swallow swords. We're gypsies, moving wherever there's work to be found. Our scrapbooks and photo albums bear witness to our vagabond lives: college years, grad-school years, instructor-mill years, first-job years. In between each stage is a picture of old friends helping to fill a truck with boxes and furniture. We pitch our tents, and that place becomes home for a while. We make families from colleagues and students, lovers and neighbors. And when that place is no longer working, we don't just make do. We move on to the place that's next. No place is home. Every place is home. Home is our stuff. As much as I love the Cumberland Valley at twilight, I probably won't live there forever, and this doesn't really scare me. That's how I know I'm circus people.

I like to throw parties for my latest circus family. We have badminton tournaments in the front yard, drinks on the long porch, and late into the night, we tell stories about how we got here—the towns we left, the schools that exploited us, the lovers we abandoned or who abandoned us. When it's just women, we talk about the babies we've delayed having, and sometimes we talk about the ones we forged but did not have, whether now is the time, will there ever be a time, can we even have them anymore? It's taken me a long time to figure out one very simple thing: The world is made up of hometowns. It's just as hard to leave a city block in Brooklyn or a suburb of Chicago as it is to leave a small town in Indiana. And just because it was hard to leave Linden Avenue in Flatbush or the Naperville city limits or Lima doesn't mean you can't ever go back. I wish I knew where my mother was so I could tell her that.

My mother always told me, *Marry yourself first, Jenny.* And I did. She also said, *When you leave, don't look back.* And I tried not to, but for some reason this nowhere place keeps talking to me anyway. Maybe every town in America transmits that radio signal, and on certain nights when the weather and the frequency are just right, we can all hear our hometowns talking softly to us in the back of our dreams.

AUTHOR'S NOTE

I WAS BORN IN Peru, Indiana, which was once the winter quarters of the Hagenbeck-Wallace Circus. Some of the circus characters in this book are inspired by real people, such as Henry Hoffman (my great-great uncle) who was killed by his bull elephant Charley in 1901. Some real places have been incorporated as well. However, all of the rest, as I'm certain the circus historians and the good people of Peru will tell you, comes entirely from my imagination.

A number of books and other historical documents were essential to my writing and research: *The Circus in America* by Charles Philip Fox and Tom Parkinson (Waukesha, Wis.: Country Beautiful, 1969); *The Circus: Lure and Legend* compiled and edited by Mildred Sandison Fenner and Wolcott Fenner (Englewood Cliffs, N.J.: Prentice-Hall, Inc., 1970); *The American Circus: An Illustrated History* by John Culhane (New York: Henry Holt & Company, 1990); *Freaks: Myths and Images of the Secret Self* by Leslie A. Fiedler (New York: Simon & Schuster, 1978); *Pictorial History of the American Circus* by John and Alice Durant (New York: A. S. Barnes & Company, 1957); *Circus Lingo: Written by a Man*

Who Was There by Joe McKennon (Sarasota, Fla.: Carnival Publishers, 1980); *Troupers of the Golden Mascot or Tales of the Yellow Wagon Shows* by Louis Wood (Des Moines, Iowa: Kenyon Press, 1904); *Indiana's Big Top* by Don L. Chaffee (Grand Rapids, Mich.: Foremost Press, 1969); *Route Book of the Great Wallace Show, Season 1895* and *Season 1899* (Columbus, Ohio: Nitchske Bros. Press); "Miami County: Coming of the White Pioneers, Their Activities Down to 1885" from *A Pioneer History of Peru and Miami County* by John A. Graham (Peru Republican Printing, 1877); *Slaves in the Family* by Edward Ball (New York: Random House, 1998); *Miami County, Indiana: A Pictorial History* by Marilyn Coppernoll (Virginia Beach, Va.: Donning Company, 1995).

I'd like to thank the curators and staff of the historical museums of Miami and Howard counties in Indiana and the Circus World Museum in Baraboo, Wisconsin, for their kind and generous assistance. My entire family supported me during the writing of this book, especially the generation who lived in Peru back "when the circus came to town" and told me their stories about those days. Special thanks to my great-aunt Margaret Hoffman, for letting me have the bullhook, and my great-uncle Joseph Shrock and my grandmother Mary Wilson, who saved everything and then gave it to me.

I started writing this book in 1991. A great number of people supported me personally and professionally during those years, far too many to name individually, but I'm grateful to all of them nonetheless. Specifically, I'd like to thank my friends who read these stories as I was putting the book together and provided invaluable editorial advice:

Liv Bowring, Jo Carney, Chris Ludwig, Nina Ronstadt, and Catie Rosemurgy. I'd like to thank all my teachers, especially Tom Chiarella and Barbara Bean at DePauw University, John Keeble, Tom Rabbitt, and Allen Wier at the University of Alabama, and Tim O'Brien at the Sewanee Writers' Conference. Thanks to my students in Alabama, Minnesota, and New Jersey for their patience and support. For the precious gifts of writing time and financial assistance, I thank Minnesota State University at Mankato, The College of New Jersey, and especially the Bush Foundation, whose generous fellowship allowed me to take a year off from teaching, during which time I wrote and revised most of these stories.

My agent Peter Steinberg has been my devoted champion, along with my editor Ann Patty, fellow Hoosier and circus person. And most importantly, I thank my family—my sister Christy, my brother Kenny Scott, and my parents, Kenny and Patty—for letting me go where I've needed to go and for always welcoming me back home again to Indiana.

ACKNOWLEDGMENTS

GRATEFUL acknowledgment is made to the following publications in which some of these stories were first published, in some cases in a slightly different form:

Antioch Review: "The Last Member of the Boela Tribe"
River Styx: "The King and His Court"
Story and *New Stories from the South* (Algonquin Press): "The Circus House"
The Southern Review: "Wallace Porter" as "Wallace Porter Sees the Elephant"
Shenandoah: "Jennie Dixianna" as "Jennie Dixianna and the Spin of Death"
American Fiction, Vol. 10 (New Rivers Press): "Boss Man"
Walking on Water (University of Alabama Press): "Winnesaw" as "Mississinewa"